A GRAND NIGHT FOR MURDER

A Grand Night
for
Murder

Emily Porter Blair

SYCAMORE HILL PRESS

Preface

My father passed away in 2011 and my mother two years later. In the massive collection of their papers I found an old carbon copy of a typed manuscript, the pages brown with age. My brother and I had no idea who wrote it or why it was in our parents' possession.

In 2015 my husband and I took a road trip to see my Aunt Maya and took the manuscript with us. Maya immediately recognized it as one my great-grandmother Emily had written but never published. We looked at each other and said, "Wouldn't it be fun to get this one published too?" And here it is.

One page of the manuscript was typed on the back of a letter dated February 8, 1930, so we know Emily wrote this book sometime after that. Her book *Three Saw the Murder* was published in 1938, and this one was probably written between those dates, although we can't be sure.

Adapting the manuscript was a fascinating experience, involving hundreds of emails back and forth between me in Pennsylvania and Maya in Arkansas. We found flaws in the plot and rewrote parts to make it work but tried to stay true to Emily's voice and vision. After we had done considerable editing we were grateful to get a second copy of the manuscript from another of Emily's descendants, her granddaughter Valerie LaRobardier. There were significant differences in the two versions, and it took many more emails to choose the best of both and merge them.

We wanted to be careful about inserting modern thinking into a story set in 1916. We didn't know, for instance, that back then it was common to refer to a single horse as a team, and fortunately we learned this before we changed all those references. Emily quoted poets, authors, and the Bible with the obvious assumption that most of her readers were already familiar with the passages. We had to Google her sources and then figure out how to clarify without interrupting the flow of the story. Emily named one of the characters A.T. We decided that his middle name was Than, in honor of Emily's oldest son, Than Oscar Porter, who was Maya's father and my grandfather. Despite searching online and contacting libraries and historical societies in Maine, we never did figure out the full context for the phrase "the much-vaunted method of the idiot who found the mule." It's such a great phrase that we decided to leave it in, but if you know the back story, we'd love to hear from you.

I never knew my great-grandmother Emily, who died long before I was born. I didn't know my Aunt Maya very well, because we lived far apart, and most of my information about her was routed through my parents. Both of us regret that it took my parents' deaths for us to develop a meaningful relationship. Working on this book has led to wide-ranging discussions, and a deeper understanding of our family. Emily has changed from a picture and a name that didn't mean much to me into a real person whose strength and ambition I can claim as part of my heritage.

We are both grateful that we came to know Emily better through her manuscript. She was a talented writer and an interesting person. We hope you will enjoy her story as much as we did.

Barbara Moyer, 2018

1916, Maine

*O*utside a lighted window, a man stood in the falling snow. From the heat from a stove inside and the sheltering angle of the house where he stood, there was little frost on the panes to obstruct his view. Inside, a woman stood ironing a baby's dress. She used an old-fashioned sadiron that she heated on the top of the stove. She ironed upon a long padded board supported crazily by the back of a chair at one end and the tank of the stove at the other. A single electric light hung in the middle of the ceiling of the big room and from the chain pull a long cord hung low, so that a child might reach it.

The woman who ironed alone so late at night was pretty, strikingly so—golden hair, a clear pale skin, long-lashed hazel eyes. Her slender form drooped wearily at her task. Her glance turned often toward the door at the right, which opened onto the long piazza at the end of the house. Pausing, she turned toward the door that opened to admit a man, stamping the snow from his feet. The man was tall and broad of shoulder. His hair, under the close-fitting cap that he pushed back but did not remove from his head, was crisp and black. His eyes were steely blue, and his thin lips seemed turned to a perpetual sneer.

The woman faced him, her back to the window, her right hand close beside the iron, now merely warm.

The man spoke, and the words caused the woman's drooping shoulders to tense with wrath. He laughed and fury spurred her. Her right hand grasped the iron and hurled it with precision. It struck just back of the the man's *temple where the cap band was pushed away, and the man swayed and fell. The cord from the light caught on the man's clothing as he fell. The light went out. The watcher outside the window turned away.*

§ § §

Out there in the snow a boy was tramping home. The night had no terrors for him, snow and wind were nothing. Just ahead he heard a muffled shout. A man came staggering out from the snowveil, behind him two others intent on his capture. The boy flattened himself behind a telegraph pole. Little more than a rod away from him, as he hid there, he saw the foremost of the pursuers leap upon his quarry. The man who was just behind carried a blanket. As the attacker pulled himself away from his victim, the other threw the blanket about the prone figure, quiet for the moment. Then two horses loomed close in the dim light that snow sheds in the darkest night.

Swiftly the blanket was wrapped about the victim, now struggling and cursing. He was carried to the side of the road and as the horses came past was bundled unceremoniously upon the long sled they drew.

The horses were urged to a run and all vanished, phantom like, into the night.

The boy stood still, shivering. The horses had not worn bells. The men had not spoken, except the victim of the assault and his shouts and curses had been muffled by the blanket. The boy thought that he knew that muffled voice. And the man who had been driving the horses, who had taken no part in the fracas; the others had been a moving blur, but the driver had been more discernible, standing by himself at the front of the sled. The boy thought that he knew that figure, too. Ought he to have interfered? What could he have done—nothing, probably.

The boy resumed his homeward way.

Thanksgiving Eve, 1916

"Wouldn't this be a grand night for a murder, Tom?" Pearl Jameson teased her friend as she smiled at him in the wintry twilight.

"Hello there, Golden Glow. What's this about murder?" Tom Wells looked with quickening interest at the vivid face haloed with bright hair beneath a close white wool cap.

Pearl laughed. "A gloomy night like this always makes me think of murder. I can't imagine a murder on a bright clear day but a night like this seems just meant for it. Not," she continued half seriously, "that I plan to do any murders, even though I do know of one that would be a blessing right now," glancing at the blonde woman standing nearby.

"Outrageous girl. If a certain party ever is bumped off, I'll know where to look to get the reward."

With the twilight, soft flakes of snow were beginning to fall, and the wind, which had been silent for a time, was gathering its forces for a night of rioting. Thanksgiving eve it was, and the snow lay deep in woods and fields. The day had been overcast and gloomy. Now the storm was beginning.

"Thought I'd take a little trip to camp. Nothing much doing in town. Be back tomorrow maybe. Want to go for a sleigh ride?"

"I might," Pearl replied.

"It seems to me that you should have outgrown the urge to come and see the train pull in. I remember that you used to be one of the gang that pestered poor old Jim Wrayley's life out stealing rides on the hack, but I supposed city life had taken that all out of you."

"We did have fun, didn't we, riding down to the station and watching the train come in, but lots of things were fun when we were kids. I'm here to meet a friend."

"Man, woman, or child?"

"Man, a detec-tiff."

"Not really."

"Yeah, honest to goodness one, name of Adam Stillman, known to his friends as Standstill."

"Going to ride home in Jim's rig?"

"Yes. I thought he would like a new experience, and I'm not so keen about driving a horse as I used to be, got out of the way of it. The snow is deep for this time of year too."

"Two feet on the level in the woods. Deer all yarded. Not so good for lumbering. No frost under the snow."

"How long we have to wait?" Pearl asked.

"About fifteen minutes."

"Let's walk outside. The waiting room is cold and there's a woman in here, also your amiable cousin. I am not particular about seeing either, separately or together, especially together."

"Nor me. We might plot that murder while we walk."

They paced the platform together, the girl with the red hair whose three-buckled black overshoes' tops met the hem of a gray-green wool skirt, which she deemed modestly long while local opinion pronounced it indecently short, and the man with straight black hair who moved with the ease of well-trained muscles and the step of an Indian. His feet were shod in leather larrigans, moccasins whose laced tops reached his knees, and on his back snowshoes were slung, long finely balanced ones whose bows curved at the toes to a particular shape. As they walked their talk ranged from gay banter to bitter complaint and almost to anger, an anger directed not toward each other, but rather toward some common grievances.

Always the snow sifted down, throwing a shifting veil between the walkers and the dark trees on one hand, and softening the ugly outlines of the little station house and sheds on the other.

A whistle sounded in the distance and a great fiery eye came swiftly through a dark tunnel of forest and night. With a wave and a quick goodbye Tom started his hike to camp.

As the train puffed to a stop, Adam Stillman stepped down to the platform, greeting Pearl with a wide smile. "It's a long, long road from Portland, O Pearl of great price. Half a dozen traveling men, youngsters, a score coming home for a feed, a woman with a crying baby, two Canucks, jabbering the patois."

"What did you expect? Society gossip or the latest theory in ethics in a day coach on a rural train? Give your bag to Mr. Wrayley. We're going down on the hack."

"What ho, me dear. What ho, we ride in the chariot, midst the falling snow. It's grand to be out of the world like this. No crimes, no troubles. All is peace and prosperity."

"What nonsense, Adam. Tom Wells and I have just plotted a murder, and don't let anyone hear you make that speech about being out of the world. This, my boy, Edenville, Maine, in the County of Aroostook, is the hub of the universe, even though most of Boston and all of New York believe it to be a region of bears and wild Indians."

"We're going along to Uncle Joe's with you, Mr. Wrayley," Pearl said as the ancient charioteer settled himself in his seat at the front of his queer conveyance.

"This is different," said Adam. "A strange sort of limousine, a covered wagon on runners."

"Did you notice a woman there in the station waiting room?" Pearl asked.

"Large and fair, a bit like a parody of one of our blonde sirens?" replied Adam.

"The same, I know who she is. She's to be connected with our murder."

"Murder is not a joke, my dear young lady. You shouldn't speak so lightly about it."

"I know, Adam. I suppose I ought not to. It doesn't seem very real to me. I haven't had your close connection with it. I'm just like most everyday people. Murder is a fascinating subject, but one that doesn't come close to a girl who spends her days at a desk, watching for shoplifters.

"Well, here we are."

Adam looked about. The house, topping the hill and overlooking the straggling village, shrouded in the falling snow, was large and gaunt yet radiated hospitality, somewhat like a raw-boned country woman standing with welcoming arms outstretched. Light streamed from windows and an opened door.

Inside, Aunt Prue, Mrs. Prudence Leeds, bustled about. She was gray-haired, plump and apple-cheeked. Mr. Leeds, Uncle Joe to all the countryside, was curiously like her, after the fashion of some people who have lived together for many years, but his hair was snowy white, and his eyes a clean clear blue, while hers were hazel brown. Adam was introduced to Jack, a lad leaving boyhood but not yet a man, and Aggie, whose status appeared to be a blend of hired help and friend.

"It does seem good to see some folks around the table again," said Aunt Prue as they sat down to a steaming meal. "When there's just Joe and me besides Jack and Aggie, it seems as though there wasn't much use in cooking."

Adam Stillman smiled and looked about. This dining room was so plainly just a dining room, but comfortable and homey. Homey, that was the word; wainscot up to the chair rail; oatmeal paper above; a sideboard skillfully fashioned from native woods by Aunt Prue's father; the table about which they sat, of the extension variety now made small to practically no size at all, according to Mrs. Prudence Leeds' way of thinking. The room was a mixture of the old and the new, which because of innate good taste had become a blending instead of a jumble.

"I saw Tom Wells at the station," said Pearl. "He was going up to his camp on the West River."

"Why would anyone go to camp now?" Adam inquired.

"Tom goes up there every two or three weeks all winter, partly to see that everything is all right, and partly because he likes it, I think," said Uncle Joe. "The mill company has camps there and keeps a caretaker on the premises. He's old Charlie Gordon, a Canuck, but he'll be going out for Thanksgiving probably."

"By damn, hallelujah," murmured Jack, and reddened under the disapproving eye of Aggie.

"Charlie is rather picturesque," the older man agreed with Jack's implication. "Halleluhah is his favorite cuss word."

"I saw Leigh Wells at the station too, and a blonde, waiting for the Bangor train, at least I thought she was," Pearl continued. "I saw Leigh's rig—he still drives the sorrel mare, doesn't he?—hitched by the sheds; so I supposed he was coming back to town."

Aunt Prue's eyes snapped little sparks about the table. "That woman is a painted hussy, and Leigh Wells is a fool. It's no use for you to look at me that way, Joseph. And it's no use trying to cover up something that the whole town is talking about. You hear it everywhere you go. Leigh has a little shame left, but not much. Why do you suppose they aren't coming here for Thanksgiving dinner? I asked them, even if I shouldn't grieve if I never saw Leigh again, but Ellen made excuses, said Leigh thought they ought to have their Thanksgiving dinner at home, and it was a job to get the children ready. Stuff and nonsense! He's ashamed to face us after the way he has carried on all the fall, and Ellen is ashamed of him. I know it, and so do you, Joe Leeds, if you'll be honest enough to admit it."

Adam reflected: So, even here in this sleepy place they had the eternal triangle, always had, he supposed.

Aunt Prue turned to her guest. "Tom and Leigh Wells are cousins. Leigh's father brought them up. Tom's mother and father died when he was a baby. Ellen is our adopted daughter. She married Leigh five years ago. It's too bad to start you right off with a family scandal, but you'd have heard whispers anyway. Might just as well bring it right out in the open first thing. Ellen and Leigh live on the Well's place. Tom built himself a place on the back road that goes to the mill. Old Mitch Therault cooks for him and does chores. Tom is a lonesome sort and likes to live that way.

"Aggie, see if the pie is cool enough to eat."

The mince pie that Aggie had found to be the right temperature having been properly disposed of, Uncle Joe announced that he must go out for a time. His wife looked out through the top of a window pane, nearly covered with thin frost. "It does seem to me, Joseph, as though you might send Jack. He's young and will go out anyway."

"It won't be so bad once I'm out in it, and I have something to do that Jack can't attend to."

"Would I be any help?" asked Adam.

"You aren't used to this brand of weather. You'd better stick by the fire tonight. I'll be back in a little while."

Aggie, in the kitchen, was accompanying the dishwashing with a doleful dirge. "*This world's a wilderness of woe—*"

Pearl cast a look at the frosted panes and shivered. "Let's go in by the fireplace." But when they had settled about the fire for a comfortable evening, she fidgeted.

"Fiddlesticks, you need a dose of calomel. It's snowing and the wind is blowing some. If you think this is a bad night you should see a blizzard out west," Aunt Prue admonished.

Pearl did not wish to see a blizzard, out west or elsewhere. She was filled with foreboding, or was it only mince pie? Aunt Prue and Adam talked. She was giving him the history of the people and place. From the kitchen came faintly, like the wail of a demented ghost, "*To save a poor wretch like me.*"

From her despondent reveries, Pearl was roused by the voice of Aunt Prue. "Now, where did Jack go?"

"I heard him tell Aggie that he was going down to meet some of the boys. Do you want him for anything?"

"I just wondered. No, I don't want him. He's a good sort of boy. Old man Lawler's son, lives up on Rt. B. The old man's new wife doesn't like Jack. He's been with us about two years now."

"You seem addicted to taking in strays. Pearl is really your niece, isn't she?" Adam asked.

"Yes, Pearl is my sister's child. Joseph and I have to have our amusement and the good Lord never saw fit to send us any of our own. Pearl, you look as if you had lost your last friend. Whatever is the matter?"

"Melancholy has marked me for her own. I'm full of foreboding or mince pie or something. It takes me right in here," placing her hand over her heart and achieving such a look of tragedy that Adam laughed.

"I see there's a phonygraft over there in the corner. Let's dance."

"I thought it was sympathy I needed. Maybe it's just exercise." Pearl's spirits began to rise to the accompaniment of music and movement.

"Put on another record, a snappy one," she laughed as she turned to see Aggie in the doorway. Aggie, whose skirts modestly covered her high shoe tops, and whose face expressed stern disapproval. In the lull caused by her appearance, she spoke. "Do you know, Mrs. Leeds, that it's after ten o'clock and that hair-brained boy isn't home. Neither is Mr. Leeds."

"They will be back before long, I expect," said Aunt Prue. "Jack is likely playing checkers somewhere. Joseph is probably buying a Thanksgiving dinner for some of the mill workers with his right hand keeping his left hand in his pocket, so it won't know what he's doing. He loves to do it and I'm sure he can if he wants to. I shan't object. Come in, Aggie, and sit here with me. Pearl, why don't you make some fudge?"

"Is Aggie a servant or a protégée?" asked Adam, as he sat by the big range in the long low-ceiled kitchen watching Pearl deftly measure and mix.

"Both and neither. She's free, white, and I wouldn't like to state her age. There are no servants in Edenville. Aggie's been Aunt Prue's "hired girl" almost as long as I can remember. She gives me a pain, sometimes. I'm sure she was disappointed in love in her youth, if she had one."

Adam glanced at her in surprise.

"I'm being catty. Don't know what ails me. Aggie worries about my soul. She's afraid New York will ruin me if it hasn't already." Pearl switched topics suddenly. "I wonder if Ellen was able to get her shopping done. Perhaps I'd better call her." She went back to the telephone on the wall by the pantry and turned the crank on the box vigorously. In a few moments she was back by the fudge. "Ellen says that Leigh was to come home hours ago and let her have the horse to drive down and buy a few more things she wanted for tomorrow, but he hasn't come home. She says she'll get along somehow. Ugh, what a night, what a night for murder."

"Murder again, my dear Pearl? Something is really bothering you."

"I can't get Ellen off my mind. That's really the trouble with me. In the three days I've been home, I've gone there every day, although I haven't felt particularly welcome. Ellen is as close-mouthed as a steel trap. I know she's unhappy. I know Leigh is meaner than dirt. I know he is hateful to her, and I don't want her to cry on my shoulder, or anything like that, but I'd like to cheer her up a little if I could. Somebody ought to beat Leigh Wells. Somebody ought to knock some sense into him. Ellen is ten times too good for him. Now she has a little boy four years old and twins, a boy and a girl. They're about a year and a half old. Of course the children keep her tied to the house. But there isn't any need of it. It isn't as though they were poverty stricken. Even in New York they would be moderately well off. Leigh can be extremely pleasant when he wants to be and he's smart."

Pearl stopped her tirade to tend the fudge and Adam moved to the window to peer out through the frosted pane into the night.

"Tell me something more about this place. It interests me a lot," he said.

"There isn't much to tell; it's a hundred and forty miles north of Bangor; most of the folks farm on their own places; everyone raises potatoes, sells potatoes, or buys potatoes, eats potatoes, talks potatoes, except for the folks who work in the mill; and they only eat and talk."

"Is it a big mill?"

"No, rather small, hardwood flooring and novelties. But this mill is only one of the Wells mills.

"Eden Township is as big as any, but Edenville is small. One main street, the North Road, several tributaries leading to station, mill,

farms, or other towns. You see, the North Road was the highway before the railroad was built or even the mill—that's over the other side of
the railroad on the river—the older places, like this one and the Wells'
place were farm homes long before there was a village here."

Adam peered again through the window. How sane and wholesome
it was there in the warm, light kitchen, where an attractive maiden
poured creamy fudge into a gleaming pan. Surely, here was respite from
stress and trouble. Then, remembering the things he had heard during
the evening, he turned away from the window. Here all might be calm
and sanity; out there in the snow the same passions beat as in the great
city where he lived, differently dressed, differently expressed, basically
the same—envy, jealousy, greed, hate.

In the Snowy Night

It was nearly eleven o'clock when Jack came in and Uncle Joe was a bit later. Both the menfolks were silent and preoccupied. Uncle Joe's mood darkened with the news that Leigh had not returned home, but he said little.

Aunt Prue, who had begun to catch Aggie's fidgets, rolled up her knitting and declared that it was bedtime for everyone.

"Sorry to have been kept away all the evening," Uncle Joe told Adam as they stood a moment, reluctant to leave the cheerful blaze of the fire. "I'll have time to visit proper tomorrow, I hope."

Uncle Joe repaired to the kitchen, there to remove his snow-wet socks and felts, and put them to dry on the rack above a long rectangular register, placed there for the purpose. Joseph Leeds was an ardent exponent of the doctrine of comfort. He had designed and superintended the installation of the heating plant in the house, saying that he intended to have heat where he wanted it and when he wanted it. Wood was, to his thinking, the only fuel to use in a country where it was plentiful. The long old-fashioned kitchen had been remodeled and its working appliances grouped at one end. At the other, far from the range and the cooking, was this odd long register and above was placed the rack. It was a great convenience, for as Mrs. Prudence Leeds was wont to say, "When there's men folks or children around in the winter time, there's just a long procession of wet socks and mittens, and I do despise them under my nose all the time."

Adam, weary with his journey, retired gratefully to the comfort of an excellent mattress and a liberal supply of soft blankets and comforters. Jack had already instructed him in the mysterious ways of ventilation in the north. "You just put this inside window up a bit and open this slide in the outside one, you'll get plenty of air, and in the morning you just reverse the process and hop back into bed. Only, of course," he continued with some embarrassment, "you don't need to do it for yourself because I'll do it for you. You can stay in bed and sleep as long as you like." Adam did sleep, long and deeply.

But Pearl found sleep hard to woo. She lingered over her preparations for bed, and before she had performed the window rite, she heard the telephone ringing, one long ring, then two short ones—one long, two short. She went to her door and heard Uncle Joe cross the dining room as he came from the bedroom beyond it to answer the call. Hesitantly, she listened.

"He hasn't come in yet, you say? Well, I wouldn't worry. There's nothing you can do tonight. He'll get in all right. Yes... yes, I will. Good night."

Now, wondered Pearl, was that Ellen? It must have been. Poor Ellen, so obstinately or proudly silent about her troubles, acting as though Leigh's delinquencies did not matter to her at all. Ellen with her slender girlish figure, despite the three children she had borne. With her delicate features and golden curls, she had been a beautiful bride, full of happy plans for remaking the ancient Wells house into a wonderful home. Leigh had loved Ellen then, at least as much as men of his type love. But Uncle Joe, how he had hated giving Ellen in marriage to Leigh. He had never denied Ellen anything she desired, but he distrusted Leigh. So long as Ellen was happy, Uncle Joe's distrust and dislike had lain dormant.

It hadn't lasted long, this happiness. It was tarnished already by the time Peter was born. The baby had been only a bother to Leigh, something that took from him the wife he owned. He had begun then to go about with other women. On the summer day that the twins were born, Leigh was on a trip to Boston, a trip that could have easily been postponed. How worried Uncle Joe had been as they awaited word from Aunt Prue as to the results of Ellen's travail. He worked repairing the potato sprayer, but the hired man had fixed the sprayer afterward with never a word about Uncle Joe's bungling work.

There had been whispers that Leigh had a woman with him on the trip to Boston. Ellen had never admitted to hearing these whispers, but she could no longer keep up the pretense of not knowing. All she could do now was pretend that she didn't care. She must have been in sore straights before she would call Uncle Joe. It would seem to Ellen like a confession of failure. It would be sensible, but it would negate Ellen's determination to accomplish what some would call skinning her own skunk.

Pearl wished that Ellen was not so strange and quiet now. She wanted to offer to go and stay with her, only it wouldn't have seemed right to go and leave Adam when he had just come. She had thought she would ask Adam to go with her when she went over there and stayed with the children, but with the snow and Leigh not coming home and all— Absurd for Ellen to be so tied by the children, absurd for her to work so hard, to have no maid to help her care for that old house, absurd and wicked, yes wicked, she hoped something had happened to Leigh. She mustn't think that—she drifted into troubled dreams. Had she heard a door or was it just the frost and the wind in the bare branches outside her window? What time was it? She had only to pull on the light at the head of her bed to see, but she lay there in the dark and shivered slightly, listening.

Again she slept and waked, this time with a definite impression of something amiss. She put on the light, donned slippers and dressing gown and crept down the wide staircase. No sounds other than the sounds of the night came to her. She snapped on the light in the sitting room. The dead embers in the fireplace showed black wet spots where spits of falling snow had come down the chimney. That absurd wide chimney where Santa Claus might have come down, long ago when she had been a little girl and hung her stockings on the mantle there. There were fireplaces all over the house, and Uncle Joe kept them ready for use. "I know there's not much heat to a fire place and they take a lot of wood," he was wont to say, "but there's a sight of comfort in them and wood is plenty round here. I have a furnace for heat, but I like the fire to look at."

Pearl smiled at the empty fireplace and crossed to the dining room door. It was closed. Odd, she thought, this door is always open.

Cautiously she opened it and crossed to the door of the kitchen. She hoped no one would hear. It was so silly to be padding around in the cold winter night, for no reasonable cause.

The kitchen door stood ajar. Pearl pushed it open and turned the light switch on the wall of the short passage. The kitchen was warm, and Pearl reflected that if she had been dropped down from the sky in the darkness and landed in Aunt Prue's kitchen she would know where she was from the message to her nose. An aroma of spice and cleanliness was always exhaled from cupboards and drawers. Perhaps there was an odor of sanctity lent by Aggie's spirit lingering there. Even the smell of the drying woolens on their rack at the far end of the room had no power to disturb the serene atmosphere of this sanctum.

For an instant Pearl stood in the middle of the room, a sense of puzzlement holding her enthralled. What was there to have drawn her from her bed? Then she became alert; on the floor leading from the door that opened to the side porch and the yard were wet footprints, and on the drying rack hung a pair of woolen stockings, on which stood beads of water from freshly melted snow. Those stockings could not have been hanging there more than fifteen or twenty minutes.

As she stood in bemused wonderment, Pearl was startled by her aunt's voice. "Pearl, Pearl, whatever is the matter?"

"Nothing at all, Aunt Prue, don't get up. I just came down to get some soda. I have an attack of indigestion. No, it's not bad," she said, rattling the cans in the cupboard. "Just that pie for supper, I guess," selecting a cup and spoon and thinking that Aggie's mince pie seemed to be supplying a multitude of excuses.

"Well, get back to bed and if you want anything more do call Aggie or me, you'll get your death of cold padding around in the middle of the night and it won't help your stomach either. "

Pearl assented meekly and crept back to her room. She dissolved the soda in water, poured it down the washbowl wastepipe in the bathroom and placed the cup on the bedside table.

Again she wooed sleep with an uneasy mind. Huddled beneath the covers, she reasoned with herself. Why should she feel so disturbed? Nothing had happened, at least nothing to worry about. She had come home for this one week of Thanksgiving, had come partly because Adam had accepted her half-laughing invitation to come and see what a real northern Thanksgiving was like. "Thanksgiving," she had said, "Huh, what do you know about Thanksgiving? Sleep half the day, hotel food, a big dinner that tastes just like every dinner in a public eating place, a show the like of which you could see any day if you had the time and the price, a late supper and dancing or a dive somewhere to finish off with and a head the next morning." And he had said he was willing to be shown any sort of Thanksgiving she had in stock, and moreover that he would make the long trip from New York to see it. Then Adam had been unable to come with her but had insisted that he would join her. She had come home alone. She had been half glad of the chance to come by herself, to see her home and to judge how it would look to the eyes of a city man. It had mattered to her then that Adam might find it crude, might be bored.

But when she had arrived here, she had found a disturbing situation. Aunt Prue, audibly and righteously indignant at a condition of affairs that aroused her forthright soul to arms, Uncle Joe deeply troubled and anxious, because that situation involved Ellen, Ellen his foster daughter and the darling of his heart, for Ellen had always been Uncle Joe's favorite. And Tom Wells at home, Tom, tall, dark, silent and indianesque—one of the girls at school had coined that word. Tom had always stirred her imagination, but she told herself, he had never known that she was alive before, not really. And Tom was as bitter as Uncle Joe was troubled, because of Ellen, his cousin's wife, Ellen Wells, Ellen Leeds, Ellen Waugh, daughter of Conway Waugh, adventurer and probably criminal.

Pearl heard the clock in the hall strike three. Those were Uncle Joe's socks, on that rack drying, and they had been out in the snow, long after Uncle Joe had come in and gone to bed, once. Well what of it, what did it matter?

As though in recompense for her troubled night, sleep came to Pearl, deep and refreshing, a good sleep but a short one, she thought as she waked again in the dark to the jangle of the telephone bell, one long ring and two short ones, repeated stridently. She slipped to the door to hear Uncle Joe's voice saying, "Yes, Ellen, it's me. You say Leigh isn't home yet? I see, yes, never mind, I'll come over and tend the stock, yes, just as soon as I can harness up."

Pearl hesitated. Uncle Joe's voice had been so different this time, different from when he answered that other call, or was she just imagining that, was the other call, earlier in the night Ellen's call, or was there someone else who was worried and had called on Uncle Joe for comfort? Should she, Pearl, offer to go over to Ellen's with Uncle Joe? It would be the natural thing to do, but did she want to go? She went down softly to the dining room and called, "Uncle Joe, I heard you talking to Ellen. Do you think I'd better go over with you?"

Mr. Leeds came from the bedroom, clothed except for the heavy outer garments that Pearl knew hung in the kitchen. "No need for anyone else to go," he said almost brusquely. "Leigh has been out all night, and the baby has been croupy. Ellen is alone and worried. Leigh may have come home by the time I can get over there. It's been snowing all night and won't be so easy to get through. Prue would go, but I told her to stay in bed. That's what you'd better do, too. I'll call Jack to tend to the fires and the chores. I don't suppose there's anything much wrong. You'll have your young man to entertain, you know."

Pearl did not share in Uncle Joe' optimistic view. In the city, men stayed out all night sometimes, so she had understood, indeed five o'clock in the morning wasn't an hour to begin to worry much, but in the country, it just wasn't done. The blonde woman, now, she had been going away by train, but all women were not blonde, there was the little Italian girl Tom had been telling her about while they talked last night, while they talked about murder and Tom's cousin Leigh.

I Have Crushed Them

Adam awakened to find grey light filtering in at the window that had been closed, and rosy light glimmering from the fireplace where a fire had been lighted. "Service," he muttered. "Wouldn't you know it, get up, you lazybones, the family has doubtless eaten long since." He felt fit, fit for anything. He whistled in the bathroom, which was warm and white and clean. He greeted Pearl buoyantly, when he had descended the stairs, to find her waiting to have her breakfast with him. "Jolly, I call this, snow without and cheer within, I feel like a million dollars. Bring on your murders, old girl, bring 'um on singly or together in lots and watch me deal with the villains and villainesses."

He looked more keenly at the girl's shadowed face. "Oh, I say, I'm being a silly ass! I just seemed to get the atmosphere one is supposed to get in country places, I half fancied myself the young laird of the manor, or something like that. Is anything wrong, is anybody sick or anything?"

Aunt Prue came in from the kitchen in time to hear his question. "There's nothing happened that needs to interfere with a body's breakfast. It looks as though Leigh Wells had skipped out. He didn't come home last night, and of course Ellen is sick with worrying about him—him leaving her alone all night with fires to tend and a croupy baby to look after. It's the little girl, she's named after me—Aggie, are you bringing the coffee?"

"Is it so very unusual then for him to stay away from home all night?" asked Adam as he and Pearl sat down to their breakfast.

"It is not unheard of for Leigh Wells to stay away most of the night," Pearl answered, "even when he has told Ellen he would be home, but there seems to be no doubt that his present fancy left town last night, by herself; he hasn't been at any of the few places he might have gone, and the horse has come home by itself. I suppose half the town knows already that Ellen is worried. That's another thing. If anyone knew where Leigh was they would let Uncle Joe or Ellen know, unless they had an interest in keeping it quiet."

"You say," Adam continued, "that the horse came home by itself. Is that unusual?"

"Not unusual for this one. She's a mare and not young. It's not hard to train a young horse, especially a mare, to go home alone, and this one was taught to do it years ago. Lately she acquired the habit of coming home by herself when Leigh left her standing too long in the snow. Jack says she's done it a number of times. It's been rather a joke on Leigh, bandied about in certain circles. You see, he would drive to the home of the blonde one, on business of course—he gave her some sort of position in the mill office—and would blanket the mare and tie her to the fence. When the visit inside became too protracted, in the mare's opinion, she would break away and go home, leaving the gentleman to get home as best he could.

"She can't get into the stable after she gets home if the doors are closed, but there's a shed just beside the stable that has no doors and she finds shelter there until someone unharnesses her and puts her in."

"Why does he continue to drive her?" Adam asked.

"I understand that years ago when she was little more than a colt, she rebelled at punishment and nearly killed Leigh. After that he felt a great affection for her. It's a curious light on Leigh's character, if it's so. I don't vouch for the truth of it.

"Last night, she came home some time during the night. She was in the shed when Uncle Joe got there. The robes were carefully tucked down over the seat of the sleigh, the reins were carefully put up out of the way. The mare was blanketed just as she would have been if she had been left out while the driver went inside, and the halter rope had been cut."

"Ropes don't get cut accidentally. Did Ellen know the horse came home?"

"She says she didn't. The driveway is some little way from the house, so she likely didn't hear anything" Pearl speculated.

Adam responded, "It's most interesting, Pearl, most intriguing. What will be done about it?"

"Uncle Joe will ask A.T. when he comes up from Houlton today."

"Who's A.T.? Why will he be coming up here today?"

"He's Uncle Joe's brother and he'll be coming up to Thanksgiving dinner."

"Pearl, O Pearl of my world's oyster, you don't mean, you can't mean Arthur Than Leeds, past grand whachamacallit of all the lodges my boss belongs to, who was once attorney general of the state of Maine, and all that sort of thing?"

"That describes A.T. pretty well. I expect it's he and no other. He's supposed to be retired now. He says he's only going to work when he wants to, but he's in his office at his home almost every day."

"And he's coming here, and I'll have a chance to meet him and see him work on a case. You didn't tell me he was your uncle."

"He isn't my uncle, he's Uncle Joe's brother. I didn't know you knew anything about him, and there isn't any case, as you call it. Leigh Wells has done some erratic stunt. I hope you don't call that a 'case.'"

"Why, Pearl, who was moaning and groaning and saying hist and hark and murther, all the night long? Didn't you greet me with a plot for a murder on my arrival and keep it up all evening until I expected my dreams to be full of corpses and blood? They weren't though, I slept like a log."

"Oh, Adam, I could talk that way last night because it didn't seem like anything but talk, but now I'm afraid. I can't bear it if there is really a murder mixed up in our own family. Whatever would we do? Think of Aunt Prue and Uncle Joe and Ellen with three babies. I tell you it is horrible, I would much rather think that Leigh has just skipped, even with a woman."

"It isn't snowing very hard now," said Aunt Prue, coming briskly into the room, "and I think you two might go to church. Joseph can't go of course and Jack is busy, doing errands, and I think I will go over to Ellen's in a little while. The baby is better, but Ellen is all upset. I can't think what has got into her. Probably Leigh has left her and if he has she ought to keep Thanksgiving Day all her life."

"Some women don't feel that way about their husbands," ventured Adam.

"Some women are just born fools," countered Aunt Prue, "and Ellen isn't."

Pearl was peering out into the snow. "The storm is letting up, and the sidewalks will have been plowed. Would you like to go to church, Adam?"

"Sure, why not? If I can't do anything to help in the present difficulty. What about the inestimable Aggie? Church ought to be her strong point."

"Aggie is a Baptist, and the services at her church are this evening. We go to the Congregational Church at 10:30. It's now 9:30. We'll get back before the train is in that brings A.T., and I really don't see what you could do. It isn't as though this were New York, or any city for that matter, where you would know what machinery to put in motion for the tracing of missing persons—even then it isn't always successful, is it?"

"Often it's not, especially when the person doesn't want to be found."

Aunt Prue, responding to the note of weariness in Pearl's voice, looked at her from level bright eyes. "Now Pearl, you are worrying your head off just for nothing. I know I say more than I should, and you know that I'm the last person to wish harm to anyone, but, if any harm has come to anyone, it's better that it should be Leigh Wells than anyone else, according to my way of thinking. I don't believe for one minute that he's dead or even hurt. This is a lot of bother about nothing. You'll see, when A.T. gets to asking questions, you'll find that Leigh had plenty reason for leaving town.

"Now you just go along out and get your mothy ideas blown away. If you take Adam to church with you it will give the gossips an extra reason for thankfulness, though goodness knows they are having a feast today anyway."

Pearl was somewhat heartened by her aunt's sensible outlook. She reflected that if Uncle Joe had been out in the night, when the rest of the household thought him in bed, at least his wife would know about it, and if Aunt Prue thought it was all right—well, anyway, she would be glad to get out for a little.

Waiting beside the crackling fire in the living room for Pearl to complete her preparations for going out, Adam heard bells outside. Aunt Prue bustled to the door, opening it to admit a tall man, coated and capped in fur, with a baby in his arms. "Tom Wells, of all things, you've brought the children over here."

"Two of them," the tall man replied, giving the baby to Aunt Prue and turning back to the sleigh for the other child. "I brought Peter and Con over," lifting the four-year-old across the snowy porch steps. "Uncle Joe thought it would be better for Ellen, and the baby will sleep better if they're away."

With skilled fingers, he slipped the boy's cap from bright curls and unbuttoned the heavy coat that wrapped four-year-old Peter, a grave and responsible lad, who addressed Aunt Prue with serious mien, "My father has not come home. Mother is very worried, and baby Prue has croup."

The second edition of childhood, having emerged from its wrappings, entered a protest. "Tookie," he squalled, "Want tookie tookie." Peter rushed to the rescue. "Hush, Con, don't cry. Aggie's cookies!" Immediately Con wriggled from Aunt Prue's embrace, grasped his brother's hand, and the pair voyaged kitchenward.

Aunt Prue rose, arms filled with the cocoon wrappings. "You folks didn't meet last night, did you, but both know who the other one is, you needn't wait for a formal introduction before you speak."

Adam smiled widely. "Needed to wait for an opening. I heard Mrs. Leeds say your name as you came in, mine is Stillman, Adam Stillman. Pleased to meet you."

The tall man smiled, a smile that somehow seemed not to alter his expression of reserve, but before he could utter the words of greeting that were upon his lips Pearl entered the room. Inside the door she stopped, eyes wide with amazement. "Why-why," she gasped, "I thought, I thought, Uncle Joe had come back." She finished the remark rather lamely, Adam thought. She might have thought the sounds of arrival she had heard in her room upstairs had been Mr. Leeds. But her disturbed amazement at the sight of Tom being presented to Adam, seemed odd.

Whatever the remark Tom had intended to make might have been, he contented himself with a hearty handshake for Adam and observed that as they seemed about to start for church he would be glad to drive them there.

"Were you headed for church?" asked Adam curiously as they slipped along to the accompaniment of tinkling bells and the falling of a few feathery flakes which marked the passing of the storm.

"Me, to church?" replied Tom. "The congregation would swoon, I haven't been in a church for years."

"Come with us, Tom," said Pearl. "It is no more than fair for you to help keep the village tongues awag."

"You can't be much more of a stranger in church than I am," Adam observed, "especially at this particular church."

Tom made no reply, seeming wholly absorbed in negotiating the snowy canyon of the street.

Adam was interested in everything around him: a white earth and a gray sky, with feathers still floating now and then, feathers from the plumage of the great gray goose which soared above them, turning to white as they floated down; a red-haired girl, distraught, seeming almost as much a stranger as the silent fur-clothed man, guiding a primitive chariot toward the little church whose belfry spire loomed before them.

"You'll come, won't you, Tom?" Pearl urged, "We're just a little late and we won't go down to Aunt Prue's pew, we'll just slip in at the back."

"Yes." Tom blanketed the horse as he spoke his monosyllabic acceptance of the invitation.

Adam had been warned that he might find the service a bore, and had thought to use the time in sorting the impressions he had received of place and people alien to his mode of life, but he scarcely finished looking about him when his attention was caught by the preacher.

"The scripture lesson for today comes from the eighteenth Chapter of the Book of Psalms, beginning at the thirty-seventh verse. *'I have pursued mine enemies, and overtaken them: neither did I turn again till they were destroyed. I have crushed them that they were not able to rise: they are fallen under my feet.'*"

Gaunt and gray, like a prophet from out of the book before him, the minister's voice sounded trumpet-like, through the hushed aisles.
Adam's first reaction was amazement; had the virus of death by violence infected the whole region? Was this a Thanksgiving service? But the reading voice was magnetic; it drew the mind. Adam found himself giving strained attention.

"For thou hast girded me with strength unto the battle: thou hast subdued under me those that rose up against me. Thou hast also given me the necks of mine enemies; that I might destroy them that hate me. They cried, but there was none to save them: even unto the LORD, but he answered them not. Then did I beat them small as the dust before the wind: I did cast them out as the dirt in the streets.

"Here endeth the lesson."

Adam, released from his mental bondage, looked at his companions. Both were like figures of stone. Pearl's face was white, set in strained passivity. Tom's was merely impassive. Not strained, not stolid. Just impassive. Adam wondered, Were they enthralled, just as he had been until that moment, by the prophet in his pulpit, thundering of a matter near their hearts?

Just how the preacher had used the scripture to bring his hearers to a realization of the beneficence of the government under which they dwelt, and their duty of giving thanks, was vague in Adam's mind ever after. But the sonorous voice of the preacher thundering the Psalm made a deep impression on his memory. Long after that day he could hear that scripture with the ear of his inner mind.

After the closing hymn, Tom murmured something about getting the team and escaped from the crowd of neighbors and friends who bore down upon them. Adam and Pearl got away as soon as they could with some degree of politeness. They packed themselves snugly into the seat of the sleigh, and headed through the frosty air toward Aunt Prue's Thanksgiving dinner.

Shut the Door

The sun was breaking through the clouds as Pearl and Adam entered the Leeds home at noon on that queer Thanksgiving Day. Tom Wells had refused Pearl's invitation to come in saying that he would go back to Ellen's house and see what the latest news was there.

"But you will be back later, won't you?" Pearl had said. "Perhaps, after dinner," Tom had replied unemotionally, and had driven away with bells ajingle in the sparkling air.

Inside by the fire, sat a man. A man, not short and not tall, a man whose shoulders stooped a little under a black swallowtail coat, whose eyes were a shade darker than Uncle Joe's and looked keenly from beneath jutting brows. His face was deeply lined and his hair was an unruly black shock. Instantly Adam knew that this man was A.T.

"So you work for the Blackton Agency, under my old friend," said A.T., when introductions had been effected. "Well, we have a pretty problem before us right now. Perhaps you will give us some assistance."

"I'd be glad to help if I could, of course, but I doubt I will be able to assist much in a case where you are at work. Mr. Blackton says if we had men like you in New York we would double our captures and convictions."

"Um-m," murmured A.T. "I'm a mere country lawyer. I should be of but little use in New York, I think, but here, where I know my ground I ought to be able to do something."

"Isn't that overly modest for a former attorney general and sometime legislator?"

"Someone has told you things, young man," A.T. accused. "I admit that I am a has been. I'd rather be a has been than a hasn't been, if you please. So far I don't know what to think. We don't know very much yet, except that there seems to have been no way that Leigh Wells could have left town, and yet he isn't here, not here alive and in the flesh, at least."

"I am all at sea," confessed Adam. "If a man wanted to go away, he could go, couldn't he? Or he could hide somewhere."

"It isn't as easy as it sounds to do either of those things here. I called the mill offices," A.T. informed Adam. "There's only one man there today. He hadn't seen anything of Leigh. Henry Delong, the night watchman, doesn't have a telephone. He lives near the mill. We'll find out whether he has seen Leigh or not later in the day.

"I've been trying the much-vaunted method of the idiot who found the mule. So far it has only led me to a potato car.

"I've figured this way. I'm Leigh. I want to go away. I want to look upon the far places, the streets of Bangor, Portland, Boston, or even your great New York. I want to go secretly so that no tiresome business, which is going to pot anyway, nor the demands of a family may search me out and bring me back before I have had a fling.

"The falling snow has closed the highway for automobile travel until such time as the plow comes through. A horse is a vain hope for reaching my distant goal. There are no trains I can take without being observed. Returning to the trains, we know Leigh was at the station when the train you were on came in and that he didn't board it to go north. I asked the station agent and the train crew when I came up here this morning. The agent is equally certain that this man did not board the Bangor train, which bore the blonde, Miss Foote, southward.

"There were no other passenger trains until morning. Then there were the freights, one went north with mostly empty heaters and box cars, and one went south with potatoes, heater cars mostly, sealed and locked after they had been loaded. There were three or four lined cars. A lined car is an ordinary box car with the inside walls lined with boards and the space between the boards stuffed with sawdust. A stove is set up inside between the bins of potatoes at each end of the car and a man goes with the car to keep the fire going and to see that the potatoes don't freeze. If I can exchange places by fair means or foul with a man who is going out on a freight train with a lined potato car, I stand a slim chance. It's a regular business all up and down the line here. I must find out who sent out cars last night."

"I sent out the only lined car," Joseph Leeds said in his deliberate way.

"So," A.T. agreed, "That narrows our guessing."

"Now suppose you were a young man, well known all over this part of the county, who wanted to get out of the state for some reason or other. If you could manage to get to one of the smaller stations or side-tracks, and could arrange to change places with a man in charge of a car, you could get to Boston, maybe, but it wouldn't be an easy thing to do. No," A.T. continued reflectively, "it's a pretty theory but it would take a lot of doing. Besides, we don't know that Leigh Wells wanted to leave town. We don't know much anyway, but we will after dinner. Have you been in the kitchen, young man? If you haven't, come on, great doings. Aggie silent, not a hymn is to be heard. Prue is directing like the general before a great battle, and the youngsters are underfoot. It's the best place in the house right now. Come on."

"One thing puzzles me a lot just now," said Adam as he rose to follow the slightly stooped shoulders. "How did you know before you got here that anything had happened?"

Laughter twinkled for a moment in A.T.'s deep blue eyes, "Filius legibus best timeo malum temporem," he chanted in a high nasal singsong. "He didn't need to sign it Josephus. Schoolboy Latin, young man, just schoolboy Latin, in a telegram I had this morning. If it had come from Timbuctoo, I should have prepared to go there as soon as possible, and find out all I could on the way. The legibus is for the sake of euphony and the filius is not exact. It makes a useful code. Folks who don't know Latin can't read it at all, and folks who do think it is nonsense. Joe and I worked out a lot of codes when we were boys. Backwards talk, hog Latin, number codes, and others. If we have occasion to send a private telegram and can't remember the approximate Latin words we substitute hog Latin. Joe wasn't anxious to have any leaks of what is purely a family matter at present, and he wanted me to keep my eyes open."

Adam was conscious of being slightly let down. These men, who played such juvenile tricks as sending each other mysterious messages done in schoolboy style, who regarded the disappearance of a man as purely a family affair, were they really capable of unraveling an honest to goodness mystery if there was one, or were they merely children at heart who lived from day to day in a haphazard manner, and achieved a reputation? At least A.T. had one of a sort, by being lucky.

This undercurrent flowed through his mind during the visit to the kitchen, where things were going on much after the manner of A.T.'s prophecy. They gathered around the long table filled with an abundance of food. Baby Conner sat in a high chair. Peter sat on *Webster's Unabridged*. The turkey was roasted brown and stuffed with dressing made from Aunt Prue's family recipe. There was chicken pie, a blend of the sweetest meat and sauces between flakey crusts. The onions were dressed with country cream, potatoes were mashed white and fluffy. Deep golden Hubbard squash was mashed, creamed, and seasoned fit for a king. Deep red cranberry jelly and green tomato pickles made the previous fall, rolls light, hot, and toothsome, celery crisp and white from the trench in the vegetable cellar; there was much for which to give thanks. Dinner was a jolly affair, and gave no indication that any of the diners had anything to concern them except the excellence of the turkey and its accompanying dishes. At least it gave no such indication to Adam. For dessert there were pies—mince and pumpkin.

Prudence Leeds knew that her husband was desperately worried. Joseph Leeds knew that his brother was mulling over the answers he had been able to give to a few hurried questions, asked in the interim between Joe's arrival at the house and the call to sit up to dinner. Pearl's heart felt like lead, a weight that pressed against her breathing and made the swallowing of food and making of small talk difficult.

The sun slanted through the windows, glinting on the icy stalactites that adorned the eaves outside.

"Well, that's that," said A.T. with a sigh as the company arose from the table, "best meal I ever tasted, Prue."

"You say that every Thanksgiving day, Arthur," answered the lady of the house with a perceptible softening of her usual brisk manner.

"And it's true every time I say it, Prue. 'Tis Prudence prompts me by her deeds.'"

The men adjourned from dining room to living room. Adam smoked a cigarette. A.T. smoked a cigar. Uncle Joe did not smoke. He sat down wearily before the fire. "What's to be done, Arthur?" he asked quietly.

A.T. responded somewhat reluctantly, "The time has come to go forth to the search of the missing.

"Let's go about in the village seeking whom we may find, and what they know. From what you tell me I gather that the situation sums up to just this. Leigh Wells is not among us, and we desire to know his present location and state of being. Here comes my friend and pupil, Tom the silent, who spent last night deep in his native haunts. No use to ask him questions. He knows nothing of happenings in the town last night and would not tell us if he did, but he makes an excellent charioteer."

"Tom would talk if he knew anything that would help Ellen," said Uncle Joe. "Tom always thought a lot of Ellen."

"The Wells are deep and silent, at least Tom is," chuckled A.T., and again Adam felt that sense of being let down. He was half disgusted with the whole matter, nevertheless he wanted desperately to go on that questioning expedition.

As though divining his thoughts, A.T. turned from the window where he had been looking out across the snow. "Want to go along, young man? Want to see how the country folks elicit information from the local inhabitants?"

Adam flushed under the gaze of those deep-set blue eyes, but he answered steadily. "I would like to go along."

"Right. We'll take Joe's team and he and Tom can trail us. Right with you, Joe?"

Mr. Leeds nodded assent.

"Looks as though you might be spending a busman's holiday in this neck of the woods," A.T. remarked as the sleigh runners slipped through the snow.

The sunlight flooded the world with a wintry warmth. Houses appeared withdrawn and remote, clothed in ragged ermine mantles, unreal, like dwellings of mysterious and alien peoples. Children playing in the snow were little gnomes, misshapen, mischievous, their shouts and laughter mingled with the sleigh bells in eerie, almost sinister chorus.

Adam roused himself from the absorption of his half thoughts to reply.

"If it didn't seem so conceited, I might think you were all conspiring to stage a mystery for my benefit. Pearl met me at the station with a tale of dark deeds afoot, said she and the deep and silent Wells had plotted a murder, but she was quite cheerful about it, and I reproved her for her frivolous attitude. Then she went into a funk, for some reason I can't fathom, and now she seems bent on communication with her alleged co-plotter and seems to fear that the plot conceived in jest might have been carried out in fact. I suppose that people in this neck of the woods, as you call it, are much the same as people anywhere else but it all seems to me like a fantastic fairy tale in an effective setting."

"Try forgetting the stage for a minute and get down to cases. Start with Leigh Wells, a young man, manager and part owner of this mill here, doing a prosperous business in hardwood novelties. This mill is only one of half a dozen strung along the railroad in a hundred and fifty miles. The Wells interests are large in all of them, and the mills are only one string on their bow.

"Leigh was always conscious of the importance of the Wells, especially Leigh. He fancied himself as a strong man, taking advantage of all of a strong man's privileges, having a strong man's simplicity of outlook. In reality he was weak and vicious, mean and egotistical. Now he has suddenly dropped out of sight, vanished overnight from a place where everybody knows everyone else and more about the other fellow's business than the other fellow knows himself.

"Then there's Ellen."

Whatever revelation might have been made regarding Ellen Wells was lost in a sudden change of front. A.T. had driven down the long lane from the Leeds home and turned into the main street of the village. Just before them, on the sidewalk, half a dozen men lounged before the drug store window. A.T. stopped with a pull at the reins and a loud *whoa*. "Well, boys," he addressed the assemblage, carelessly, looking past them at the display in the drug store window, "What d'ya know?"

"Hello, A.T. How's tricks?" answered a thin man whose mackinaw coat, unbuttoned at the neck, showed a red and black plaid wool shirt.

"Fair to middlin'," A.T. responded.

The man in the plaid shirt moved closer and lowered his voice. "Tryin' to get a line on Leigh Wells?" he asked.

"I'm some curious about him, Paul. This," nodding toward Adam, "is the lad who is visiting up at Joe's place, name's Adam Stillman. Adam, this is Paul Spencer, deputy sheriff round these parts. Heard anything, Paul?"

"Not much, but it might be something. One of the boys saw him driving into the Mill Road last night along after ten o'clock. I figured he might have gone to the mill or he might have stopped at Delong's place. Might be that if we went over that way we could get some track of him."

"Not a bad idea," assented A.T.

Paul Spencer stuck himself to the side of the sleigh. At least it seemed to Adam that he did, and with a "So long, boys" to the group on the sidewalk, which had maintained a studious obliviousness of everything except their own affairs, the quest was again taken up.

Down Main Street, across a wooden bridge, far below which patches of black, swiftly moving water showed through the partial covering of ice and snow, up a hill, across Elm Street, short and tree shadowed, and into Mill Road, they trotted sharply; the deputy sheriff, perched upon the side of the sleigh like a grotesque genie, talking disjointedly to A.T., who grunted a comment now and then. The sound of bells behind them told Adam that Mr. Leeds and Tom Wells followed.

A few roads beyond the turn A.T. stopped the horse. "Looks like hard sledding," he observed.

"M-m," said Spencer. "Looks like they didn't break out this road today. We can make it, no drifts, I'll walk ahead. We'll stop at Delong's place. You know Leigh was pretty sweet on the Delong girl before the Foote woman cut her out."

While the mill buildings still loomed some distance before them, they came to a small, bleak, frame house close by the side of the road. Except for the smoke that spiraled now and then from the chimney at the back, the house looked untenanted. The depression in the snow that marked the path to the kitchen door was unbroken by recent footprints.

The door was flanked on either side by windows whose blinds were closed inside. As the men approached, Spencer, who was in the lead, stopped and pointed silently at one of the posts that supported a discouraged fence at the corner of the house. The fencepost bore its little tuft of snow undisturbed upon its top, but tied below was a bit of halter rope, and its free end had been cleanly cut.

A gentle knock upon the door brought no sound from within; neither did a brusque and heavy rapping. Spencer turned the knob and pushed open the door.

A man sat before the stove, feeding it fuel from a box at its side. He looked up as the men trooped in. "Shut the door," he said. "She's cold!"

The room was hot. It reeked with steam and the smell of burning wood mixed with a heavy acrid odor of burned cloth.

The man was nondescript—neutral skin, hair, and eyes merged with gray and faded clothing into a colorless whole. He shook as with a chill and stuffed the stove with another stick of wood.

"For Godsake, Henry, what ails you?" Spencer's careless manner was gone. His voice crackled in the dim room.

"S-hh," urged the man. "Shut the door. She's cold." Adam felt horror creeping along his spine. The man was daft. Across the room they could see, as their eyes became accustomed to the gloom, a narrow bed upon which lay the form of a girl. Blankets had been heaped upon her, leaving only the face upon the pillow uncovered. Rather a beautiful face, Adam thought, clustering dark hair around it. A still face, immobile and cold. Yes the girl was cold—cold and quite dead.

She's So Cold

Adam's glance strayed to the telephone on the wall. A.T. questioned Paul with a nod in the same direction. "No use," Paul answered, "only goes to the mill office. Suppose I take your team and go. Better than telephoning, anyway."

"Yes, we'll wait right here till you get back. Mind if I have a word with Henry while you're gone?"

"Good idea. I'll have to telephone to Sheriff Bruger and Doc Rush anyway," Paul answered.

The man by the fire who had appeared to take no notice of what was going on, muttered as Paul stepped outside, "Shut the door! She's cold."

The air in the room was close and oppressive. The men had only unbuttoned their overcoats, now they removed them. Adam and A.T. seated themselves in straight-backed kitchen chairs that they moved from their places at the kitchen table. Uncle Joe stood looking thoughtfully at the man by the fire. Tom Wells, his face somberly impassive, made coffee and placed a mug of the hot, black liquid on the shelf of the stove beside Henry Delong. Uncle Joe took the bowl of sugar from the table and said, "Do you drink your coffee with sugar, Henry?"

The man by the stove shook his head, and drank from the cup beside him absently, as though it were an involuntary act, a reflex.

"How did it happen, Henry?" asked A.T.

"I don't know," answered the man, tonelessly.

Tom Wells had slipped into the other room of the house and the air in the kitchen where the men sat was becoming cooler and cleaner. Adam looked about in horrified curiosity. It wasn't that they sat so calmly in the room with the dead girl and the man who was half insane. It was rather the queerness of the whole situation. It was bizarre, unreal. They had driven to a house to inquire about a missing man. Had found what appeared to be evidence of the man having been there. Had come upon the dead girl and this man, and now they sat quietly in a chamber of death and asked futile questions.

"What time did you get home this morning, Henry?"

"I don't know."

"About the usual time, was it?"

"I suppose so."

"Was Bea like this when you got here?"

"I don't know."

"Was anyone here when you got home?"

"No."

"Did you find Bea on the bed there?"

"I don't know."

A.T. leaned forward as spoke sharply. "Henry, Leigh Wells was here last night sometime. Did you know it?"

The question roused the drab little man, color crept into his face. He swore vindictively.

"No, I didn't know that black, -------- stinking sonuva had been here. I will kill him now. I will kill him like a rat. I'll burn his blasted mill to the ground."

"What has he done to you, Henry?"

"What has he done to me?" cried the man, his voice now shrilling to a scream. "He killed her. Killed my girl while I watched his mill. I knew he came here, I told him to keep away. Then I came home this morning to find her still and cold outside the door." His voice had sunk to the toneless level of his first answers, he sank back into lethargy. "Still and cold," he mumbled, "She was so cold."

In the silence that followed Adam heard as though it was some new foreign sound the steady tick, tock of the tin dipper clock on the shelf behind the stove. His eyes strayed about the room. He noted the stove, four covers, a reservoir for hot water at the back, a tank, he had heard the people call it, an iron tea kettle steaming lazily on the top, a shelf or hearth, knee high from the floor, in front of the fire box. He never remembered seeing a stove just like it. It stood to the left of the door through which they had entered, a long time ago it seemed. In front of the stove sat the silent drab man, sunk in his grief and hate. Behind the man, in the corner of the room were cupboards, tall cupboards, their lower sections jutting out in chests of drawers, the top of which made a space for cooking. Completing the circuit of the room his glance strayed over an iron sink, a door, a window, the table near which he sat, a table whose leaves dropped down on either side, hinged to the rest of the top. A red and white checked cloth was spread upon it. A sugar bowl, spoon holder, salt and pepper shakers of ugly glass sat in its exact center.

Then, on the side wall the couch, with its pitiful burden. Adam's eyes did not rest long there. He was not unaccustomed to death, even death in much more gruesome guise than this, but he felt a distinct uneasiness in looking on that calm cold face.

At the foot of the couch was the door, through which Tom Wells had gone to raise a window or open some other door. It stood half open and beyond it Adam could see part of the foot of a bed of white iron twisted in curlicues and whorls.

The glimpse into the room was blotted out by the figure of Tom Wells. He had come in as silently as though his feet had been shod in moccasins. Adam thought his face had darkened in its expression, if a face so immobile could be said to have expression.

The door from the outer world opened and Paul entered alone. "The doc can't get here for an hour," he said.

A.T. said, "I'll tell you what, Paul, let's go over to Leigh's place. Leigh Wells connects up with this somehow, and he's missing. You can tell Bruger that I'm looking for Leigh and asked you to help. We can be back here before Bruger arrives," he added grimly.

"Someone needs to stay with Henry," Joe said.

"Will you stay here, Tom?" asked Paul as the others put on their coats.

"Yes, I'll stay," Tom answered, not moving from the doorway.

A queer situation, Adam mused as they left the little house in its shroud of snow. A silent, inscrutable man, another man half mad from shock and grief, and a dead girl.

Again Adam found himself riding with A.T. in a world more unreal than before. The winter twilight was breathing a sharper chill into the air. The sun, low in the west, cast fantastic shadows. Even the voices of the bells seemed modulated to sadness. The row of electric lights along Main St. gleamed palely like stars come forth too soon.

"It is all only half real to me, still," he told A.T. moodily. "Do you think this Leigh Wells went there last nigh and killed this girl, unintentionally perhaps, and then got out of town somehow?"

"I'm not caring to think what happened, yet," said A.T. "I'm only feeling sorry for poor old Henry Delong."

"Not for the girl, only for the old man?"

"I'm sorry for the girl in a way, too, of course. It's a pity that she should have lived a short and unsatisfactory life, only to end it in such a way that she'll be remembered with the sort of pity that we are giving her now. But her father has lived an unsatisfactory life for twice as long, putting all his hopes on her, hoping to retrieve himself in her. He doesn't know it, of course. If you had asked him about it, any time in the past ten years, he wouldn't have known what you were talking about. We who live here, back in this corner of the world, are inarticulate.

"Do you know, young man, why I can swing a jury the way I want them to go, do you know why any man anywhere, can move men by speech? It is because I know the things these folks hold deep in their hearts, and can make them live in their minds. It is because any man who moves people by speech, speaks out the things they desire to think, so that he moves them. Only you must know the things men hold deep in their hearts, and present them in such a way that they will be glad that they are as they are, if you would have men agree with you. Henry Delong is a baffled unsuccessful man, condemned by his own inefficiency to be a night watchman in the plant of a man who circumstances placed in a position above him. He's fifty years old, a widower, and he had this one daughter.

"Beatrice was a good girl, ordinarily good, ordinarily smart. Given the right chance she would have married a man of her own caliber and they would have been moderately prosperous and contented. She didn't have that chance. Instead she had only the chance of marrying—if she did marry at all, and there is little chance to do anything else, for girls placed as Bea was—of marrying some boy of even less caliber than her own, having neither sins nor virtues sufficient to make him attractive. It is no wonder that she fell captive to Leigh Wells' bow and spear."

"But she knew he was a married man, didn't she?"

"Of course she knew it, but haven't you heard the lines married men hand out to girls? Since the time Lilith refused to submit to Adam men have been complaining, 'I'm unhappy, I'm misunderstood, my wife is cold, she no longer loves me, or if she does I'm tired of her.' Men string those lines in all corners of the world, and women are caught on them. Some of the women help the men string it and some of them string it for the men. It's another case of telling people what they want to believe. But I'm sorry for Henry."

"You don't think that Wells might have gone there last night and this Delong found him there and killed him, do you?" Adam propounded the question diffidently. He was quite sure that A.T. did not think so, but it seemed to him that there was some chance that it might have been the case.

"No, I don't think that's what happened. Henry would be very unlikely to come home from the mill, and he's not a killer."

"I thought he was rather wrought up to the point where he might become one, for just a minute this afternoon, and that he might be subject to those periods of excitement."

"Possible, but very unlikely. Besides he would have to dispose of the body, and I can't picture Henry Delong doing that."

"I noticed that it isn't so far to the river from his place."

"No it isn't a great way, but I can't see Henry dragging or carrying a dead man that far—alone."

"Suppose—here's an idea—suppose Wells comes there, expecting to find the girl alone. She's sick, and the old man hasn't gone to his work or has come back from it to see about her. The old man goes wild and raps Wells over the head with something and puts him out for keeps. Then when they find they have killed him, or the old man has, he and the girl, between them carry the body to the river and throw it in. I saw myself that there were only patches of surface ice. The girl is sick anyway and the exposure and shock are too much for her. Old Henry finds he has not only murdered his employer but killed his daughter as well. That would account for his being partially unbalanced from shock. God, that 'Shut the door. She's cold' got to sending the chills up my spine, and my spine isn't so sensitive either."

"It's plausible, but I don't think it's true. I only hope the sheriff doesn't think of it. He can't do anything anyway unless he finds the body. If the body were found in the river it would help support such a theory as that, but no body has been found yet and it's not much use to speculate on a murder unless you know it's been done, is it?

"We can't be sure that Leigh was there last night until we compare the pieces of the cut halter rope. You know of course that it will not do to jump to conclusions. When we meet the sheriff tomorrow—I doubt that he will be able to get here tonight—it would be better, I think, not to give him any ideas that the facts we already know will not bear out. He will have theories aplenty of his own, and will try to make his facts fit them. It's not his business to detect criminals, nor to be honest, is it mine, but since he makes it his business to detect, I shall make it mine to protect innocent persons from the harm his zeal may do them.

"He and the county and state attorneys have been elected by the better element. My son, beware the better element. They are much too apt to become self-righteous. Just ahead here is the Wells place. I want to see Ellen before Bruger does, but we'll only stay a few minutes. I want to get back to the Delong place by the time the doctor gets there."

"Is this doctor your coroner?"

"No, he doesn't act as a coroner. Bruger will bring Dr. Little, the county medical examiner with him, probably."

On the right, as they drove along, tall somber spruces threw long black shadows across the road. The twilight was opalescent and as they turned into the driveway, following the line of an untrimmed cedar hedge, the western sky before them showed streaks of slate gray, ruffled with amethyst and aquamarine, gifts of the setting sun.

The house was low and old-fashioned. A long shed connected it with the barn which was so big that it dwarfed the dwelling of the humans. Adam learned that this was typical of farm buildings at the time when hay and grain were stored in great quantities to feed stock through the long winters.

Someone had shoveled a path to door, which opened on a piazza at the side of the house. Joe stopped the horses to let A.T., Adam, and Paul Spencer alight and then led the teams into the shelter of the barn. A.T. knocked on the door. Pearl Jameson answered his knock, her bearing faintly hostile.

"You want to see Ellen, I suppose," she said as they entered the long, low ceilinged room. "I'll tell her you're here."

They stood, an awkward group, for a moment, looking at the wide boards of the floor. Then Ellen Wells entered.

She came from the room at the front of the house; her blue dress and golden hair were rumpled, her face showed traces of tears, but she was quite self-possessed. Her greeting for A.T. and Paul was friendly, and she was politely cordial to Adam.

"If you don't mind sitting in the kitchen," she said, "we won't disturb the baby. Mrs. Grimes has been helping me nurse her and she's sleeping quite well now."

"Do you think you could spare Mrs. Grimes, then?" Paul Spencer asked diffidently.

"Why, yes, I think so. What—"

But A.T. spoke quickly, "Ellen, Bruger will be up here in the morning to see if he can help find Leigh. Will you just tell us now, about last night?"

Adam saw a look of fear in Ellen's eye's. She looked past them as though searching, until Uncle Joe came in from the shed.

A quick glance that passed between Ellen and Uncle Joe, but Adam could not read its import; sympathy, encouragement, warning—it might have been any of them.

"I really don't know that there's anything to tell," said Ellen and her voice was steady. "Leigh stopped in at 11 o'clock and then was gone again about 15 minutes later. Little Prue had croup the rest of the night, so I didn't get much sleep."

"Do you usually wait up for Leigh?" asked A.T.

"No, but last night I thought he would be home early, he had said I might have the team to drive down and get some things at the stores. Then when he didn't come and I knew I couldn't get to the stores anyway, I just kept working around."

"Doing what?" The question was abrupt but A.T.'s voice was gentle.

"Mending and fixing the children's clothes. There's always so much of that to do when you have children, you know."

"Then early this morning, you telephoned to Joe?"

"Yes."

"You didn't telephone to anyone else, or see anyone else?"

"No."

"Why didn't you call the doctor, Ellen, if the baby was sick?"

"Leigh didn't believe in having the doctor every time anyone was a little bit sick. I knew he would be angry if I called the doctor."

"Then you expected him to come home?"

"Yes, I expected him all night."

It seemed to Adam that the big blue eyes widened yet more and that something of terror was hidden in their depth. Something she hasn't told, I suppose, or something she's lying about, he told himself.

A.T. rose, signifying that they should go. "That's all I wanted to know, Ellen," he said. "Bruger will want to know those things and maybe some others I didn't think of. If you answer him as clearly as you have me and remember that all he needs to know about or has any right to question you about is this disappearance of Leigh, it'll come out all right."

"Whoa!" was Adam's inner comment, "I should call that pretty plain."

"Oh, yes, Ellen, one thing more." A.T. twisted his soft felt hat diffidently. "Was there anything in your domestic life that would cause Leigh to leave you?"

"Nothing," answered Ellen.

"Umm... if you could spare Mrs. Grimes, Mrs. Wells, Dr. Rush would like to have me bring her over to Delong's place," Paul said.

"I'll let her go if they need her. Who's sick?"

"Henry's sick and Bea's dead," blurted the deputy sheriff. Then it did seem that nerves already strained taut would snap. Uncle Joe turned upon Paul, his mild eyes ablaze, but A.T.'s steady hand upon his arm quieted him. "It's just as well for you to know that, Ellen. We should have told you in any case before we left, although not so baldly perhaps. Now you know about it because Paul told you, when he came to get Mrs. Grimes to take her over to Delong's. Adam and I will be going along. Paul and Joe can wait and bring Mrs. Grimes with them."

Pearl, who had remained invisible since notifying Ellen of her callers, now came into the room for a word of farewell.

"You don't look like you're getting so terribly bored," she said to Adam. "Shall I be considered inhospitable if I leave you to the others tonight?"

"I shall be quite all right," said Adam. "Stay here if Mrs. Wells needs you, and I shall have your company another time."

"Beautifully put," retorted Pearl. "You needn't confess, I know you had forgotten all about me."

"Never," lied Adam. He was secretly amazed that what she had said was true. He had forgotten, temporarily of course, that Pearl existed. Night had come while they had been inside. A.T. slid the blanket from the horse's back with an expert touch. "We have to be getting along," he said, and forthwith getting along was what they proceeded to do.

They talked little as they sped along. A.T. only said, "I do hope Doc

Rush doesn't rush too fast," and chuckled at his own joke.

It was evident as they neared Delong's house that someone had arrived just before them. It proved to be the doctor and he was about to use the piece of rope that dangled from the fence post as an anchorage for his horse, as they drove up. "Don't do it, Doc," begged A.T.

"Why, A.T., what's the matter with it?"

"It may be important evidence, when the sheriff has seen it."

"That so? Well, they won't find my finger prints on it. I'm wearing gloves. What are you doing here, A.T.?"

"Just sticking around," replied A.T., and followed the doctor into the house.

In the hour or more that had passed since they had driven away, nothing appeared to have changed in that dreary room. Henry Delong still sat by the fire. Tom Wells sat by the table, and the dead girl lay on the narrow bed. Time or the coming of night had brought a calmness that was almost peace to the atmosphere. An oil lamp burned upon the table.

"Is Spencer bringing Mrs. Grimes over?" Dr. Rush asked A.T., having acknowledged Adam with a cordial if absent-minded handshake. "Well, I can't wait for her. I'll have to get on."

He went to the bed and stripped back the blankets. The dead girl was clothed in a nightgown, bloomers, stockings, overshoes, and a coat. The outer garments were damp. The doctor turned from the lifeless body and looked about him, puzzled.

"Henry," he said, "Where's the child?"

Searching

"Child?" Henry Delong repeated vacantly. "What child?"

"The baby Beatrice had last night," the doctor answered with calm directness.

Henry Delong, still sitting there by the fire was shaken as with a chill. "I didn't see no baby," he said.

Since the doctor's questions brought no explanation from Henry, A.T. told of the earlier outburst of speech, including Henry's belief that Leigh had a role in Beatrice's death.

Dr. Rush stated, "I can tell you right now without any further examination that Beatrice died from exposure, or the effects of it. You can see that she had been out in the snow. And I know that she has given birth to a child very recently, yesterday or last night, I think. If by some miracle the child is still alive, it has to be in this house or the barn."

Without further discussion, Adam, A.T., and Dr. Rush began a search of the property, while Tom searched the house and then joined the others outside. Though the chance of success was remote they hoped to at least find the child's body or some evidence of what happened. They found nothing.

Back in the house they resumed their discussion. A.T. mentioned the cut halter rope's part, or supposed part, in the night's misadventure—that its being there was their only ground for thinking that Leigh had been thereabout the night before.

"Mmm," Dr. Rush murmured, "I may be able to help you there. I had a call up the North Road at 10:30 last night. I met Leigh on the bridge, driving this way. He spoke to me, and I thought he seemed nervous. I wouldn't have thought anything about it, only that when I came back, I met him again on the bridge, going the opposite way and going as fast as he could. I yelled at him again and that time he didn't answer at all, just shoved along as fast as he could in the snow.

"It snowed pretty hard all the rest of the night, must have. There's a foot and a half more than there was yesterday, and at midnight there was only about six inches of it. It was snowing hard then.

"This," he continued with an abrupt change of subject, "looks to me like a case for the medical examiner. If the baby was born dead it's possible that she was temporarily insane and wandered out with the child and lost it in the snow. Or it might have been some way we can't guess yet. It isn't up to me to figure it out, anyway. It would be better to move her into the other room, but I want to leave things as nearly the way they are as I can for Dr. Little. This bed is narrow; I think we can move it right through that door."

The moving had been accomplished and a Morris chair of imitation oak, upholstered in a bilious green, had been brought into the kitchen when Joe, Paul Spencer, and Mrs. Grimes came. The doctor had taken Mrs. Grimes with him into that mysterious front room to talk to her privately, and Paul had asked Tom in a low voice if they had found anything. "Nothing I can find in the house or barn," Tom had answered, in a voice almost as monotonous as that of Henry Delong.

They had come away and left the quick and the dead in the care of the ample and efficient Mrs. Grimes.

The Leeds home, when the men approached it that night, stood like a haven of refuge from an unfriendly tossing sea of white. The gaunt old elm writhing in the rising wind only made the warmth and light inside more welcome. Supper was awaiting them, and with it Aunt Prue, sitting before the fire, with a book upon her knees.

"Well, for goodness sake," said she, as they straggled in having given the horse into the care of Jack, "you look completely beat out. What happened?"

A.T. briefly recounted the afternoon's discoveries.

"Dear, dear," murmured Aunt Prue, tears of quick sympathy in her eyes. "What a dreadful thing. Where's Tom?"

"He stayed at Delong's place. Said he was going home after he was sure there was nothing he could do there. Henry doesn't have any horse, you know."

"Set right up and have something to eat. I wish Tom had come over too, long enough to have supper. Aggie has gone to a prayer meeting. The children are asleep. I'll keep them here tonight."

"Food sounds good to me," averred A.T., "even though I didn't expect to be hungry again for a week after all that turkey, has it only been five hours ago? It doesn't seem possible."

Uncle Joe talked very little, and ate sparingly. A.T. talked much, although he too did not exhibit so much appetite as he professed.

Adam found his thoughts returning over and over to that moment in the lonely house in the snow, when the doctor had looked up from his cursory examination of the dead girl to ask about the child. Now they sat about Aunt Prue's dining table, attended by that good lady in person, Aggie having gone to attend her Thanksgiving prayer meeting. Jack, too, was absent and Adam might have felt himself very much an outsider, had it not been for the quiet way in which he was included in the family circle.

Seated once again before the fireplace, the talk turned inevitably to the subject uppermost in all minds—the dead girl, and the whereabouts of Leigh Wells, and the baby no one had seen. Adam was somewhat surprised to hear no words of condemnation for the dead girl. These were a Puritan people, he knew, and yet they were a kindly and charitable people, not at all like the popular idea of a narrow and righteous sect.

"You will stay over until this mess is cleared up, Arthur?" Aunt Prue's remark following a lull in the conversation, was both statement and question.

"I'll stay for a while, Prue. I hope we'll find some solution of the situation tomorrow, but that's not likely. Bruger will not welcome my assistance, but fortunately Tom and I fixed up a little deal, and as attorney for the Wells interests I'll be on deck for the search.

"I think," he continued, turning to Adam, "that if Joe introduces you to Bruger as a rising young detective from New York who is really quite dumb and can be shown up by a smart country man, he will take you on. No one can keep Joe out of anything anyway, and Paul and I won't give either of you away. I am assuming, of course, that you want to have a hand."

"I do, and if everything seems as strange to me tomorrow as it has today I'll be able to give a good imitation of a rather dumb city smarty, without having to make any effort except in the smarty line."

"You'll catch your stride tomorrow," A.T. prophesied. "The newness will have worn off the externals and you'll be able to grasp essentials." The conversation was interrupted by the advent of Aggie, an Aggie who bore all the earmarks of suppressed excitement. Her greeting to the group by the fire was sketchy and her manner begged Mrs. Leeds for speech, away from the opposite sex.

In the silence that fell upon the menfolks as Aunt Prue stepped through the door to the dining room, partially closing it behind her, Aggie's stage whisper was heard. "Miz Leeds, is it true that that Eyetalian girl was Leigh Wells' mistress and now she has killed herself and her baby to hide her shame?"

Mrs. Leeds did not trouble to whisper her reply. "Agnes Jones, you make me tired. You've been reading *Comfort*. Beatrice Delong was only half Italian. I can't imagine applying mistress to her and it's true that she's dead and no one knows what happened to the baby, but if anyone needs to hide their shame it's the people in a civilized community who let the poor girl die alone there. If you must gloat over it, go to bed and gloat by yourself. Goodnight."

"Aren't you a little hard on Aggie?" asked A.T. as Prue popped back into the room, her eyes snapping and her lips firm set. "After all, she's voicing the opinion of seventy-five percent of the people."

"Mistress, shame, poppycock," sputtered the good lady, "and Aggie, being smug and enjoying it. Joseph, you needn't look so downhearted. You can't be expected to look after every unfortunate in the county. You'd better get to bed too. It's time everyone went. We had all better get some rest. Tomorrow is another day."

Adam stood a moment at the window in his room before adjusting the ventilation system and peered through rifts in the frost coat at the world outside, a world of white and surprising beauty. The moon high in the heavens, infinitely distant, scudded through a drift of flying cloud. Its light seemed only an added whiteness from the snow. Afar, across the whiteness, stood spruce and fir, dead black like sketches done in India ink.

He thought of Pearl, (absurd name for a red-haired girl), and as he adjusted the blankets about his shoulders, he murmured, "Yes, tomorrow is another day."

Questioning

The household was up betimes, on that Friday morning. The sun shone. Aggie caroled in the kitchen, making pancakes, to the tune of "Onward Christian Soldiers."

As they were about to sit around the table, Jack came in from the kitchen and informed Uncle Joe that Ike Jennings was asking to speak to him.

"I have something to say to him, too," said Uncle Joe, shoving back the chair he was about to sit on, and hurrying to the kitchen. "Don't wait for me," he said over his shoulder.

Adam and A.T. attacked their pancakes.

Aunt Prue came out of the bedroom, the baby in her arms and Peter trotting by her side. She tied the baby into the high chair and helped Peter to his seat upon *Webster's Unabridged*, while good mornings were being exchanged.

"What did Ike Jennings want?" she asked when her husband had come back and helped himself to the hot fritters that Aggie provided.

"I expected Ike to go out with that car of potatoes Wednesday night, and he was unavoidably detained elsewhere, so he didn't go," Uncle Joe answered drily. "He came over to explain."

Aunt Prue, being a genuine country woman, was first concerned about the car of potatoes. "What did you do about the car then?" she asked.

"Telephoned to Harvey Monroe at Houlton and got him to take it from there."

"Do you know that Harvey took it?" A.T. broke in anxiously.

"I'm reasonably sure he did. He said he would and Harvey is dependable. Why?"

"I had a wild theory floating around in my head, but it is probably pretty wild and the morning train is just about in with Bruger and Little on it, I suppose. I think we had better get going and meet them at Delong's place. I figured that they would go there first and if they don't

Spencer will find some way to let me know. I've done Paul a good turn now and then," he explained to Adam, "and he doesn't care too much for Bruger's methods. A good lad, Paul, and reasonably clever."

Adam was inclined to agree with him. Paul Spencer, deputy sheriff, impressed him as a comprehending and likeable young man.

He was to have this impression strengthened during the day as he watched Burger. Paul was in the picture, quiet, unobtrusive, doing the right thing. Bruger was a man who might have been a success as a ward boss in some small city but was out of place in his present surroundings. His first move when he reached the Delong place, after a none-too-cordial greeting and acceptance of A.T.'s party, was an attempt to bully Henry Delong.

They had found things much as they had left them there except that Henry was lying back in the Morris chair and looked a trifle less dazed.

Dr. Little went into the front room to perform the duties of the medical examiner.

Bruger planted himself before Delong, his burly legs wide apart, and began. "Now, Delong, I want a straight story out of you. Who killed your girl?"

Spots of red appeared in Henry Delong's cheeks, but his voice was a colorless as ever. He sat straight up in the chair and answered, "Leigh Wells."

"How did he kill her?"

But that brief answer had been just a flash in the pan. Delong sank back into apathy. "She was so cold," he muttered.

The sheriff roared, his voice seeming to thunder in the small room. "How do you know he killed her? How do you know anyone killed her? Are you sure you didn't kill her yourself?"

"Yes."

"Yes, what? Yes, you did?"

A.T.'s voice, sharply cut across the torrent of words. "Go easy, sheriff, I'm Henry's attorney and I refuse to allow him to be led to make incriminating statements."

"He could say he didn't kill her, couldn't he?"

"Perhaps if you will let him he will make a statement. What about it, Henry? Begin with Wednesday night."

"I went to work Wednesday night the same as I always do. Bea said she wasn't feeling well and would go to bed early. I come home about daylight and she was there dead. She didn't speak nor move, and she was cold. I guess after that maybe I was seeing things, I don't just know what I done, only I got her on the bed there and made a fire."

"When was Leigh Wells here?" Bruger took over the questioning again.

"I don't know. I didn't see him."

"Then how do you know he was here? How do you know he killed the girl?"

"They said he was here. I know he killed her."

"I asked you if you knew he had been here."

Interpolated A.T., addressing the sheriff, "When Leigh's mare came home last night she had her halter on and the rope had been cut sharp off. There's a piece of halter rope, with the end cut hanging on a post out here. Doctor Rush met Leigh about midnight last night. He might have been coming from here. We don't know that he was here. We don't know where he is now."

"Do you think he killed the girl?" Bruger asked A.T.

"I have no opinion as to whether he did or didn't."

"Well, I have. I don't believe he did. I think this bird right here knows more than he's telling."

Dr. Little came out to make his report. He confirmed Dr. Rush's statement: Death had been due to exposure following the birth of a child. He said that because of the circumstances of the death, the cold where the body had lain for several hours, and the heat it had been subjected to for several more, it was difficult to determine the hour of death, but it was probably between the hours of one and three on Thursday morning. The child must have been born only two or three hours before the death of the mother, but he had found remarkably little evidence that a birth had taken place and speculated that Beatrice must have either burned some bedding or disposed of it outside. He could not say for sure whether the baby had been born in the house or somewhere else.

"I suppose you found no indications of any other cause of death. The girl hadn't taken poison or anything?" Bruger's question was intended to sound shrewdly impressive.

"Good God, no," answered the doctor impatiently. He was a big and bearlike man. Little was a misnomer.

"How much do you suppose it takes to kill a woman? This isn't a melodrama. It's plain everyday fact. There isn't the faintest sign of poison or of any external injury, no marks of blows, no bullet holes. The girl was confined, alone and under bad conditions. Then she put on clothes, I doubt that she had help even for that and went somewhere or came here in a blinding snowstorm. That much is plain to a fool. If it isn't cause enough for death, I don't know what is."

Bruger turned to his deputy. "Was this house searched yesterday?"

"Yes."

"Who searched it?"

"Tom Wells searched the house. He, Adam, A.T., and Dr. Rush searched outside."

"Tom Wells searched the house and Tom Wells stayed here alone with this Delong while you went riding around. You suspect Leigh Wells has been here and been up to some skullduggery and you give his cousin every opportunity to cover up his tracks. A hell of a fine deputy you are. Where is this Tom Wells?"

The door had opened silently as he talked and in answer to his question an even voice said, "Here, Mr. Bruger." ·

Bruger turned, amazement making his fleshy face clownish. He scowled. "What are you doing here?"

"I came over to see if there was anything I could do."

Paul Spencer saved the sheriff's face. "I hunted all over the place this

morning, and so did Mrs. Grimes. We found just nothing. If we're going to make a search for Leigh, Tom will be able to help. He knows all
the camps around here, and he can telephone to them from the mill. I
can go with him if you want me to."

It was quite clear that Bruger had little idea of just how to go about
a search for a man, dead or alive, in the vast snow-covered country all
about them. Clear, too, that he did not wish to acknowledge it. He
pondered the situation for several minutes.

"He can tell me first what he knows about the disappearance of his
cousin and *business associate.*" The last two words were an accusation.
One could not miss their meaning. But the impassivity of Tom Wells
was not ruffled. His voice was as even as when he told the sheriff that
he had known nothing of the disappearance until he had arrived at
Ellen's house on Thanksgiving morning, having spent the preceding
night at his camp up the line.

"Anybody with you at camp?"

"No. I met Charlie when I went in and when I came out I saw several
people at the siding."

"So you haven't any alibi for that night?"

"No."

"You could have been somewhere, helping this cousin of yours to get
out of the country?"

"It might have been possible."

"Were you?" The sheriff thrust forward his slightly recessive under
jaw, in a palpable effort at pugnacity.

"No."

"Well, you and Spencer can go do the telephoning. You can watch
each other. I don't trust either of ye."

"I'm leaving you right here, Henry, and you'd better not make any
move to git away. I'll see you again, before I'm through with ye. I'll
likely take ye back with me to board on the county."

Obeying a scarcely perceptible nod from A.T., Adam rode with the
sheriff toward the Wells home, A.T. and Uncle Joe following.

The sheriff talked. Adam gathered that he fancied himself a super sleuth and was pleased to have a chance to cover himself with glory. "We may be pretty slow around here, but we're sure, specially so since we got a good attorney. A. T. was great on prosecutin' so long as he was in office, but since he's bin out he is always defending some crook. Seems like the crooks don't hold any grudge against him either. They go to him and pay good money to be defended just as though he never had been attorney for the county and ridin' 'em hard. Looks funny, I say.—I ain't always lived around here, I been out and seen the world. But I don't put on airs. I'm as common as an old shoe."

"I'm sure of it, Sheriff," Adam agreed.

There was much more, of the same order. Adam listened with half his mind and busied the other half with thoughts.

The approach to the Wells place made under the brilliance of day lost much of its mystery but little of its gloom. The tall spruces, the somber cedar hedge, were still sinister.

This time they entered by the front door, a paneled door strong yet gracious, with narrow lights of glass down either side of the doorway. It was so elegant, Adam looked instinctively for a brass knocker, but there was none.

Ellen, wearing a fresh blue dress and with hair carefully arranged, ushered them into the living room at the left of the wide hall. Pearl sat near the ugly stove which had been installed before the bricked-up fireplace, with the baby in her arms. A stray sunbeam touched her ruddy hair, lighting it to flame. She looked weary, but she smiled, a secret satisfied smile. "A fire opal, not a pearl," sped through Adam's mind before he turned his attention to the interview between the sheriff and Ellen. Last night might have been a rehearsal, Adam thought. He caught again that secret glance between Ellen and Uncle Joe; more, he felt sure that A. T. had seen it and wondered if he understood more than Adam did.

When Bruger had finished his questions, even to the one about there being any misunderstanding that might cause Leigh to leave his home, and Ellen had answered, "Nothing," he had gone on with his investigation by requesting that he be allowed to search the house and barns. He had been embarrassed, almost apologetic, and Adam had wondered at this delicacy of feeling until he discovered that the embarrassment came from having no warrant for a search and being obliged to request permission instead of ordering the search to be made. It was just after the sheriff had made his request that Adam had intercepted the look.

"No need for us all tramping over your house, Ellen," A.T. had said, "Adam and I will just sit here until you get ready to go out to the barn. We want to see that halter when we go out there."

The search of the house was brief. The rooms were cold, and although the closets were huge old-fashioned affairs, convenient for the hiding of bodies, none were found, living or dead.

Ellen had accompanied the sheriff and Uncle Joe on their tour of the house but said she would rather stay inside than go to the barn, so the men had filed out of the back door of the kitchen and turned sharply to their right to go down a narrow flight of stairs into the woodshed. This shed was long, nearly thirty feet from the foot of the stairs where they stood, to the door at the other end which afforded entrance to the great barn. A narrow boardwalk extended along the right side and across the ends. At the left a small door opened from the walk at the near end and toward the far end were great doors that were rolled back for the annual storing of wood in the unfloored bay that occupied the greater part of the space.

"Say, Sheriff." A.T. halted their progress at the foot of the stairs, and his voice dropped to the tone of one conspirator consulting another. "You didn't search the cellar."

"We will, right now," Bruger affirmed and started back up the steps.

"No, no, not that way," insisted A.T. in a stage whisper, "we'll go in here." He opened a door at the back of the stairs and led them into damp darkness, striking matches, tiny flares that served to make the darkness deeper by contrast. "Hist," he said when they had made their way across one dark room, where the damp earth was soggy beneath their feet. "I'll turn on the light." He darted up stairs and turned the switch. One small bulb was lighted in the midst of yawning caverns of darkness, for the cellar extended under the entire house and had been divided into some half-dozen bins or rooms. An ancient and disused furnace occupied one end of the room in which they stood and the yawning openings about them had a shivery and unwholesome look.

Uncle Joe touched Adam's arm and together they moved to stand upon some planks close to the wall. A.T. was darting about peering into corners, lighting matches and holding them as near the cobwebbed beams above as he thought prudent, all the time, speaking in a husky whisper, "Look there, Bruger. What's that, Sheriff, 'Hush, how like a tomb?'" Adam felt again that slackening of admiration, that sense of being let down.

"What does he do it for?" Adam whispered the question.

"Partly because he enjoys it, and partly because he wants Bruger to think he's a fool," replied Uncle Joe in the same way.

Tired of his buffoonery, at length, A.T. announced, "Nothing here," and led them back to the shed. "I'll tell Ellen to put that light off," he said and went up the steps to the kitchen.

Uncle Joe led the way along the walk at the side of the shed. Just before they reached the barn they passed a door in the wall. The door was on their right and was closed. Bruger stopped and regarded it. "Where does that go?"

"Just out into the grove there," Uncle Joe told him. "It isn't used very much, even in the summer time." Bruger turned the latch and pushed, but the door stuck at the bottom. A more determined push sent the snow down upon his head as the door opened so suddenly as almost to precipitate the sheriff into the drift beyond it. Bruger closed the door in no better humor than before. A.T. joined them as they entered the barn.

"Before we look in all the cow cribs, Sheriff, let's take a look at that halter with the cut rope. Where did you put it, Joe?"

"I hung it on a hook back of the stall here," said Uncle Joe leading them to where the horse had stood. "I didn't think then that we would find the other piece of rope so soon." The light was not very good there in the stable and Uncle Joe looked, and looked again, at the hook where he had hung the halter, before he stammered, "It-it's gone."

"Think, Joe," begged A.T., "are you sure you put it there? We'll have a look for it anyway. Where did you hang the harness?"

But diligent search through the big dim lit barn did not disclose a halter with a cut rope.

The Smell of Death

The sheriff roared uncomplimentary observations on all the stupid folks who dwell in the country. Uncle Joe stood peering about in puzzled wonderment, saying, "It was here. I swear I left it hanging on that hook."

"Where anybody that took a notion could have taken it," Bruger said sourly.

"Who does Leigh's chores?" A.T. asked.

"Old Mitch Theirdult," his brother replied. A.T. nodded reflectively. "Mitch cooks for Tom, doesn't he?"

"Yes, he lives at Tom's place and comes over here to tend to things."

"Tend to things," sneered Bruger, "Whadya mean, tend to things?" It was evident that he knew A.T. had been having a little fun with him back there in the cellar, and that he was half afraid someone was trying to put over a more subtle hoax now. A.T. answered calmly, "Curry the cow, comb the horse, milk the hens, and do a bit of dusting now and then. You know, Bruger, some of your travels must have led you through common barns and stables. Were you never a simple farmer lad, up with the pigs in the morning and down with the chickens at night?"

Uncle Joe, feeling that the baiting of Bruger had gone far enough, filled the pause in his brother's question by asking one himself. "Shall I go over and ask Mitch to come here?"

"No." Bruger was suspicious of everyone now. "I'm going to run the rest of this investigation. There has been bungling enough. How do you get to this other Wells castle? This one is a swell dump, I'll say not."

Uncle Joe's face flushed, but he made no answer. There was no need. A.T. was as ever quick with words, and his manner was bland, almost to the point of approbation. "Just around the corner, Sheriff, you will find a beaten path. I don't know that Tom or his henchman make mousetraps, but the path will take you to their door." He pushed one of the big awkward doors open a little way and stepped back, bowing low and murmuring, "After you, my dear sir."

The snow in front of the big doors had been trampled and pushed aside so that a space was comparatively clear, but at the corner of the barn around which the path was supposed to be was a drift waist high. Bruger eyed it unfavorably. A.T. continued to be blandly urgent. A.T. wore overshoes and, after the manner of countrymen, had tucked the bottoms of his trousers legs well inside their tops. Bruger also wore overshoes but after the manner of the town dweller who seldom wades in deep snow, he had not jeopardized the crease in his trousers by tucking them into his boot tops. He hesitated to wade into the drift. "Are you sure there's a path?" he asked of Uncle Joe. "Yes," said Uncle Joe, "Just around the corner there."

"I'm coming, Sheriff, and you're a younger man than I am," A.T. insisted.

Bruger undoubtedly suspected that he was being made the goat, but the challenge in A.T.'s manner was not to be refused. Scorning to change the arrangement of his trouser legs he plunged into the drift and struggled through, half buried in the cold smother of light snow. A.T. followed.

Uncle Joe and Adam, standing by the big door, heard the sheriff's harsh voice say, "We could have come out that door there and been right on the path, and I believe you knew it." And A.T.'s surprised answer. "Why, so we could, Bruger, I must have forgotten that door. I always go this way."

Uncle Joe chuckled and led the way back into the stable to a small door in the west wall. He opened it inward and disclosed a path across a snowy field. Trees masked the far end of the path and through them could be seen dimly the outlines of a small house.

"Bruger isn't really the fool he's appeared to be today." Uncle Joe spoke in apology for the man who had treated him with so little consideration. "Arthur rubs him the wrong way, just as he irritates Arthur. Then he envies Arthur his hold on the people of the county, who would have kept him in office, if he had been willing to stay. The man who was sheriff when Arthur was attorney for the county had died, and Bruger is popular with enough people to elect, or so it seems at least."

"There would have been a lot of friction with Bruger as sheriff and Arthur as county attorney. There is going to be a lot of friction anyway, looks like."

"What's your county attorney like?" Adam was only mildly interested in the answer to his question but much interested in the answerer. The great shadowy barn, with its lofts for hay, now almost empty, its long row of stalls for horses and tie-up for cows, with only one gentle-eyed jersey and the mare that Leigh Wells had driven on that strange Thanksgiving eve, was, he reflected, a fitting background for this man. Both symbolized a passing order.

"This new man is all right," Uncle Joe said slowly. "He is an able man in prosecution and aims to be a terror to wrongdoers."

They had turned from the dimness inside and now stood outside of the great doors, doors through which racks loaded high with hay had often passed in the days when the Wells farmlands had been broad and the lumber business only an adjunct to farming. The climbing sun was melting, ever so little, the snow where they stood.

A grotesque figure, human or not Adam could only conjecture, emerged from the edge of the woodland that stretched away to the westward, and waddled across the broad white field in their direction. Watching, Adam saw the figure resolve itself into that of a woman, old, broad of figure with a breadth which came of petticoats and outer garments, hunched up to avoid the snow. Socks of white wool and men's boots covered her feet and her waddling walk was the result of wide-toed snowshoes on which she traveled atop the drifts like a misshapen, web-footed bird.

"Who and what is that? Am I seeing things?"

"Just Hulda, an old woman who lives by herself in the woods. She's a bit cracked, but harmless."

Adam shuddered. Something in the old hag's approach bred distrust, but Uncle Joe seemed to think he had given a full explanation of her and Adam would not ask the questions that filled his mind.

Hulda came to the edge of the driveway, and Adam saw that her face was tanned and shriveled into a thousand wrinkles, but that her hair was dark and abundant, covered by a woolen "fascinator" the top of which was decorated with glass beads. In one hand she carried a stout staff or cane, and under her other arm was tucked a woolly white poodle.

She put the little dog down upon the snow, bidding it not to stray in the tone one uses to a child, then she turned upon the men and spoke in a sharp shrill voice, "I smell death," she said. "This place reeks of it, the very trees stink with it, you smell of it too, Joe. Who's dead?"

The sheriff and A.T. came in through the stable door. With them came Mitch, little, old, bent, skinny.

As though their coming was a cue for the actors to assemble, Tom Wells and Paul Spencer drove into the yard, and looking over his shoulder, half blinded by the sunlight on the snow, Adam saw Ellen's golden head and Pearl's flaming locks advancing from the gloom of the shed. Hulda leaned on her stick and looked about her, a malevolent norn, spinning destinies for all of them. She reiterated her query, high and shrill, "Who's dead?"

"Beatrice Delong is dead, Hulda," A.T. answered, "and we suppose her baby is. We haven't found it."

"A girl and a baby, over there," she replied, nodding vaguely in the direction of the Delong place. "But I smell death here. Toto smells death, too," she said, looking at the dog cowering against her boots.

Ellen's face was as bloodless as the snow about them. Uncle Joe had moved to her side. Tom Wells stepped from the sleigh as though he, too, would stand there. The others were like people bewitched. Hulda's eyes were on Ellen. It was as though she pointed at her with a flaming sword. "Where's your husband?" she shrilled, and Ellen's voice whispered, like the ghostly echo of the voice of Henry Delong, "I don't know, I don't know."

"He's dead," cackled Hulda. "He's dead. Some of you know it already. Some of you fear it and some of you hope it. The smell of death hangs around those black spruces a long time, when it's sudden death, sudden and cruel murder."

She stooped and gathered the little white fuzzy dog in her arms.

"I need some grain for my hens," she remarked conversationally.

"I'll leave some just as soon as I have a chance," Tom Wells answered in the same way.

Hulda turned and walked toward the woods from which she had come. Once more the sun shone on a commonplace dooryard and a group of people waking from amazed unreality. Ellen and Pearl turned back to the house, speaking no words of greeting or farewell to the men there. Bruger had nothing to say. Even A.T. seemed bereft of ready speech. Only Mitch muttered under his breath, "Sacre," more muttering, "Mo Je" and a low murmur, "Nom d—"

Bruger turned to him, fiercely, "Shut off that, you old goat, and tell us what you did with the halter Mister Leeds says he hung there on a harness hook."

"Halter, I have not seen heem."

"If it ever hung there you must have seen heem."

"Ef Mist' Oncle Joe say he hang, he hang. I have not seen heem."

"And if I had my way, all you birds who don't know a thing and haven't seen a thing would spend enough time in jail to remember what has happened in the last day or two. Spencer, we're just wasting time, asking questions. What about getting some real men and doing some hunting on our own? Hunting," he continued, "for a dead man, not for a halter that likely never was here at all."

"Pooh, Bruger," A.T. scoffed, "What reason have you for looking for a dead man? You surely don't accept Hulda's pronouncement as gospel."

"Maybe I don't. But you've got to admit that Hulda's the only person yet who has any information to give out. What she says about Leigh being dead sounds reasonable to me. You yourself said that it would have been hard for him to leave. Maybe the old lady was right, too, when she said some of you knew he was dead and all that. I've had that idea all along. That's why I searched the premises. I can't see that any of you have been lending much of a hand."

"Now that's where you're wrong, Bruger. We're just as anxious to find Leigh as you are. As to Hulda's rigamarole, it isn't worth so much as the wind that blew it away. You sorta surprise me, sheriff, jumping to conclusions as you do. I only said I didn't see how Leigh could have got away."

"Well he ain't here anyway. And it's dollars to doughnuts that he is buried somewhere under this snow. Come on, Paul."

Bruger and Spencer departed to organize their hunt. Uncle Joe, Tom, and Mitch went into the house. A.T. stood in the big barn doorway, his face puckered in a frown of concentration. Adam watched him.

A.T. plucked his soft felt hat from his head, ran his fingers through his dark thatch of hair, and patted his head thoughtfully before replacing his headgear. He went to the grainery, now converted to a garage and returned with a jointed rule. Adam followed him to the open wagon shed where the sleigh that Leigh had used Thanksgiving eve still stood.

It was, he pointed out to Adam, a sleigh and not a pung. "A pung," he said, "is a lowly vehicle. It is little more than a sled with a low body and a seat or seats. We came over here in a double-seated pung. The names are used frequently without discrimination, just as 'team' is used to designate any sort or rig. We even say horse and team sometimes. We are a curious folk and often say what we do not mean and keep the things we mean to ourselves. But I don't think that we are as mean as Bruger makes out. Now this vehicle has not been disturbed since Joe found it here. I thought the sheriff might look it over, but since it has no interest for him, suppose we see what it can tell us."

Adam said, "It's too bad it was snowing so hard that the tracks were covered."

"True enough," said A.T., but there are other ways of guessing how far the mare traveled." A.T. then poked the rule in at several places, and found the snow covering the seat to be about 2 inches thick. "Now," he said, "here is a little problem of natural science. About 15 inches of snow fell between eight o'clock Wednesday evening and eight o'clock Thursday morning. But as you know, it wasn't snowing hard when you arrived, and Joe said it had let up considerably when he came over here at five o'clock. Rush says it was snowing hard at midnight when he met

Leigh on the bridge. If we say two inches per hour between midnight and four in the morning we won't be entirely out of reckoning. Allowing for some snow to have melted and settled down, I would estimate it was something over an hour from when these robes were spread over the seat until the mare got home and sheltered herself here. Five miles an hour is a liberal estimate of travel for the mare as conditions were that night. Therefore, it seems to indicate that Leigh left the team and sent the mare home at some point, and that point should be in a radius approximately five miles from this spot.

"And to what conclusion does that lead?" Adam asked.

"It leads to nothing as strong as a conclusion. It is another variation of the idiot-donkey method which lead me to the box car. That theory seems to be a washout, though there are points about it that still intrigue me. Assuming that Leigh drove his team to some point five miles or a bit more, we draw a circle. First to the north, since Leigh was going that way. Nothing there except farmhouses. I can see nothing there that would draw him in that direction. To the east, if he turned off the North road in that direction, is Canada. A lonely point in the province of New Brunswick. He might have crossed over at night without being observed at the border. But where he would go in the middle of a stormy night, on foot, in a country where houses are more scattered than on this side of the line, is beyond the imagination of an idiot. Well, unless he had arranged to meet someone, but then why the secrecy and the midnight departure? South the same conditions prevail as to the north, and west are woods and more woods. Unless he went to one of the lumber camps, I doubt he went that way.

"If it were Tom we were trying to trace, west would be the proper direction to look. Tom, if he were fleeing, would take to the woods. It would be possible for a woodsman to travel right through to Quebec. Few would like to try it though, and certainly not Leigh."

Adam looked to the west. A little way beyond the railroad tracks, fields gave way to forests clothing ridge after ridge of hills. The hills grew into low mountains where they met the sky. In the heat of summer, they might call, invite. In the cold of winter, they would have little allure to a man such as Leigh.

Pearl came out clothed for the outer world. "Uncle Joe is going to stay with Ellen," she said. "I'm going to go back home with you for lunch."

"Dinner, young lady, dinner," A.T. corrected. "Don't try to show off your sophisticated city ways. You breakfasted this morning. You dine at noon. When the afternoon is past you have supper."

"I'm squelched," Pearl said, "I am obliterated. I stand corrected."

"Apology accepted." A.T. strutted toward the team. "How is Ellen feeling now?"

"She was greatly disturbed by Hulda's talk. Much more than she needs to be, it seems to me. No one pays much attention to what Hulda says."

"Bruger, our excellent sheriff, was impressed," A.T. said. "He thought her assertions sound. He allowed that they coincided with his own ideas on the subject of Leigh."

"She was impressive in a way," Adam said. "Now Pearl, don't sniff disdainfully. I only meant that as a scene her act was good. In a show, it would go over big. But who or what is she? Is she insane?"

A.T. answered, "Who is really sane and who is not is a question that cannot be answered in this world. Sometimes I think that a lunacy commission, if such a thing could be found, would find two thirds of the people in the world a wee bit off center. Hulda is just a queer old woman. If she were moderately wealthy she would be eccentric. As it is, she is merely ex centric.

"Let's wash his face in snow, Adam," Pearl said. "That remedy is old fashioned enough for even A.T."

"He should be punished," Adam agreed and laughed. He had always disdained plays on words as a cheap form of wit.

"I am punished," A.T. said serenely.

No. 3 Camp

Tom Wells approached as the three were laughing and diffidently suggested to Adam that he could ride with him to check out the No. 3 camp. "Perhaps you would like to come down to my place for dinner. It's getting along toward noon, and Mitch here can fix us something. Cooking is his business."

Adam was of two minds. He would like to share Pearl's company. He was really her guest. But there was an appeal in the idea of fresh contact with Tom of the reserved silence. This seemed to be a heaven-sent opportunity. "Will you make my excuses to Mrs. Leeds, and accept them yourself, if I go with Wells?" he asked Pearl.

"Yes, we will excuse you, and perhaps Tom will come with you and have supper with us. Aunt Prue wanted you to come last night, Tom. She will expect you tonight."

"Mitch can go back by the path," Tom said, "but we'll drive around by the road."

Driving around by the road proved to be taking the way they had come from the Delong place, past that small and secretive dwelling standing amid the snow banks, across a little bridge that spanned a brook and left into a road that paralleled the brook. They had come, Tom explained, around or nearly around a rough square. The path to the big barn cut off the remaining corner. To their right, the railroad ran and beyond were forest, hill, and stream, broken only by the mill, behind them, with its yards and tracks, and deep in the forest the woodsmen's camps and cuttings.

The house faced the railroad track and the forest. At its back was the brook and the grove that nearly filled the square around which they had come.

The house was small, square, comfortable, and attractive. Shingled and stained a weathered grey, its exterior blended with its setting of trees, so that it seemed to be akin to them, a growth of the forest. The inside, too, was like a camp in the woods, but a surprisingly luxurious one. It spoke of ample means, and the exercise of good taste in their use. More than ever, Adam was puzzled, puzzled and intrigued by the situation. Here was a man who was, so far as Adam had heard, not wealthy, but doing himself rather well in the way of comfortable living, and back there in the house which "reeked of death" lived the family of a man who was if not extremely wealthy at least well up in the ranks of the well to do. What was it Pearl had said that first night when she talked of Ellen and Leigh? That they would be counted as wealthy even in New York.

Adam wondered if it would be politic to ask Tom about the woman they called Hulda. His host seemed to be in what was for him a genial and responsive mood. He had answered questions without reserve and had even volunteered several bits of information about local matters.

"Yes," he said in answer to the question Adam finally asked, "Hulda has lived down there in the woods alone as long as I can remember. She always carried that cane and many a time have I run from it, when I was a boy. We used to make fun of her after the manner of children, used to yell after her, and whistle at her dog. She always had a dog, a little dog. She has some sort of romantic life story I understand, and she didn't always live alone. She gets more and more peculiar as she gets older, and she was old when I was a boy. Nobody minds her. Folks are good to her and she has three grown sons, step-sons who send her money and would give her a house in the village, but she prefers the woods. I can't say that I blame her. I can understand."

After this lengthy speech, Tom sat in silence. Detached, Adam decided. Detachment was the thing that set Tom Wells apart, not reserve, aloofness, or stupidity: detachment.

The midday dinner Mitch served them was excellent, eaten in friendly silence. Adam noticed a picture of Tom in football togs and asked him where he played. They sat before the field-stone fireplace, watching the flames. Tom answered, courteous but uninterested, that he had played on the University of Maine team during his second year. "I wasn't able to stick it," he admitted, "Two years finished me. Too much talk and too little woods, I guess. Speaking of woods, we had better start for the No. 3 camp."

"I'd like that," Adam said.

They drove back to Mill road and turned west toward the deep woods, passing through the mill yard where the whirr of wheels and the drone of saws came faintly on the afternoon air.

"Interestin' place, a mill," Adam volunteered.

"A saw mill is, yes, but this cutting spools and clothespins isn't much so. It's not my end of the business anyway."

"How will the disappearance of your cousin affect the mill?"

"It won't make any difference for a time, but if he doesn't come back there will have to be adjustments all up and down the line, someone appointed to take his place, I suppose. I don't know. A.T. looks after all our legal business."

"Do you think he'll come back?" Adam felt that he was asking a question that was not tactful and perhaps ill advised, but he was anxious to hear Tom's answer.

But Tom merely said, "I don't know," and went into the silence. Adam felt a glimmer of sympathy for Bruger. "I don't know," was a stone wall across the trail at every turning. He turned his attention to the world about him. Cedar, spruce, fir, maple, and birch trees and brush crowded close on either side of the narrow roadway over which they traveled. The birch and maple limbs were bare and their tops traced a delicate network across the sky. The evergreens still bore tufts and flecks of snow on their spiny branches.

They stepped where a trail of snowshoe tracks joined the road and Tom hung a sack with grain in it in the crotch of a maple.

For nearly a mile more they rode, before Tom drove into one of the infrequent turnouts at the road side and stopped. "From here we have to go on snowshoes," he said. "At least, I shall go and you can come if you will. It's only a short walk. Not enough to lame you." He took snowshoes from under the seat of the sleigh as he talked. "This road we are on doesn't go on to the camp. It's used by a wood cutting crew, pretty near Beaver Brook. If you would just as soon try these things I'd like to have someone with me when I look at the camp. Bruger would hate to take my word, unsupported by expert testimony."

Adam found the snowshoeing feat not difficult but was glad that he had to travel no great distance.

They found the old camp empty and forlorn. It was evident that neither Leigh or anyone else had been in any of its log and plank structures for a long time.

Tom dropped Adam back at the Leeds house with the promise to return for dinner after he delivered the grain to Hulda and checked on Henry. Aunt Prue said, "Now Pearl, you take Adam into the parlor and show him the family album, or play 'Love's Sweet Song, or if you must, be modern and play parcheesi. Aggie and I are taking the children home. Jack has joined the searchers and A.T. said he is going to theorize and deduct."

Pearl led the way across the hall. "Which shall it be, Adam, the album, the song, or the game?"

"You have an album?" Adam asked.

"Yes. An album of undoubted age and veracity with bewhiskered males and hoop-skirted females, and children in pantalets."

"The album then, by all means first, and the rest of the program later."

If Adam expected the traditional parlor of haircloth chairs and antimacassars he was pleasantly disappointed. The old prints hanging on the walls gave it a mellow air of age. Instead of an overstuffed davenport there was a day bed with ends of spooled wood. Pearl brought the album from one of the tall cupboards that flanked the inevitable fireplace.

From its pages they gleaned much laughter. One of the more recent pictures showed Ellen and Leigh on their wedding day. Adam studied the face of the man whose disappearance was causing so much speculation. A handsome face certainly, but Adam felt the lips showed more of a sneer than a smile.

Pearl sighed and said, "Ellen should have married Tom."

"Really?"

"I doubt he ever asked her. I'm sure Tom wanted Ellen. But Leigh was always the popular one. He was a few years older than Tom, and

Tom was always shy. Leigh made sport of him, used to call him dumb. It's possible that Leigh courted Ellen to prove he could get whatever Tom wanted."

A.T. came into the room to say that Paul Spencer had telephoned to ask him to go over to the Delong place. "It seems that the sheriff having spent the day searching and found nothing, is determined to take Henry to the county jail. Paul thinks I may be able to persuade him to let Henry stay here until after Beatrice is buried. Pearl, would you mind if Adam accompanies me? We'll be back for supper."

Pearl, seeing no graceful way to refuse, chose to send them off with wishes for success in their endeavor.

As they drove, A.T. told Adam that two dozen men and boys, directed by Bruger and captained by Paul Spencer, had searched along the river as far as a rocky bend three miles below the town and had found nothing. Nor had a search of roads and the railroad track been more productive. Men on snowshoes had combed the village and the surrounding area looking for mounds of snow unnatural in appearance, or any other traces of the missing man. An ancient, disused mill pond was searched, as were the mill buildings. Questions had been asked at all the houses in the village. It seemed as though Leigh Wells had driven furiously across the bridge in the midst of the sleepy village with no word of answer to the greeting of a fellow wayfarer and had thenceforth vanished into snowy vapor, leaving his horse to make its way back to its stable.

A.T.'s investigations had been equally fruitless. Telephone calls north, south, and east had netted no more information than had the calls Bruger made to the wood camps to the west that were active and connected by telephone to the mill. A.T. had been hopeful of results near the border. There were a few establishments along the circumference of his circle that might have sheltered Leigh, but his inquiries had yielded nothing.

Paul met them outside the Delong house and asked Adam, "Find anything at the No. 3 camp?"

"No."

"Didn't think you would."

"You haven't found anything either, have you?" Adam asked Paul.

"Not a thing," Paul admitted cheerfully, "and Bruger is sore as the devil." Turning to A.T. he said, "I really hope you can persuade him to let Henry stay here until after Bea is buried tomorrow. If he could just take Henry back to jail with him, he'd feel that he hadn't wasted a whole day when he might have been sitting around and swapping yarns with the turnkey or telling the ladies of the temperance society about the evils of liquor in the county. He really hasn't got a thing on poor old Henry either."

The light of the day was beginning to fade. Already the sun was streaking the heavy clouds on the western horizon with angry crimson when they knocked on the front door of the home of Delong. The sheriff answered, but after a brief greeting, his gaze shifted behind the three men. Coming along the road, the angry sky and the somber wood behind her, was Hulda, walking somnolently. The white poodle ran beside her and in her arms was a shapeless and sodden bundle wrapped in newspaper.

She held the bundle toward the Sheriff and said, "Here's the baby."

A Gruesome Package

"Where did you find that?" the sheriff asked brusquely.
"Back there in the brook."

Bruger took the bundle from Hilda, grunting in disbelief. Then as he lifted it toward him to look inside, he recoiled from it, thrust it back into Hulda's hands and said, "Take it into the house."

The old woman grinned at him, leered, and chuckled, and led the way into the kitchen where Henry Delong still sat in the green Morris chair. Adam wondered if the man had slept or eaten, or if he had been sitting like that ever since they had seen him hours ago.

They cut the string that tied the gruesome package, pulled off the sodden paper, unwrapped the piece of faded grey blanket, and disclosed a tiny naked corpse.

"Little will have to see this," Bruger grumbled, "and he went home this noon. I don't see why someone didn't find this before."
"You may be able to catch Little by phone, so he can take the 6:30 train tonight," A.T. suggested.

"You go and telephone," Bruger instructed his deputy, "and tell him I'm going home tonight and going to stay there. I've got enough now on this bird to take him with me too," indicating Delong, who had sat unnoticed and unnoticing, like an actor on stage who was in the scene but not a part of it.

The men looked at each other in consternation. None felt that the cause of justice would be served by having Henry taken to jail on the day before his daughter's funeral. Then A.T. showed that his talk of controlling men with words had not been idle chat. He appealed to Bruger's magnanimity, and surprisingly, the Sheriff had responded and agreed not to send Henry Delong to jail. Just how A.T. did it Adam confessed to himself that he didn't know, except that he felt the glow in Bruger, induced by the subtle flattery of attributing to him a generosity of soul that he didn't have.

Uncle Joe was near to collapse. His face was gray and drawn as though he suffered physical pain. Adam wondered why he should have seemed so much more affected by what had happened than the others. A.T.

had looked upon the same scenes, and become deeply thoughtful, but in no wise beaten. Tom Wells? Who could say whether he was moved much or little. Hulda's tirade earlier in the day, ending with that incongruous statement that she wanted grain for her hens, had moved him not at all after that first protective gesture toward Ellen. At the noonday dinner he had been almost genial with a quiet sort of friendliness that had lasted all during the ride in the woods. At the Delong place he was once more silent and self-contained. It might have been that Uncle Joe was a more tender-hearted man, that the ills of others oppressed him to a greater degree. He appeared like a man who was beaten by circumstance.

Adam, A.T., and Tom returned to the Leeds house for supper. Aunt Prue gave her tired family the food she had cooked, food that was hot and comforting to chilled and wearied bodies. "Aggie's a good soul," she said, as they sat around the supper table, "and I'm used to her ways and I wouldn't be willing to change and have a new girl to fuss with, but there are times when I just can't have her underfoot. She's just been in atwitter, all day, and hearing about that poor little baby was too much. I suppose it wasn't right to saddle her on Ellen either, but I did it, and I told Ellen to keep her so busy she just wouldn't have time to talk so much and that's a job that will keep Ellen busy, too."

"Who told you about the baby, Prue?" A.T. inquired.

"Jack was nearby when Hulda found it. He came over to Ellen's and told us. Do you think they will find Leigh too?"

"Your guess is as good as mine, Prue. It's a bad business altogether." As they rose from the table, A.T. put his hand gently on his brother's shoulder. "Are you about all in, Joe?"

"I'm all right, Arthur," Joe responded, and then more quietly, "That poor mother and baby."

"Now, Joseph," Aunt Prue said as she began to clear the table, "you go right straight to bed, and forget all about this business. There is no need of making all the trouble in the world your own."

Pearl had put her arm around Aunt Prue and shepherded her firmly to the door of the living room. "I'm going to be domestic," she said. "Adam may be domestic too. It is good training for any young man.

You never can tell when it will come in handy."

"Being domestic with you will be a pleasure," Adam said, beginning awkwardly to gather up the plates. He had no experience in housekeeping arts, nor had he desired to have any until he saw Pearl deftly clear the supper things away.

"If you smash any of Aunt Prue's pet dishes there will be no fun at all," Pearl said. "You better do the heavy-looking-on as we say up here."

"I'm good at that," Adam admitted with a grin. "I've been doing the heavy-looking-on since I came."

In the kitchen Pearl allowed him to dry the glassware and the thin old silverware. Their task had a pleasant air of intimacy there in the working end of the big kitchen, an air which Adam sought to foster. Once the kitchen was clean enough to meet Aunt Prue's standards, they spent the evening on the delayed game of parcheesi, and then retired for the night.

The Leeds household was up betimes the following morning. Aunt Prue was busy with Saturday tasks. Putting beans to bake. Preparing the brown bread for its steaming. Jack brought the new milk in from the barn and separated it in the milk room off the kitchen. Uncle Joe drove away to Ellen's to help make the house ready for a short vacancy since he was to bring Ellen and the children back to the Leeds home for a few days. A.T. inveigled Adam into a game of cribbage and won the game handsomely. Pearl prepared for the return trip to New York.

After Ellen and the children arrived, Joe, Prue, and A.T. departed for the funeral for Beatrice Delong and her baby. Pearl helped Ellen install the effects she brought in the rooms above the parlor, while Adam busied himself with a book.

Presently Pearl came to Adam. "Put on a coat and come with me," she said. "I have a morbid desire to see the procession go by."

They went to a small balcony that opened off the upper hall. From this vantage they watched the short procession that followed the bodies of Beatrice Delong and her baby, as it passed by the Leeds home and on to the hillside cemetery north of the village. Henry Delong was slumped beside Tom Wells in the seat of the sleigh that followed the hearse. Paul Spencer and three other men were in a double-seated sleigh. "The bearers," Pearl said. Uncle Joe and Aunt Prue, A.T., and, curiously enough, Dr. Rush were driving together. Pearl pointed out another couple driving just behind Tom Wells, as the minister and his wife. There had been no church service, just prayers at the barren little house where they had found the dead girl on Thanksgiving Day. A few people had gathered there, moved by pity or curiosity.

"Were the Delong's so friendless?" Adam asked. Pearl answered that few were friendly to trouble, and misfortune found people mostly alone.

"I would think digging a grave would be difficult at this time of year," Adam said.

"The snow came early before there was much frost. The ground isn't frozen much under the snow," Pearl explained.

After the funeral was over and a rather subdued meal was eaten, A.T. had proposed that Pearl and Adam join him for a sleigh ride.

"What, A.T., are you hatching up?" Pearl asked.

"I don't know that I will hatch a thing," A.T. replied. "Do you remember that there was a camp where Leigh and his cronies held revels once upon a time? It's probably of no importance, but it comes within my circle of investigation, and Paul tells me it hasn't been searched yet. Adam, are you any good at winter sports?"

"I have used skis sometimes on jaunts to winter resorts."

"Good, we have a pair you can use. I am too old for such capers, but I do know the way. I will be the coachman and when we get to the proper place, I will hold the horses and you two shall fight the battle." Pearl said, "You mean the road to camp will be drifted full, so you want us to ski in and give the camp a once over?"

"Correct. I thought you might enjoy it."

In good time Uncle Joe's span was hitched to the double-seated pung and they were ready to start. Pearl wore breeches and a sweater under a fur coat; larrigans were laced high over woolen hose and a blue beret tried vainly to eclipse her hair. The sun, partly obscured by clouds, was on its western slant. The wind had been at work carving the snow into fantastic shapes, piling miniature drifts on the lee side of each little projection of hard snow and ice in the road before them. Several times they met cars traveling to Edenville to do Saturday shopping. They might, A.T. said, have used a car themselves but he preferred the team and the others agreed with him . Adam had been glad for the protection of the extra overcoat and mittens he had been supplied with for the outing

A.T. had said many things that interested Adam. The medical examiner had said that the infant whose body Hulda had found was undoubtedly the daughter born possibly prematurely to Beatrice Delong; that she had been dead when she was thrown in the stream. She died after birth from the lack of proper care and attention. She had probably lived an hour and then had given up the struggle. Paul Spencer had taken Henry Delong to the county jail, just after the funeral. Paul had hated to do it but Bruger had decided that he would have it done. The Bangor papers had the story of Beatrice Delong and her baby. They had already printed the tale of the disappearance of Leigh Wells, but so far they had made no connection between the two stories. The reporter did not know of the missing halter and the cut rope end. "He only knows what Bruger has told him," A.T. had said, "and even Bruger isn't going to cast aspersions without due consideration. In the unlikely event of Leigh's turning up safe and sound, or the more likely one of his being dead and never being found, the whole affair will be forgotten in a few years." A.T. poked his head turtlewise from his collar.

"You think there's no doubt that there is a connection between the disappearance and the death of the girl?" Adam had asked.

"I don't think there is any doubt that Leigh Wells was the father of Beatrice Delong's baby," A.T. had answered grimly. "You figure out yourself whether there is likely to be any connection."

"What do you think happened?"

"I think that Leigh went over to see Beatrice last Wednesday evening," A.T. had said slowly. "I know that after the train had gone taking the Foote woman away hence and forevermore, I hope, Leigh went to old man Gordon's place and had a lunch. It may be that he had something stronger than coffee with it, I don't know and don't care to know about that, then he went to see Beatrice. He hadn't paid her any attention since early spring when the Foote disease followed him here from Boston where Leigh had been on business. It's possible that he didn't know of Bea's condition and it's certain that if he did he didn't care. He might have even forgotten it. He was like that. I think that when he got there he was frightened or shocked and that he cut that halter rope and got away as fast as he could. But where he went or what happened to him I have no idea. It seems impossible for him to have left the country without being seen, and on the other hand it seems impossible that he or his body is hidden anywhere about."

"He was quite generally disliked, it seems to me, from what I have heard," Adam had observed.

"He was and he wasn't. Joe and Prue never liked him. I never had much use for him myself. The men at the mill, most of them, disliked him, some of them hated him, I guess. You see, he was away from the time he was eighteen until he was twenty-five or six. He went to college and traveled some after that. When old man Wells died Leigh came home to settle down and manage the property. He and Ellen were married before he had been home two months, a quiet wedding on account of his father's recent death, or so he said. They went to live at the home place. And Leigh suggested that since they wanted to have a new house with everything exactly to suit them that they do nothing to the old house for a little while. He was all enthusiasm for a new place and they were going to start it in a few months."

"But then he never built the new place or fixed the old," Pearl said bitterly.

A.T. nodded and continued, "It was only a few months after the wedding when he began to change. I don't know what came over him, I don't know that anything did. Just his native mean streak coming to the top, I guess. He began chasing other women, used to go away for days at a time and leave Ellen by herself, lost interest in the new house but refused to do anything for the old one. When I say he used to go away, I don't mean that he left entirely as he has now. He would go to some place nearby and stay at a hotel, driving to the mill office but somebody always knew where he was.

"Ellen is proud, she would never let on that it hurt her. She's kept everything bottled up inside her for five years. For all that Prue and Joe love her just as though she were their own, especially Joe, Ellen can't even find relief in talking to them, and they can't do anything about the situation."

"How does Tom feel about Ellen?" asked Adam.

"Tom has been half in love with Ellen, maybe more than half, ever since they were kids. He has seen how things were, but can you imagine his saying or doing anything about it?"

Adam could, not saying but doing. He could imagine that easily. He could imagine Tom Wells giving his cousin Leigh the punishment he deserved with his fists, doing it silently and efficiently.

"Outside the family and the mill employees, there were some people who liked Leigh. A man who has money to spend and who spends it freely, if he has the nerve to carry it off, can get away with more than a poor man."

While A.T. had been talking they had turned from the main road into a woods road where the shadows came straight toward them in long slanting lines. Adam had been pursuing elusive thoughts set in motion by something A.T. had said. He had asked when there came a pause in A.T.'s discourse if Leigh Wells had ever been a devotee of the woods and dwelt in camps as his cousin Tom did.

"No-o," A.T. had answered, "but he used to use a camp sometimes for parties and so forth. We're going there now. It's old No. 1 camp. Woodsmen haven't used it for years, but Spencer and I talked it over and decided that as it was the only unoccupied camp that hadn't been visited and the one Leigh used to use besides, that someone ought to have a look at it. There isn't much chance of anyone or anything being there. Teams drive by it every day."

There had been silence then for a quarter of an hour. The sleigh bells jingling made so little impression on the consciousness that they only increased the stillness of the forest. The wind ceased to rake them there in the shelter of the evergreens on either hand.

At length A.T. reined the team to the side of the road at a spot where the banks were low. The young folks donned their outer wraps and put on their skis. As they moved through the forest they forgot that their errand had a serious purpose and gave themselves over to the enjoyment of the sport of climbing each gentle rise and gliding swiftly down the following slope. Pearl went as though she loved the going and Adam, watching her skill, admired her.

They came to a clearing, ringed with tall spruce and stunted cedar. The camp was a ramshackle affair with only the main building still intact. It was quite evident that no one had been near the place since the storm two days before. They had pushed the heavy door inward upon its shaky hinges and stepped inside. The light was dim, but the place was bare of any sort of furnishing except the remains of a bunk against the far wall. On the end of the bunk was a dark furry mass. Pearl walked over and picked it up. It was a man's fur coat. "Now what do you know about that?" she exclaimed. "I can't believe it, this looks like Leigh's coat!"

"Are you sure?"

"Well, he certainly owned one that looked exactly like this."
They looked around the rest of the camp but found nothing more of any import. Their backward trip was swift and quiet.

A.T. received the coat calmly. "If that isn't Leigh Wells' coat I'm a Dutchman. No marks on it that I can see. We'll take it to Paul."

Paul Spencer met them on their return to the village and confirmed the ownership of the coat. He had often seen Leigh wear it. Dr. Rush had said that Leigh was wearing a fur coat Wednesday night in the storm. So far as anyone knew he had been the last person to see Leigh.

Traveling Through the Night

The sun was setting when they gathered for their Saturday night supper of baked beans and brown bread. The table had enough people around it to suit even Aunt Prue, and the meal was a pleasant one. A.T. had been in fine form, saying, "We live and move and have our be-ans."

Since there were no Sunday trains, Adam and Pearl were starting back to New York that night. For them the Thanksgiving holiday would end with a long train journey. A.T. had a much shorter train journey back to Houlton.

Uncle Joe brought the double-seated pung once more to the door. Adam shook hands all round and received good wishes and an invitation to come again. Pearl distributed kisses to the women and children and gave Jack a smile and an admonition to be good. A.T said, "Adieu, adieu, kind friends, I can no longer stay with you."

As they said goodbye to Uncle Joe on the station platform, Adam saw a glint of tears in Pearl's eyes. When they were seated on the train, A.T. said, "Well, Adam, what do you think of Aroostook and its inhabitants?"

Pearl arched her brows and shook her head. "A.T., dear almost Oncle," she mimicked Mitch's pronunciation, "Don't be embarrassing."

Adam laughed. "I like the place and people immensely. I am being wholly serious when I say that I can't find the proper word to apply to your brother and his wife. Fine goes without saying, and superior doesn't express the right feeling."

A.T. smiled, and said, "You'll do, young man, you'll do."

He bade them a jaunty farewell when his station was reached, urging Adam to come for another visit soon, and telling Pearl that she must come home more often lest she become too much of a New Yorker.

Swept along through the wintery night, Adam Stillman lay in his Pullman berth and tried to sleep. Saturday, midnight—had it been only three days since he had met Pearl on that wayside station platform, for the purpose of spending a real Thanksgiving holiday, three days, a lifetime, or only the few moments of a fantastic dream? It had been snowing then. It was snowing now. He imagined the soft swish of the flakes, cinder-tainted against the car window. He heard rattle and clang of wheels on rails, all the little sounds of a train in rapid motion crackled in the cold wind, a cacophony.

He turned again uneasily and tried to relax. He saw again in fancy, the misshapen figure of Hulda, with that bundle in her arms, wrapped in newspaper, wet pulpy newspaper, just as she had fished it from the icy water of the little brook below Henry Delong's house.

Step by step, scene by scene, Adam went back over the time from that moment on, hoping to cast off the tension of his confused mind. Perhaps if he got all the lines straight, the pattern clear, he might sleep, and he was very tired.

Were any of the people he had met in the land of snow and restraint, murderers? Ellen? Uncle Joe? Tom? Henry? Had Leigh Wells been killed by disgruntled workmen? Had Leigh Wells been killed at all? Was Leigh responsible for the death of Beatrice and the baby and therefore ran away? Did he run away to meet up with a woman? Was Leigh trying to find Tom in the woods? Why would Leigh leave his coat and turn his horse loose? Where did the disappearing halter come in? What did Hulda's oracular pronouncement mean, if anything? Was Leigh irresponsible enough to abandon his wife, children, and business, and run away?

What was the good of all this? Of what use was it to lie here and try and piece the thing together? Adam groaned and swore, telling himself that he must stop remembering and thinking. He breathed deeply of the smoky air. He would fix his mind on the work he was going back to, and then perhaps he could sleep.

He turned again to another position and thought about Pearl: Pearl as he knew her in New York, a clever girl, working at a desk watching for shoplifters in order to study the people who went in and out day after day, fitting herself for a career, planning to be a great woman lawyer some day, getting a slant on the psychology of petty criminals or near criminals; Pearl as he had seen her that night of his arrival in this strange land from which he was now speeding away. She had been gay then, just a lively girl on a holiday; later she had been apprehensive, bewildered, distressed but still courageous; later still as he had seen her at Ellen's with a baby in her arms and a stray sunbeam glinting in her bright hair. She too was speeding back to New York, in a berth just down the car a bit. Did she sleep or was she too thinking, thinking?

Before the berths were made up they had sat together and talked. They had talked around and through, over and under the happenings of the days just past, but had avoided direct comment on the disappearance of Leigh Wells and the death of Beatrice Delong and her baby. Why? Because Pearl had wished to have it so. She had said that Ellen had talked with her that night when she had stayed at the Wells house, and that they had resumed the footing of sistership, which had been theirs in the days before Ellen was married and Pearl had gone away to college, but other than that reference to the matters in mind, their talk had been only of the country and the idiosyncrasies of its inhabitants.

Now that Adam thought about it, he felt less well acquainted with Pearl than he had been before he had visited her northern home. She had changed, from that hour in the little church when the parson's voice was dinning in their ears, "I have pursued mine enemies, and overtaken them: neither did I turn again till they were destroyed." She had washed the dishes after the supper at Uncle Joe's that Friday night—just last night?—and Adam had helped awkwardly. She had not gone to the funeral Saturday morning; she had stayed at home and Adam had stayed with her, but even then he had sensed a change in their good comradeship. Back in New York he would resume the old relationship of good friend. He vowed this to himself. He did not intend to lose Pearl.

Adam wondered if he would annoy any of his neighbors in the sleeper if he smoked. He would like to have a cigarette and he did not want to go to the smoking car. Surely everyone was asleep by now.

The train stopped and there was a confusion of shifting about from track to track. Someone had rung for the porter. Adam was not the only sleepless one, then. He peered through the opening in the curtains and asked the porter where they were. "No'ther'n Maine Junkshu, Boss. Ain't yo sleepin good?"

Adam distinctly wasn't. He tried to peer out into the night. All he could see was a blur about a light. His mind went back to its treadmill. The train was in motion again. Adam found a place close to the window where a breath of clean and cool air trickled in. He stood in the great shadowy barn, a halter with a cut rope in one hand, a fur coat in the other. Clutching them tightly he walked without effort up a towering ladder to the very peak of the dim barn roof. He spread the coat out upon the air like a magic carpet and on it floated down, down, fathoms deep into sleep.

Dead or Alive?

Pearl Jameson was at home, at her northern home with Uncle Joe and Aunt Prue. She had been there since January and now it was springtime, May, and the snow had gone. Small dirty patches of what had once been winter's white garment still lay in sheltered places, but the earth was bare and brown, spreading a carpet of smoky taupe and tan, flecked with the yellow of sunlight on sere grasses and the green of sprouting plants, as far as the eye could reach, looking from an upper window of the house on the brow of the hill. The distant woods, dark against the blue of the spring sky, were a mingling of deep evergreen and faintly purple bare tree branches. A nearer maple was a fantastic bouquet of ruddy twigs.

It had been a long winter, a winter of dread and anxiety. Aunt Prue and Uncle Joe were indefinably changed. It had not been the extra work and care of having Ellen and the children there, Pearl reflected. Both of the older people had been glad to have them, yet they, and more especially Aunt Prue, had wanted Pearl to come home and had leaned more heavily upon her youth and spirits during the long cold months. This in itself was disquieting. Aunt Prue's subscription to the creed of letting every tub stand on its own bottom had always been wholeheartedly lived up to by that positive and energetic soul.

Pearl found when she arrived home that Aunt Prue had not been exaggerating when she said that Ellen had changed. It was not that she moped or complained. She was feverishly busy from morning till night. She said, when asked if she felt ill, that she was perfectly all right. But there was strain in her eyes and her slender form had become so very thin that Aunt Prue said she looked as though a puff of wind would break her in two. A sudden noise would start her shivering, and any mention of Leigh caused a haunted look to come into her eyes.

But now, it was spring, really spring. Pearl wandered through the sparkling clean upstairs rooms and breathed deeply of the air from the opened windows. The willows along the river bank were showing a faint new green. It was spring and Adam Stillman was coming tonight. She was glad he was coming. She had missed him and other friends in the great city as well as the constant movement and occupation.

"*I'm a pilgrim and a stranger passing over*" came from the region of the kitchen and Pearl had a whimsical picture of Aggie, pilgrim and stranger making rolls in a spotless kitchen as she sang. Even Aggie was touched by the magic breath of spring.

A car came up the drive and Pearl ran down the stairs to meet Ellen, Aunt Prue, and the children who had been for a ride. "It's a heavenly day, isn't it?" she said as she lifted little Prue from the seat beside Grandmother Prue. "Did you have a good ride?"

"Yes, the old bus runs pretty well," Ellen answered, with a sidelong glance at Pearl's new green dress.

"You look real nice in that dress, Pearl," said Aunt Prue. "Why don't you and Jack take the car and drive out to the swamp to get some pussy willows. We saw them but we weren't shod for that sort of business. Jack could get some, though. You'll have lots of time before A.T. and Adam get here."

"I'll go if Jack can. He is 'round back raking up leaves." Pearl flew away. Her feet were winged today. She came back with Jack following more slowly behind her. "We'll bring you pussy willows, oodles of them," she cried as she seated herself beside Jack who had elected to drive.

"There are muddy places in the swamp road," Ellen called after them as they drew away.

"As if I didn't know all about the mud in that swamp," Jack muttered, shifting gears with unnecessary vehemence.

"Have you been there lately?"

"I have and so has everybody else who could walk or ride, there and everywhere else all over the bloomin' place. Folks are awful interested in the country this spring."

The brilliant spring day had been suddenly dimmed for Pearl. She shivered.

"You came away without your coat, and now you're cold," said Jack. "You ought to know by this time that it isn't safe to be without a coat this time of year."

"Ellen's coat is here in the car. I'll put it on. I am cold. Are people looking for, for—"

"—Leigh's body," Jack finished, as grimly as an eighteen-year-old boy could.

"Jack, you don't like Ellen. Why?"

"Mostly I just don't. I didn't know her much, until this winter. She was married and away most of the time, when I came to Uncle Joe's."

"But Jack, you mustn't judge her by this winter. She has been terribly upset. It must be horrible to be kind of a widow and not know whether, as A.T. would say, you were grass or sod."

"Don't you believe it, Pearl. She knows all right. She knows it is sod, or mud, and she knows people are hunting everywhere for Leigh's body, and Uncle Joe knows it and so does Aunt Prue. Can't you see how worried they are?"

"I can't believe it, Jack. You don't know these things, you just surmise them."

"I don't just surmise. People are talking."

"People always talk," Pearl said. "Leigh got away. He's probably living the life of Riley with a woman he didn't bother to marry. It's the uncertainty that worries Ellen. Uncle Joe is starting to feel better because he is beginning to think that Leigh won't come back."

"Folks are saying that Uncle Joe and Ellen both know he won't come back alive,"

This wasn't news to Pearl. She had heard whispers. But she knew that talk would die down after awhile. "Who's talking?" she asked.

"The fellers that work at the mill mostly. Bruger keeps encouraging them to hunt for Leigh's body. Paul Spencer has got orders to hunt but he gets angry at some of the talk. He pasted a feller on the jaw last week for saying that Ellen knows what happened to Leigh."

The odor of spring was in Pearl's nostrils and the willow bushes in front of her eyes, but she smelled the aroma of Aunt Prue's kitchen and saw the drying rack above the register. "What do they say about Uncle Joe?" she asked.

"Everybody knows that he hasn't any use for Leigh, and he's crazy about Ellen. Some folks feel he'd do anything to protect her."

"What about Tom?"

"No one really knows Tom all that well. It makes it easy to believe what you want about him. Then there are those that think Leigh got lost in the woods and froze to death. Some think he was robbed and killed."

Pearl said, "So lots of talk and nobody really knows anything."

Jack asked, "What is this New York friend of yours, this detective, coming here for? It isn't just to see you. Yeah, I know that would be a good excuse, but why get off at Houlton and see A.T. first? Why isn't he in the army like Tom and all the other fellows?"

"Don't be such a kid, Jack. Tom and most of the others who are in the army now were in the National Guard. They were mustered right into service and went into camp, but Adam wasn't, and he has important business to clear up before he can go in. He'll be going, as soon he can. I wish we really did know what had become of Leigh. Then perhaps things would settle down."

Carefully avoiding a mud hole where the winter frost had cracked the surface of the roadbed, Jack pulled up and got out to cut the braches of catkin-laden willows bushes.

"I'm driving back," Pearl announced as he returned to the car with arms loaded.

"I don't think you're right about what you said about Ellen," Pearl said as they started on their return, "but I'd like to know what makes you think so."

"Well, you see, Pearl," Jack began, watching the road before them as closely as though he still had the wheel. "Some funny things happened that night Leigh went. Suppose he had planned to skip out, the way A.T. said a feller might, on a potato car. Suppose when he got his plans all made, Ellen found out about it and was so mad she killed him; and suppose Uncle Joe found out about that, and helped her get rid of the body. You know he would. He'd just think that anything he did to protect Ellen was right, wouldn't he, Pearl?"

"It is all supposing, just supposing, and you don't really know a single thing. I think it is wicked to suppose such things."

"Maybe I don't know a single thing and maybe I do know more than one single thing, but you tell me why Leigh arranged to have Ike Jennings kidnapped and taken out of town that night when Ike was planning to take a lined car out for Uncle Joe."

"Ike Jennings made that story up, kidnapped and taken out into the country that snowy night. It is a likely story now, isn't it?"

"Likely or not, I know the kidnapping part is true."

"How can you know, Jack?"

"I do know, and I know something else too, something nobody else knows, unless Aunt Prue knows, about Uncle Joe, and if they do find Leigh's body and start questioning folks, I might have to tell it. That's why I wish this Adam of yours wasn't coming up here. He didn't seem to catch on too much last winter, but he's a detective, isn't he? And you say he's a pretty good one. I'm going down to Houlton and enlist. And if something does come up, don't you tell a word I've said. You won't, will you Pearl? You won't let it out to that feller, because if I'm gone nobody will think of me maybe."

The mild spring day had indeed grown cold for Pearl. The wind that blew across her face had the chill of ice and snow in it. If they did question people, she might have to tell of finding Uncle Joe's wet footgear at two o'clock in the morning, but had it been at two o'clock? She couldn't be sure, she couldn't swear to it. What did Jack know, what she knew, or something else, something more condeming to the old man who had been so good to everybody all his life.

"I think," she said, aware that she was giving advice she would not follow herself, "that if anything comes up and there is an inquiry that you ought to tell all you know to A.T. You know that he will see that no harm comes to Uncle Joe."

"I know he would try to. A.T. is a brick of course, and he's smart, smarter than your Adam maybe."

"He isn't my Adam, Jack. It isn't fair to call him that. It isn't fair to think he would do anything to hurt Uncle Joe, either. He's human even if he is a detective. Besides, Leigh's body hasn't been found and perhaps it won't be. You don't know that anyway. You don't know he's dead. Oh dear, I just hate murders and mysteries. I used to think they were fascinating, but now I'm off that sort of stuff for the rest of my life. But I won't tell, Jack, I won't ever tell a single soul."

A Ruby Ring

When Adam stepped from the train to the station platform at
Houlton that spring day, A.T. was waiting to greet him with
a hearty handshake. Hack drivers were offering their services to other
arrivals, their cars, a motley collection, backed conveniently near. A.T.
led the way to his car and when they had become one with the straggling procession that wended its way toward the town's center, having
disposed of the usual amenities, he asked with an effect of brusqueness,
"Just what brings you to these parts?"

"My immediate business is looking for Footeprints," Adam made
answer.

"I suspected something of the sort, and having been interested myself,
and traced them when they were fresher than they are now, I should be
able to give you material assistance."

"I had counted on that. Also on help in the other business which is
believed to be connected with it."

"Have you any scruples against going fishing on Sunday?" A.T.'s question, apparently irrelevant, caused the younger man to smile.

"None," he answered.

"Good. It's a bit early for fishing, but I've been getting the fishing fever
and tomorrow if you have no objections we'll try our luck at a brook
I know of."

"If you say fishing, we'll fish," Adam agreed. "I'm following your
lead."

"Well, your cue now is to observe and to admire, being the stranger
within our gates. You're seeing the shire town of the potato empire, the
oldest town in the county, at one and the same time a progressive and
up-to-date city and an old-fashioned and conservative town; rich and
poor, blue-blood and red, high and low, the honored and the dishon-
ored, all in one mighty—um, sometimes I am moved to finish that
sentence with 'sepulcher.' Take a look, because in a very short time we'll
be shaking the dust from off our tires and on our way to Joe's where I
grant you will find someone more interesting to see than all this."

The wide public square was alive with traffic. Parked cars lined all the curbs and a double line extended the full length of the center. "Why all the excitement?" Adam asked.

"Saturday afternoon," A.T. answered, successfully avoiding a woman and three small children who elected to cross the street in front of them. "All the folks from far and near come to town to do their trading."

"Market day?"

"A bit the same, yes, except that it is the country folk who buy and the town folk who sell. In a few hours now the Square will be black with cars and people. Saturday night is an institution here."

On either hand the new shouldered the old, modern brick structures abutted on ancient ones of wood, hotels, stores, banks, the last closed now. Farther out, away from the business center, schools, churches, hospitals, fine well-cared-for homes, and over all, lining the streets, grand old trees. All these things Adam saw pass before him as they drove about. When A.T. stopped before his low, white, tree-shaded house beside a small park, he pointed to a group of red brick buildings, on a little hill before them. "Court house and jail," he said.

Their stay at A.T.'s home was short. "If there are things to be looked into here," A.T. said, as they started again on their way toward Eden-ville, "we can do it better the first of the week. Now for the hills and dales, and the merry wood which will be green some day."

The road was good, broad and level surfaced it led, up and down, up and down, ever north, with broad fields lying to the east and west. Farmhouses, with great barns nearby, mostly with a connecting shed between, courted the highway, as though always conscious of the long months of snow that fell to their lot each year. And ever, far to the westward, rose the line of tree-clad hills that marked the domain of the sentient and silent forest.

A robin trilled from the top of a wayside elm, and Adam said, aware that he voiced nothing new, but constrained to speak, "Spring is a miracle."

"Spring, and youth, love and service of your country, all are miraculous if you have the second, necessary element of miracles. Don't think that I'm cynical or that I fail in sympathy," A.T. went on as Adam did not reply. "It's only that time deadens the response in some of us. Pearl, now, will be feeling much as you do, and Jack's young breast is likely to be savage. Even Ellen will be feeling the call of the springtime, and her life is pretty much shadowed now; but Prue and Joe and I only know that the call is there. We're old, young man, old and should have a philosophy to live by."

"Has anything new come up in regard to the Leigh Wells business?" Adam asked.

"No, there's nothing new. The usual spring crop of dead bodies has been reported on different water courses. Only two this spring, both identified as men who were drowned by going through the ice last winter. Leigh was reported seen here and there, but nothing came of it. Bruger thinks that Leigh was killed. He's been on the hunt for three weeks. He doesn't think that Leigh decamped, deserting Ellen for another woman."

"Pearl wrote me that Henry Delong was not held for the grand jury," Adam said.

"No. There was no evidence that Beatrice was murdered. Little's report was that she died of exposure. Such evidence as there was indicated that Henry was at the mill all night and came home to find her dead. The mill fires showed no signs of being neglected."

"What's Henry doing now?"

"Living at Tom's place with Mitch. Two old derelicts safe in port. Henry's gone back to watching the mill at night."

"Is Delong satisfied that Leigh had nothing to do with the girl's death?" Adam asked.

"You'd think that his going back to the mill indicates that, but it doesn't really. Henry and Bruger are both tenacious in their beliefs. Bruger still clings to his first interpretation of the halter rope, that it shows that Leigh was there and Henry discovered him there. Henry says the rope shows that Leigh was there for no good purpose and that he was responsible for Beatrice's death."

Adam next asked about Tom.

"He spent most of the winter in the woods as he always does. He refused to take over the mill end of the work. Says he is not fitted for it and will stick to the woods end. One of Leigh's henchmen is looking after the business end of the mill for now.

"Tom's in Army camp down state. The declaration of war has changed the plans of many of our young men. Before he went away he told me something you'll want to know. There's no wood in this region suitable for use in the construction of airplanes. Tom was responsible for the rumor that there was suitable wood because when he knew what the Foote woman was after and that she was no friend of our country, he lied to Leigh in order to mislead her. Leigh always depended on Tom for the woods reports, that being Tom's end of the business. And when Tom knew that the woman was getting at Leigh for a purpose he told Leigh that there was wood here that has been said to be found in only one place, in the West. But Tom told me about it, and I'm sure he spoke truly when he said there wasn't a single tree of the wanted variety in all this territory."

"That is one Foote-print traced, at any rate," Adam said.

"There are more of them. The Foote woman was undoubtedly an agent working to accumulate information. She worked Leigh as well and got a tidy sum from him. That night when she left here she dropped off the train at Houlton, drove to the C.P. Station, and went across the state line. At Debec Junction she was met by a man who posed as her husband and they went into hiding at some remote farmhouse. Later when they attempted to leave the country they were apprehended and jailed.

"This, just ahead, is country you might recognize. The Wells place on our left."

Adam shivered, just as Pearl had when she rode with Jack; perhaps the spring wind was cold.

"Those dark trees give the place a sinister look," Adam said. "If the place were mine I'd lop those things all off and let in some light."

Down the hill and across the bridge, and up the hill on the other side and once again Adam approached the house, in its setting of tall elms, which Pearl called home.

Standing on the steps, her arms full of the pussy willows she had just taken from the car, she called gaily, "What ho, welcome to man and beast."

"Which is which?" challenged A.T.

"Both are both, I supposed," she answered, smiling, and led the way to the living room where Aunt Prue hastened to welcome them, her mind preoccupied with the food that was ready for them.

"I smell beans and brown bread, most excellent Prue, and I'm famished," A.T. greeted his sister-in-law.

"Joseph just came in and we're all ready to sit down to supper. If you want to wash up, you go right away and do it, so's we can eat."

Supper was a pleasant meal. Uncle Joe talked of the farm and assured A.T. that the new man and his wife who had been hired a short time before and were installed in the house at the foot of the hill were good help. Aunt Prue contributed to the general fund that the asparagus bed was coming along well and they could have asparagus in a few days, also that the rhubarb was looking promising, and that the daffodils would bloom soon if the wind did not blight the buds.

Ellen observed that she would like to know how the things were doing around her house and said that she would like to go over there and look about the next day.

Then upon this peacefulness, this well-being, obtruded Hulda. She entered without knocking and sat upon a chair, offering as greeting a high-pitched chuckle.

Aunt Prue offered her food, which she refused. Ellen gathered the children about her and left the room. Aggie said "humpf," and went to the kitchen, sniffing.

Hulda looked on and again she chuckled. "You, Joe, and you, A.T., come with me," she said. "That young feller and Jack can come too, if they want."

"Where do you want to go, Hulda?" A.T. asked calmly.

"Where the black spruces hold the smell of death," croaked the hag. "It'll be dark there, Joe, get a lantern."

They said no more, but followed. Uncle Joe's car was still parked where Jack and Pearl had left it. Jack slipped behind the wheel. A.T. motioned to Adam to get in beside Jack. The others got in behind and Jack drove straight away to the Wells place on the other side of the village.

They stopped before the tall closed doors of the big barn, and followed where Hulda, like an ill-conditioned gnome, led them. The yellow light of the lantern illumination only their feet and a circle of earth about them.

Around the corner of the barn went Hulda, a few steps along the path to Tom Wells' house, around the opposite corner of the barn, along its end, and around the next corner, to where in the angle made by the wall of the long shed there was a sheltered spot. A patch of muddy snow, the tag end of the winter's drifts, lay there, and stooping near it, Hulda cleared away a little pile of leaves. "Look," she said, "he didn't rest well."

The lantern light fell on a hand, clenched and rigid, pushing up from the frosty earth and rotting leaves. A ring with a blood-red ruby dimly glowing through a film of dirt, gleamed from a finger.

There was a moment of shock—a numbing moment, of minds startled, shaken from accustomed grooves.

A.T. bent and touched the ring. "Leigh Wells' ring," he muttered. "Leigh Wells' hand."

A Shallow Grave

A pall of stillness smothering thought and action descended on the group standing in the gloom of early night peering at the spot where the red stone glowed in the lantern light. Uncle Joe broke the spell with a groan. A.T. placed his arm across his brother's shoulders with a rare gesture of affection and protection. "We'll have to send word to the sheriff," he said, voicing the obvious, cloaking emotion with the commonplace. "You come with me, Joe, to Tom's place. We can phone from there. The boys will stay here. Hulda—" He turned to question the woman, but she had vanished into the night. "It doesn't matter. She can be questioned later," he said and turned, groping among the dead grass and tangling raspberry creepers toward the path at the back of the barn, leaving the lantern there to evoke that ruby gleam.

Adam wanted to be away, wanted above all things to go to Pearl, to be the first to see Ellen Wells when the news was carried to her that her husband's body had been found, buried in her own back yard, but he could not leave Jack, alone there in the gruesome night, the grave of a murdered man at his feet and the empty house behind him. No, that would not do. This boy was already laboring under great emotional strain. Better for him and for all concerned that he should not be left alone there.

"Do you have any idea who buried him here?" he asked, not realizing at the moment that the question might be an added shock, following his own line of thought aloud.

"No, Unc—anyone might bury him here, but not, not—"

"I understand," Adam broke in on the boy's stammering reply. "Jack, I know what you have in mind. You think this looks bad for Mrs. Wells and for Uncle Joe. It does on the surface but stop suspecting them. Do you think for one minute that Joseph Leeds could conceal a murder, would help cover up a murderer even if it was one of his own household?"

The boy was miserable, but he stuck to his guns. "Yes, I do. And so will everyone else in the county except A.T. He won't, or if he does he just won't let himself. Don't you see? Uncle Joe would do anything for

Ellen, anything at all. She couldn't bury a body on a snowy night with two feet of snow and two or three inches of frost to dig through, but Uncle Joe could. It wouldn't be so awful hard to do. I could do it. You believe it yourself, don't you?"

"No, I don't," said Adam flatly. "I don't believe Mr. Leeds knew where this grave was, or even that there was a grave. I'm not talking the way a detective should to you and I don't want to be quoted. I'm telling you this for your own private ear, because I want you to get that preconceived notion out of your system, and be of real help to A.T. in the investigation that will follow this find. I can't stay here. I wish I could, but I'm not my own master in the matter. Don't start by thinking you know just what happened on that stormy night when I was here before. You may know some of it, but you can't know it all, and if you start out by thinking that you know, you'll be sure to fit everything you find out to your theory.

"You can fit ideas, you always can, if you ignore part of them. That's what your sheriff will do, if I'm any judge of men, and to find out what really happened, how this body came to be buried here, is going to be no easy task. When you think about it, just keep the people you think about straight in your mind. It's one thing to recognize that possibly Uncle Joe might conceal a murder or an accidental death, thinking he was protecting his foster daughter. It's another thing to be convinced that he did so until you have proof."

"I wish I had enlisted a week ago." Jack refused to be comforted by Adam's efforts. "I wish Paul Spencer was here, he's a square shooter. I wish Tom Wells was here, he'd know what to do."

"Buck up, boy, buck up. If you're man enough to go to war, you're man enough to face things here. A.T. will know what to do. Put your faith in him. Tell him everything that's on your mind."

"How can I tell him things that will harm Uncle Joe?"

"You can tell him the things you think will harm Uncle Joe, in fact you would be much better to tell him. He'll have to know them anyway, and if he hears them from you he'll be ready to deal with them when he hears them from someone else."

The beam of a flashlight shone through the trees. Uncle Joe and A.T.

returned, accompanied by Mitch, carrying a powerful light of the sort that might be used as a lantern or a torch. He flashed its strong light over the ground at their feet. It was evident that a grave had been made there. Adam was puzzled about the reason for only a hand showing above the brown earth, "as though it had sprouted there," he thought, and shuddering, turned to listen to A.T's. directions for further procedure.

"Will you drive Joe home, Adam, and tell the folks about this? It's better that they hear it before it has spread through the place and grown all out of proportion. Then come back for Jack and me. I'll get Burger, and he'll bring Little with him. Paul Spencer will get over here as soon as he can."

Uncle Joe spoke not at all, on the brief ride home. To the group of nervous women waiting about the fire in the living room for their news, he announced briefly that Leigh's body had been found just back of the shed at the Wells house, and without waiting for reply from anyone passed through the dining room and to the bedroom beyond. Aunt Prue's wholesome face twisted with pain and reluctant tears filled her eyes as she followed her husband. Pearl's cheeks whitened so that the sprinkling of freckles the spring sunshine had spattered upon them stood out like tiny mud spots.

Aggie gasped with an open mouth, shocked, not altogether unpleasantly. Realization of what the discovery would mean to those about her would not come instantly to Aggie's mind, tuned to receive the sensational. Of all who heard Uncle Joe's words, Ellen was the most outwardly composed. She paled as Pearl had. Her eyes became enormous, dwarfing her other features. She whispered, "So that's where—" and then shut her lips firmly.

Adam felt awkward, and a little exasperated. How could these people take so startling an announcement so calmly?

"I'm going back there," he said.

Ellen and Pearl moved as though his words had broken a spell. "I want to go with you," Ellen said.

"I think you'd better not. At least you'd better wait until I ask A.T., and if he says for me to I'll come back and get you."

Ellen was about to insist upon going but Pearl said quietly, "I think it would be best to wait. If A.T. wants us to come, he'll send for us."

So Adam drove back alone. A slender crescent moon showed in the eastern sky, but the west was black with clouds, presaging a storm.

He found the situation much the same as when he had left. Nothing could be done until the arrival of the sheriff. Old Mitch had a vile pipe going full blast. Jack smoked cigarettes nervously.

When Adam told A.T. of Ellen's desire to come back with him, A.T. only said, "Just as well for her not to see this," and scanned the cloud bank in the west. "Mitch," he said at length, "do you think you could find Sam Terrio?"

"Sure I find heem, you want heem?"

"We will need light here, when Bruger comes. It looks like it will storm here before midnight. You see if you can find Sam and tell him to bring as many big lights as he thinks he can connect with the house wires. Tell him to hurry and to keep his mouth shut."

"Yes, Mist A.T., I tell heem." And Mitch moved away, using the powerful flashlight he carried.

"Taking that light away makes it pretty dark here," Adam remarked looking at the feeble rays of the kerosene lantern at their feet.

"That was Tom's flash," Jack informed them. "He gave it to Mitch when he went to war."

A.T. peered at his watch. "Almost half an hour since I telephoned. Bruger ought to be here soon."

By common consent they ignored the pile of snow at their feet and watched the cloud mass gather in the west, each busy with his own foreboding thoughts.

Adam chided himself for his unreasonable exasperation when his news of the finding of the grave had been received so calmly. What had he expected these folks to do, scream and tear their hair? From what he knew of them, he most certainly expected nothing of the kind. He himself had been, still was, unduly excited. He tried to analyze his own state of mind. Nothing so unheard of in finding the hiding place of the body of a murder victim. He remembered other cases, one in particular when he had helped fish a dismembered body, tied up in gunny sacks, from a shallow pool. His flesh had not crept along his spine as it crept now, here where the most menacing thing seemed to be the rising storm that sent wind gusts moaning through the tall black spruces, a requiem for the dead.

"Wish they would hurry," Jack muttered for the third time in as many minutes. And as though his wish had become effective at last, a car drove into the yard. A few moments later, Bruger's burly form appeared around the corner of the barn, lighting the way with a flash for Dr. Little and two deputy sheriffs who accompanied them.

Greetings were casual, incidental to the business in hand. A.T. pointed to where the ruby gleamed. Bruger swore softly. "Whadder you suppose they left that hand stickin' up for—advertisin'?"

"Frost plays queer tricks sometimes," Dr. Little observed, and waited for Bruger to make the first move.

"Well, I don't see how we can do much tonight. How can we dig that up in the dark? God, but this is a hole. Where can we git a canvas? Hafta cover this place and set a guard."

"I took the liberty of sending Mitch for Sam Terrio, to see if he could rig lights to work by," A.T. said. "I think they are coming now."

"Can you get enough light here for anyone to work by?" Bruger demanded of Sam, who stood looking about, now at the ground, now at the dim wall of the building before them.

"Sure, I can have plenty of light for you in fifteen minutes, maybe less, but you'll have to work fast. That's a rip-snortin' thunder shower workin' up there," pointing a capable hand to the west.

"Whadder ye think, Little?" Bruger asked the medical examiner.

"Get on with it, man," exclaimed Little impatiently. "Get on with it. You will have a pretty mess on your hands, canvas or no canvas, if you wait until after it rains."

"Go ahead then, Terrio, and make it snappy. Who found this, anyway?"

"Hulda."

"Hulda, huh? She's got the habit! Where is she? Why didn't ye hang onto her?"

"She's rather elusive," A.T. replied. "Slipped away before I thought to detain her."

"Who knows about this? Who's been here?"

"Joe, Jack, Mr. Stillman, and I came over with Hulda from the house."

"Where's Mrs. Wells? Has she been here? Where's Joe Leeds now?"

Adam stepped forward. "I took Mr. Leeds home, a little while ago. Mrs. Wells wanted to come back with me, but I thought she had better not."

Bruger looked Adam over in the dim light. "Johnny on the spot, aint ye, young feller? Who paid you to think? Winn," turning to one of his deputies, "go over to the Leeds place and bring Joe Leeds and Mrs. Wells here, PDQ." He blustered as the deputy, a mild-looking man, hesitated.

A.T. made a startled movement, as though about to interfere, but contented himself with drawing Jack to one side. "Think you could find Dr. Rush?"

"Yes."

"Find him and tell him to get here right away."

Jack vanished into the night as silently as Hulda had an hour before.

Bruger turned to Brown, the other deputy who he had brought with him and including Greenleaf with a gesture, said, "You boys, go hunt up some tools to dig with. Orter be some in the barn there or over to Tom Wells place."

Dr. Little was annoyed. "What's the idea of all this hocus pocus of getting the family around now, Bruger? I don't see any sense in it."

"Maybe you don't, but I do. It's my business to find out who murdered the man that's wearin' a ruby ring on his finger, aint it? And that man is buried right in his own dooryard. If that don't say family to you, it does to me."

"Better go a little slow with it," The doctor advised. "You have a hand and a grave here, by the looks of things, but you my not have Leigh Wells' body. You can't be positive of what is here until you dig."

"Its Leigh Wells' body here, I'll bet a hat, and I want to see who it is that knows about it."

Light from several makeshift leader wires, running from the barn and the shed, flooded the spot where the earth showed evidence of having been disturbed, just as the deputy Winn came around the barn accompanied by Ellen and Pearl, Uncle Joe, and Aunt Prue.

Uncle Joe appeared ill. Aunt Prue was plainly indignant. Ellen was quite calm, indeed she seemed detached and mildly interested in the scene before her. She did not flinch when Bruger pointed to the hand and asked if she knew the ring upon it.

"Yes, that's Leigh's ring," she said, her voice steady.

"Now everybody is here, you," indicating the family group, "stand here." He indicated a spot just within the circle of light, "and you boys," addressing the men who had come up with the spades, "dig."

Adam looked at A.T., but A.T. was listening. Pearl was holding her hands clenched tightly before her. Uncle Joe seemed swaying on his feet. How very white his hair had become, Adam thought, looking with compassion upon the old man, sharing the indignation apparent in every line of Aunt Prue's round body.

A ragged bolt of lightning split the western cloud bank, and the roll of the thunder drowned out the sound Dr. Rush made as he approached.

"Bruger," he yelled, coming to a stop just facing the sheriff. "What do you mean by exposing a sick man to such a show as this? Mr. Leeds is my patient, under my care. I demand that you send him home at once."

Dr. Little added his voice to the din of the rising wind. "Rush is right, Bruger. No sense in all this damned melodrama. Send the folks who have no business here home and let's get about this business quick. Can't you see that storm brewing? It'll be here in half an hour."

"Everybody can go now, for all I care," Bruger agreed, grumbling, "I've seen 'em, and right on the spot, too."

The men fell to work with spades, swiftly yet carefully moving the layer of snow and then digging into the earth, and soon only A.T., Adam, Jack, and Dr. Rush, who had returned to talk in low tones to Dr. Little, watched the men engaged in their gruesome task. Old Mitch hovered about the fringe of the light. After a time, Henry Delong joined him.

Adam wondered that the happenings of the night had drawn no curious spectators to the scene. "Not many people about," he said to Jack. For answer, Jack took a flashlight from Mitch, who was passing, and swept the trees behind them with its beam. Startled eyes in peering faces reflected the light. Like coyotes, waiting in the dark, Adam thought. Curious but cowardly.

Before the first scattering raindrops fell the men had uncovered the body in the grave. It was clothed in a business suit. A knitted wool sweater taking the place of the vest beneath the suit coat, overshoes on the feet were buckled over the trouser legs confining them closely. A fur-lined cap was pushed well down on the head and the face was covered with handkerchiefs, now stained and soiled, but still tied tightly about the head.

"Its Leigh, all right," said Bruger. "Where should we put him, Doc?"

"Take him in through that door and on into the house. Rush will help me make the autopsy there."

So Leigh Wells came back, in a sense, into the house where he had lived.

Adam and A.T. followed the men who carried him in and stood about awkwardly while Bruger and Little made their plans. They followed the doctors as they left the house, and heard Dr. Rush, say quietly to his colleague, "Do you think that blow on the side of his head killed him?" and Dr. Little answer half impatiently, "Can't say until we can make a thorough examination, but if you want a guess, I'd say he was strangled."

A Sunday Walk

Adam and A.T. hurried to the parked cars. Jack was huddled in the back seat. Rain and thunder made the night vibrant.

"When we get a thunder shower this time of year, it's usually heavy but brief," A.T. said, and that was the end of conversation during the ride to the Leeds home.

The car halted before the barn doors. After Jack darted through the rain and swung them wide, A.T. drove over the threshold. As Jack closed the doors behind them the noise of the storm was muted to a steady squish accented by rolling thunder.

In the living room the fire burned brightly, hissing as raindrops came down the chimney, not dousing its cheering flame. The family was gathered there, all but the children, who slept, quite as though no storm could touch their childish lives. Another had been added to the group, in the person of Mrs. Grimes, the nurse. A.T. greeted her cordially. "Now this is what I call something like it. When did you blow in?"

"Just before the shower," Mrs. Grimes replied composedly. "I had just come off a case and needed shelter for the night." She smiled, and Adam, seeing a faint reflection of that smile on Aunt Prue's face, realized that even that strong soul had need at times for moral support. Pearl's eyes questioned them, but the question did not reach her tongue.

Aunt Prue said to her brother-in-law, "Arthur, will you sleep on the couch in the parlor or have your room in the attic?"

"I'll have the couch, Prue, if one is as convenient as the other. Joe, do you remember the night Mrs. Everett slept on the little bed in the corner of the attic?" A.T. turned to Adam without waiting for his brother to reply. "Mrs. Everett was one of our local character folk. She was what we called a weaver, meaning that she had some sort of nervous affliction that caused her to move from side to side continually while she talked or listened to others talk. She was not exactly a pauper or a beggar, a sort of itinerant guest at the homes in the countryside. There is a meeting house not far away that was then a community affair, called the Union Meeting House. Special meetings were being held there one summer and a shower came up along in the evening, a humdinger of a shower. People sought shelter at the few scattered houses that were around here then. Mother had the house full and overflowing. Joe and I had one bed in the attic, which was then one big unfinished room, where the rafters ran from near the floor to the peak of the roof and the knots in the boards made fantastic pictures to look at on a summer morning, when I was so fortunate as to lie in bed. Joe and I slept there a lot that summer.

"Mother and Aunt Jane slept in the other big bed that night, and when everyone had been placed, Mother discovered that Mrs. Everett had not been provided for, so she made up a little bed that stood in the far corner of the room, hung a sheet from the rafters in front of it to give a little privacy, and tucked the poor old lady away for the night there. When the lamps had been blown out and all was still, Joe piped up in a piercing whisper, "Mother, Mother, did you hitch her?"

"Mother only said 'shhh.' She had remarkable self-control; we boys buried our heads in the bedclothes to stifle our giggles."

Aunt Prue said, "You and your stories," but she gave A.T. a grateful look as she rose to announce that it was time they all went to bed, advising them to go to the kitchen for a snack if they felt hungry.

"There's cookies and milk all set out," Aggie said in a subdued voice. Pearl drew Adam into the kitchen but they did not eat. "Sometimes," she said, "I think they will make me scream with their 'business as usual' ways. Ellen like a stick. Uncle Joe and Aunt Prue so calm and A.T. with his yarns. If they were picnicking over a volcano which might erupt any minute they would talk about the weather and A.T. would tell about something that happened fifty years ago."

"A.T. would get them away from the volcano if he could," Adam responded. "If he couldn't, he would entertain them while they waited for it to blow."

Adam found himself presently saying good night and going to bed with the picture in his mind of the gleaming ruby, the ghouls at work in the glare of unseemly lights, overshadowed by the picture of an elderly man, whose hair was iron gray, whose face was lined with kindness and humor, whose shoulders under their dark coat stooped a little and whose eyes were keen and far seeing.

That story now, not so very funny, not so very clever. It had carried a message to his brother's heart. It had said plainly, "We are brothers, one family, standing together to the last ditch." What parade of heroics could have been so effectual?

The morning was bright. The sky arched distant, blue, and cloudless. Robins in the elms discussed the weather, "Pretty wet, pretty wet." As Adam descended the stairs, strains, subdued but unmistakable, floated from the recesses of the kitchen, *"O-o-over the hi-i-lls where spi-i-ces grow."*

A.T. stood in the opened front doorway. He drew Adam into the room at their right, the parlor where he had spent the night.

The embers of a fire lay on the hearth. The rumpled couch had been pulled before it. A.T. looked at the bed and smiled. "I don't suppose there's another cot like this in a good many days' journey. Joe cut an old bedstead down to make it." He lifted the very modern box spring aside to show the frame of an old-fashioned corded bed. The side pieces of hardwood three inches square were tensioned to fit mortises in the stringers of the end pieces, and both sides and ends were pierced at intervals of eight inches with holes through which rope was corded. The head and foot were low, of spooled wood. The remodeling from a full-sized bedstead had been cleverly done. Adam looked at it with interest, but his mind was on other things. He looked at A.T. wonderingly but received only a quizzical glance.

"Not a real antique," A.T. said as he replaced the spring and straightened his stooped shoulders, "but sorta interesting. After breakfast will you go for a little walk with me? Our fishing will have to be confined to the house mostly, it seems."

Breakfast was a surprisingly cheerful meal. Ellen and Mrs. Grimes were occupied with the children and had not come down, for it was still early. Adam looked at his watch and compared it with the clock that ticked away before them. What might the day hold in store?

As Adam and A.T. took their hats from the rack beneath the stairway in the hall, Pearl came from the dining room. Her eyes were wistful but she merely said, "Going for a walk?"

"Want to come?" A.T. countered.

"Yes."

Adam was pleased and yet displeased. He wanted to have Pearl's company, but he wanted a chance for unrestrained conversation with A.T. A third person, even though that person was Pearl, might be a bar to plain talk. He made no objection, however, and the three set out, A.T. leading the way up the hill by a path through trees and field, avoiding the highway, and talking not at all. Adam too, became entranced with his own thoughts, finding himself presently standing with his companions at a gap in the fence of the cemetery at the top of the hill north of the house. He became conscious of the stillness about him; of the Sundayness of the atmosphere. This was Sunday. Down there where the smoke from clustered chimneys drifted in the morning air, it might be that doctors were making minute examination of a murdered man's body. Perhaps the houses sheltered a killer. It might be that he had sat at a meal with such a one, but here in the open where man's observance mattered not one atom, it was Sunday, all seemed peaceful and calm.

A.T. was speaking softly. "'Yet a few more days, and thee, the all-beholding sun shall see no more in all his course, Nor yet in the cold ground where thy pale form was laid, with many tears, nor in the embrace of ocean, shall there exist thy image.' I always thought a hilltop a fitting location for a cemetery. I want to show you something."

He led the way through the gap in the fence and along the lower side to the right, to a grave where the smooth earth showed no sprouting green, but had been freshly worked and planted. A headstone had been lately placed, a stone of rough granite, dressed only upon the face that bore the inscription "Beatrice Delong and her infant daughter," and the dates, June 8, 1899—Nov. 24, 1916.

For a moment they stood looking at the stone in silence. Then Adam, moved by the atmosphere, continued with Bryant's immortal poem, "'Earth that nourished thee shall claim thy growth, to be resolved to earth again.'"

Pearl gestured to include the many graves. "'All in one mighty sepulcher.'" She sighed deeply. "We're all the same in the end. We live, we die, we're buried."

A.T. responded, "Yes, but I intend to live so that when my summons comes I will be ready to 'lie down to pleasant dreams.'"

"I wish Beatrice and her baby could have had that opportunity," commented Adam.

"I thought this area of the cemetery belonged to the Wells family," Pearl said with a questioning look at A.T.

"This secluded corner," said A.T., "is a part of the Wells family lot. Tom sold it— yes, he had a legal right to dispose of this part," he explained, in answer to Adam's questioning look, "to Henry Delong, for the traditional sum of one dollar. I'm telling you this and more, in confidence. I do not want you to give your information to others.

"Tom also established a fund to care for the lot and to place this headstone. He gave to Henry Delong and to Mitch a life lease of his house, and decreed that Old Charley should live at his camp in the woods as long as he wished to do so, and that he should be properly cared for elsewhere in case of illness. It isn't a dark secret, but I understood when I drew up the necessary legal papers that Tom wished nothing said about it, which was perfectly natural, when you think of Tom, the silent."

"What do you make of it?" Pearl asked.

"Nothing except that Tom was philanthropically inclined, and did not wish these people, old and lonely, to suffer any further misfortune."

"Then why did you bring us here and tell us about it?"

"Perhaps to give point to my morning's sermon. I'm not skilled as a preacher. There's room for three more graves here."

A.T. led the way back to the path down the hill, but paused again at the fence gap.

"When were these arrangements made?" Adam asked.

"First of the year," A.T. humped his shoulders in that familiar gesture. "Tom said they were New Year's resolutions. He told me he made a will too."

Pearl made a restless movement. "Do you mean to imply that Tom feels he is in danger of being killed too?"

"I'm not implying anything of the sort. I'm only telling you what

Tom did."

Adam said. "If Tom knew something about Leigh's death and concealed it, he might think he was in in danger."

"If Tom concealed anything about Leigh's death, he did it for good reason," Pearl asserted positively.

Adam was annoyed at Pearl's quick championship of Tom. The realization that he was annoyed was an annoyance also. "Being involved in Leigh's death would be an excellent reason for concealment," he said.

"Tom was at camp that night. He was miles away when Leigh was killed, " Pearl reminded them.

"Trouble is," A.T. commented, "we don't know when Leigh was killed, where he was killed, or why."

Pearl insisted, "Tom was here all the rest of the weekend. We found the coat on Saturday. It must have been there before the storm was over. Leigh must have been killed before then. Besides, why should Tom kill Leigh? Just because he didn't like him?"

"Loving Leigh's wife might have been a motive," Adam said.

A.T. said thoughtfully, "That might be a motive if we had here the typical triangle. But we have only one side of the triangle. I think it is true that Tom loved Ellen since they were children, but we have nothing to show that Ellen returned that love or that Leigh had any knowledge of it."

The three moved slowly toward the path beyond the fence gap. A.T. continued, "I agree with Pearl, that it seems Tom had no opportunity to murder Leigh. But I agree with Adam that there are indications that Tom knows or suspects more than he is telling.

"I'm not sure what Dr. Little will have to report after the autopsy today, but I want to ask a lot of questions from various people before the report and before Bruger begins to take action. I want to begin with you, Pearl. I want you now to tell me everything you can recollect about last Thanksgiving eve, everything, mind. Do not assume Jack's juvenile attitude. Do not condemn anyone in your own mind because you observed something you have thought significant of guilt."

Pearl's face became almost as ruddy as her hair. "I want to ask you one question first."

"Spill it," said A.T., lapsing for a moment into the gamin role he loved.

"If you find that someone you love is guilty of this murder will you help to have them punished or will you help to get them off?"

"Pearl, I'm surprised at you. You're doing exactly the thing I warned you against, but to set your mind at rest, I will tell you that if I should find that Joe killed Leigh Wells, I would try with all my might to see that justice was done."

Pearl looked hard at the face of the man before her. Away back in the depths of his eyes the gamin still lurked, but Pearl was reassured.

"You wiggled out very nicely, and I'll tell you the whole story. Where shall I begin?"

"With the conversation you had with Tom at the station."

"I can't remember exactly what we said."

"Tell as much as you can."

"Tom greeted me cheerfully and wordily, for Tom. I was just a bit surprised and a bit flattered. Tom never took much notice of me. I decided that the city had improved me, and that I was making a hit. I suppose that was what made me make that smarty remark which seems so insane to me now, that it was a grand night for murder. Once I brought the subject up, we couldn't seem to keep away from it. Then Leigh was there at the station with the Foote woman and I had been hearing a lot about their affair, a lot of it from Aggie. You know how she would revel in it, without even knowing that she did. That led Tom on to tell me about Beatrice Delong, how Leigh had been going there and all, until the blonde woman came on the scene. Tom didn't say anything about Beatrice expecting a baby, just that Leigh had been going there a lot and that Henry had found out about it and warned him to keep away. We talked some about Ellen and how she held her head up and never seemed to admit that Leigh was such a skunk, and that's really about all."

"Did Tom seem vindictive toward Leigh?"

"He was angry, I know, and much disturbed in his mind, but he didn't make any threats or anything like that. He said one queer thing. I don't know that it was so queer for him either, only I had never heard him express it before."

"Yes?"

"I was joshing him about leaving town on Thanksgiving eve, when there would be so many good things to eat the next day and he said, almost apologetically, 'You know I can only stand houses and people for so long and then I have to go to the woods. It's a sort of disease, I guess. I find healing in the woods.'"

"So he went to the woods," mused A.T., "but came back the next day, early."

"Yes, I never got to talk with him again. He went back into his shell." Pearl was half regretful.

A.T. brought them back to the subject in hand. "And that night what did you see or hear that disturbed you?"

"I couldn't seem to get to sleep. I had been depressed all the evening, although I shouldn't have been." Pearl smiled at Adam. "I heard the telephone ring and Uncle Joe answer. Then after a while I slept some but woke up later feeling very much disturbed. I thought I had heard something. I don't know just what I did think. I got up and went downstairs. In the kitchen I found Uncle Joe's socks and felts all freshly wet from snow. It was about half past two in the morning. That's all, truly."

"And just because Joe had been out that night, without finding out where he had been or why, you have been accusing him in your own mind of being a murderer or accessory to murder. Don't you think you have been rather foolish?"

"It does seem silly, when you put it that way. But I wasn't accusing him myself. I was only thinking how it would look to Bruger and to other folks. Why, Bruger had poor old Henry Delong in jail for weeks with less to go on than that."

A.T. laughed and there was grimness in his laugh. "Don't worry yourself over a 'Brugerboo.' He won't keep Joe in jail."

Pearl sighed in relief. "I feel better to have told you. Sorry I was so silly about it, Where do you suppose Uncle Joe had been. Do you know?"

"No, I don't know, but Joe will tell me when I ask him. He was probably on some innocent errand of mercy and has never connected it with anything serious. Still, Prue has been worried too, and she must have something more to go on than you had, or she wouldn't have been."

"No," Pearl replied as her face clouded again. "She hasn't worried because she thought Uncle Joe might have killed Leigh. She has worried because she fears the construction that may be put on whatever took Uncle Joe out of the house that night, and because she is afraid Uncle Joe thinks that Ellen may have killed Leigh. I think that is just what Uncle Joe does think. He isn't worrying about what will come to him. He's afraid for Ellen. Ellen said that Leigh was not home after after Dr. Rush saw him at midnight, but if it could be proved that she lied, there would be a bad case against her."

A.T. picked up the story. "Ellen had motive, Leigh's treatment of her. If he came home she had opportunity. She might conceivably commit murder, or manslaughter, given sufficient provocation. Aunt Prue knows this. She would almost be capable of it herself under certain conditions. She would not condemn Ellen; Aunt Prue is one of the best women I ever knew, but she is the least bound by accepted codes of action of any I ever knew. She would not plot to kill, but if she knew that a man like Leigh had been killed impulsively or accidentally I can just hear her say, 'Good riddance.' Have you anything to offer, Adam, before we go to the house and ask more questions?"

"Nothing much. If you're not in a hurry to go in, I wish you would tell me a little more about Ellen. Why did you say that she might conceivably commit murder?"

"Let's move on," A.T. interjected. "The sun has not sufficient strength to dispel so much cold as the earth has absorbed in the last six months."

"I'll go back a bit in time," A.T. continued as they moved slowly along the path. "Ellen's father, Conway Waugh, was a mad Irishman and Joe's best friend. Con was attractive and brilliant. He had many good qualities, but he was wild, with the real wildness that loves adventure for its own sake. As you may imagine, there was little in the ordinary life of the country farmer that appealed to him.

"He followed the log drives in the spring. He hunted and trapped, but he hated the lumber camps in the winter. He drank and gambled not because he was vicious, but because he loved the excitement. For all that, he was very fond of Joe. I think Joe represented to him something he was bright enough to admire but to know he couldn't achieve. On the other hand, Joe loved his brilliant wit, and stuck to him with that streak of stubborn loyalty which is so much a part of him. Con drifted away in search of adventure. Occasionally he came back. Sometimes prosperous, sometimes broke. Joe always had a welcome for him, would have helped him in a material way, but Con would not have it. 'Money, Joe,' he would say. 'What's money? I can get that anywhere. You give me what I have never found in anyone else. You will never give me money.'"

"So an independent, adventurous sort," Adam said.

A.T. nodded. "When the Klondike rush was on, Con went in search of gold. We lost track of him, didn't hear from him for years. Then he sent Joe a letter with Ellen, a baby about a year old. Mrs. Grimes brought her. The letter said, 'I'm done for, Joe, killed a man in a fight. No good to cry. You'll be a better father to Ellen than I could ever be, and I know that Prue's heart is big enough. If you never hear from me again, you'll know I'm out for good.'

"Joe never did hear from him again. Con sent enough money with Mrs. Grimes to provide for Ellen's childhood, but Joe has never used it. He would have given it to Ellen when she married, but she wouldn't have it either. It still stands ready for Ellen's use at any time. I have often wondered that she didn't use it, or part of it, since Leigh gave her so little, but I can see that it's due to her pride."

"Mrs. Grimes, then, is not a relative?"

"No, she's just what she seems to be, a nurse who was hired to bring Ellen east. She has stayed on and become part of the community. She could tell us nothing about Ellen's mother, except that Con said she was dead."

"Do you believe so implicitly in heredity that, because of her father, Ellen might be a murderer?"

"Yes and no. If you mean, do I believe that because Con killed a man, Ellen might do the same, I do not. But if you mean do I think she has inherited enough of her father's makeup so that she might, under some circumstances, kill, I do, because I've watched Ellen grow up. She's rather fine, finer than Con ever was, to my way of thinking, because she has had different training, different care, but I know that she has much of her father's essential makeup, and I believe might be wrought up to the pitch of anger where she would kill."

"Then if she were brought to trial, all her father's past would be raked up and it would tell against her?" Adam made a statement although its form was a question.

"Yes. That's Bruger's car driving up to the house. Let's go in, and Pearl, get hold of Jack and keep him away from Bruger, until I have a chance to talk to him."

Frozen Solid

"Well, Bruger," A.T. greeted the burly sheriff, "has Dr. Little anything to report yet?"

"Not a thing, and he won't have either, not right away. That body is nothing but a block of ice. They got a hot fire in the stove and Little and Rush are waitin' to go to work. They're playin' pitch and Doc Rush is hopin' nobody sends for him. First time I ever knew a feller to be killed in his own place, buried in his own back yard, and thawed out by his own kitchen stove. Can't do a thing until the thawin' is finished so's the docs can get to work. I thought I'd come over and talk to the folks here. Hate to waste all day."

"Does seem a pity to waste so much time," A.T. agreed blandly. "I suppose you looked the body over this morning. Did you hear Little or Rush say what the cause of death might have been?"

"No. They both shut up as tight as clams. Said they couldn't tell a thing about it now. That's all bluff, of course. It's plain enough to see. There isn't a mark on him except that one on his head. Somebody hit him a wallop with something and then took him out and buried him."

"That's a simple and convenient theory, certainly." A.T.'s acquiescence would have seemed suspicious to a more subtle mind than Bruger's. "I wonder why Hulda vanished last night. Have you seen anything of her this morning, Sheriff?"

"No, I haven't seen her, nor heard anything about her."

"Well, Sheriff, it seems to me that there's something mighty mysterious about Hulda. She's too apt at finding dead bodies. Doesn't it strike you as queer that she should find Beatrice's baby so easily just where people had been looking for Leigh's and then find Leigh's where no one had thought to look for it? I believe Hulda is the person you want to question right now. She ought to be able to throw light on this whole thing. The folks here won't run away, you know."

"Besides," as the sheriff hesitated, "I don't think you can talk to anyone here just now, or in fact until after the autopsy."

"I'd like to know why not," Bruger bristled.

"You have nothing to question them about until after you know that

Leigh Wells was murdered." A.T.'s answer was mild and calm, but it failed to turn away Bruger's wrath.

"Know he was murdered!" he sputtered. "Think I was born yesterday? Anybody except a natural-born fool would know he was murdered. You know it, too. And let me tell you, Mr. Arthur Than Leeds, that because it happens that you're a lawyer and that your folks are upper crust around here, Joe Leeds can be a murderer just the same, and he can be sent to Thomaston, or his folks can be sent there, just the same as though he was a poor man, with no friends to his name. I'm sheriff of this county, I'll have you know. You can't put over any of your high and mighty stuff with me. I'm goin' to do my duty."

"Go right ahead and do it, Bruger, and in the meantime I'll be attending to mine. You may think yours is to question the folks at this house. I know that mine is to prevent you from doing anything so ill-advised. How would it look to the state attorney, if you should question a man you suspected of murdering another man, before you knew what you were talking about? You know he was buried, but you don't know how he died. Now if Dr. Little says that Leigh died from foul means, and not from natural causes, people will have to be questioned to find out, whatever there is to be found out as to how the killing was done. Right now, all you have to work on is that Leigh's body has been found in what can be considered suspicious circumstances, and of course you haven't neglected Hulda altogether."

A.T.'s shoulders had become more rounded while he talked in an even and reasonable tone. He peered up now at Bruger, with his head a little to one side, looking much like a bright-eyed, inquisitive bird.

Bruger had asserted himself and felt better for it. Watching him, Adam, who had stood beside A.T. listening to the exchange of words, knew that the sheriff felt his inferiority most acutely, although unconsciously, and had compensated for it to some extent by his outburst.

Bruger continued, "Of course I haven't neglected the old hag. I sent Brown down there this morning. He ought to be back now."

"I would like to go over to the Wells place and take a look at the body, if you have no objection, Sheriff. Do you think Dr. Little would object?"

"I don't see why I should let you poke into this business. You act as though you wanted to keep me out of everything." Bruger still smarted from a fancied wrong.

"No reason at all why you should, Sheriff. But we all make mistakes and seeing what's left of Leigh might influence me to agree with you about the murder business," A.T. said amiably. "Want to come along, Adam?"

Bruger led the way, A.T. and Adam following in A.T.'s car. Adam wondered just what line A.T. was following in going back to the Wells place; was it just a ruse to get Bruger away from the Leeds home, to defer the questions that would be asked sometime? He wanted to talk about the whole matter, but A.T. looked tired, worried, and Adam had no wish to add to his burden. If Joseph Leeds had not killed his son-in-law, would A.T. be able to prove that he had not? If Joe had, would A.T. be able to avert the punishment meted to killers, to save his brother from a living death inside the gray walls of the state's prison?

All the world outside seemed now strangely remote, unimportant. Even the business that had brought Adam to Edenville seemed trivial now. Strange, the effect this tragedy had. How all-important it had become to him, a stranger in a strange land. Adam felt that a spell had been laid upon him, a spell deepened by entering the long, low old-fashioned kitchen. Bare and unlived in, it seemed dead like the corpse, lying on the makeshift trestle of planks near the range.

The sound of their entrance brought Dr. Little and his colleague to the door of the sitting room at their right. Dr. Little's keen impatient face softened a little as his eyes met A.T.'s. A.T. smiled faintly in answer to his look, and spoke with seeming diffidence, "The sheriff thinks that there isn't a doubt of this being a murder case, but I am sorta dumb today and he thought that he might convince me by showing me the body."

Dr. Little cleared his throat and frowned portentously. "Sheriff, you may think whatever you want to about this case, but remember that it's not a murder until I say it is, and I can't say until I have performed an autopsy. You will not let your zeal lead you to make undue haste, I'm sure. I would feel it a slight upon my office if you assumed murder before I had determined it."

Adam put his hand to his eyes with a gesture of perplexity. When had they made the transition through the looking glass into this topsy-turvy world where responsible men ignored the body a few feet away from them, bearing witness to violent and gruesome death and bandied silly words about with an air that smacked of the pompous? Then looking at A.T.'s face lined with worry, and back to the watchful eyes of Dr. Little, comprehension filled his mind.

The face of the dead man had been cleansed of the soil that clung to it from its burial. The features showed only the awful composure of death, not marred in any way except for the bruise near the temple on the right side of the head.

"I wonder where he got that?" Dr. Rush said, looking intently at the face.

"Somebody handed him a good one, and not with a fist either, and still I'm told to wait and to putter around, while the person who did this cooks up a good defense, but I'll get him, or her, before I'm through with this." This plaint was from Bruger, who still thirsted for vengeance and glory.

"Say, Bruger," Dr. Little interjected, "when you get hold of Hulda, I want to talk to her. I know she is half crazy, I know it as a medical man, not just as you know it from observation, and I want to see if I can determine what is true, and what is her meanderings."

"I don't think Hulda is important. Do you?"

"Most certainly I think she is very important. Why, man alive, it may be that your whole case will hinge on Hulda."

Brown the deputy let himself through the door, unceremoniously. "The Hulda woman has flew the coop," he said.

Immediately, Hulda, unimportant heretofore in the mind of Bruger, became the one person the sheriff desired to see and question. He became all activity at once. "Get the deputies together and hunt," he directed. "I'll be right along myself. That woman must be found."

Bruger's departure brought relief to A.T.'s look of stress. "We'll be getting back," he said to Adam, and "Thanks, Little."

"S'nothing," Little replied.

"I hope Bruger has luck with his rabbit stew," was Dr. Rush's cryptic addition to their leave taking.

Once again speeding toward the Leeds home, Adam threw off the mood that inhibited conversation and asked one of the questions that had been clamoring in his mind.

"If you are sure Mr. Leeds didn't have a hand in the killing of Wells, why were you so anxious to keep Bruger from asking questions?"

A.T.'s keen blue eyes swept Adam's face in a swift comprehensive glance. "Joe has been under a terrific strain all winter. This business is piling it up worse than ever. I just don't want him badgered, and I want to go over the ground first, before anyone else messes it all up. You have suspected men of murder, some who were guilty and some who were innocent, no doubt, but have you ever been suspected yourself, or had anyone near and dear to you suspected of being a murderer?

"No, thankfully I have not had that experience," Adam replied.

"I'm sure that Joe didn't do it. I'm getting a pretty good idea of who did, but I haven't a shadow of proof of guilt or innocence. Now, young man, I'll probably do a lot of things in the next few hours that seem illogical to you, but I want you to observe and remember all you see because I expect to use you and to use you to advantage a little later. I am going to talk to Jack, Ellen, Joe, and Prue. I want you to listen."

Jack's story was soon told. Coming home from a call on Thanksgiving eve he had seen the kidnapping of Ike Jennings. He had kept still about it because he was pretty sure his father had been the driver of that ghostly team that had carried Ike away into the night. He had gone to bed but couldn't sleep, had heard Uncle Joe go out and had heard him come back, later, much later. About two o'clock, he thought, but could not be sure because he had not cared to look at the clock in his room.

"Why?" A.T. asked, when Jack confessed that he had not wanted to know the time.

"Oh, I suppose I was just foolish. I just wanted to know only what I had to know. And why should I? I don't keep track of Uncle Joe's actions. There's plenty of reasons for him to go in and out that don't concern me."

"What did you think anyone wanted to carry off Ike for?"

"It might have been lots of things. It might have been just a joke on Ike, mightn't it?"

"It might, but you really didn't think that, did you?"

"No."

"I don't think so either, Jack, but on the other hand, I don't think it's anything you need to worry about or that you'll be asked about it at the hearing, which will probably be held tomorrow. Did you think that Joe went out and killed Leigh and buried him, that night?"

"No, I didn't, but someone telephoned before he went out and I thought it might have been Ellen. I heard him say, 'I'll be right over.' If Ellen had banged Leigh over the head and killed him, I thought she would send for Uncle Joe and then he would bury Leigh, so folks wouldn't know about it."

A.T. hunched his shoulders like a bent old man's and said reflectively, "I really thought better of you than that, Jack, Your mind and Bruger's have been hitting about the same speed; neither one is exactly perspicacious. To be sure, Bruger doesn't know about Ike. I'm willing to make a guess that because Ike was kidnapped just before he was to go out with that car of potatoes for Joe, and Joe was called up to see what should be done about the car and went to the station. Joe can tell us himself."

A.T. went to the door of the parlor, which had been put to rights and was now in use for consultation. "Joe," he called, "Hey, Joe!"

It was Mrs. Leeds who answered, "Joe went to sleep. Do you want to see him right now?"

"You will do instead, Prue. I wanted to ask Joe something but I'll do it later. Prue, I want you to tell me about that night when Leigh disappeared. I want to get all the facts I can about that night."

"I suppose you knew Joe went out?" Aunt Prue sat down, and did not wait for an answer. "Joe went to the station to see about that potato car. He fixed that up all right and it didn't take him very long. Then when he got back to the turn of the road, he decided to drive over by Ellen's. It was after ten when she told Pearl that Leigh wasn't home yet. Goodness knows, Leigh Wells had stayed out nights lots later than that without Ellen worrying. Anyway, Joe drove over there and the house was all dark. There wasn't anybody up, at least there wasn't any lights and Joe just turned around and drove along home. You know how it snowed that night and it had begun to snow hard before Joe went to the station, so the drive over to Ellen's and back from there took a lot of time. He didn't get home and get to bed again until about half past two. There wasn't a bit of sense in his going out at all that night anyway, but you know how Joe is, thinks nobody else can look after anything as well as he can.

"What puzzles me is that there wasn't any light at Ellen's," Prue continued. "She says she had a light on but that it was shaded and that she had the curtain down over the window in the bedroom, but Joe says there wasn't a sign of a light to be seen. If Joe had seen the light and gone in, Ellen would be able to say that he was there, and Joe would be able to say that Ellen was there. But it sounds like a silly story to him to say that he just drove over by Ellen's place long after midnight and came home without seeing anybody. No one will believe it, but then no one would believe if he had talked to Ellen either. It's as bad one way as the other. Nothing else happened that night except Pearl prowling around with the stomach ache."

"Dr. Rush met Leigh driving this way about midnight. If he was killed that night it must have been after midnight, and I don't see how it would be possible for anyone to bury him there back of the barn, before Joe drove by there, so it must have been done after one-thirty or thereabout, if it was done that night," A.T. said thoughtfully.

"Suppose," he continued, "Leigh drove away on some errand or other and met a man accidentally or by appointment and as the result of an argument the man struck him. Knocked him out, as he thought, got him back into the sleigh and drove him home, found that he had killed him and selected the nearest spot where he could bury the body. Question, who did it? It wouldn't have been premeditated; anybody might have done it, given the opportunity. That is, it's possible. But what did our hypothetical murderer hit with, and if that theory is true he must have been left-handed."

Uncle Joe stood in the doorway, the boy twin, little Con, on his arm. "See," he said, placing a capable hand on the child's stomach and holding him at arm's length in the position of a swimming frog, chubby arms and legs waving, "Isn't he a good one?"

The diversion brought an answering smile to the faces of those in the room. "He is that," A.T. said. "Joe, how many left-handed men can you think of right away?"

"Half a dozen, I suppose. This baby's grandfather was left-handed. Paul Spencer is left-handed, and so is Henry Delong."

Aunt Prue murmured, "So many things don't make sense."

"The cut halter rope." A.T. and Adam voiced the same thought.

"And," said Aunt Prue, "why would Leigh be driving away from there at midnight and then go back again?"

"I don't know why but the time would fit all right," A.T. said. "He might have just gone a little way and turned back, then gone on down to Henry's place and found Henry at home. Henry had reason enough to hit him."

"You mean," said Uncle Joe, "that after Dr. Rush met Leigh driving north on the bridge, Leigh might have turned around and gone back to Henry's place and met Henry and been killed?"

"Yes. It's possible, isn't it?"

"It's possible, yes, but it also might have been possible for Leigh to turn around and drive back toward home in time to meet me."

"But, Joe, he didn't, you know he didn't," Aunt Prue, sputtered the words impatiently. "Besides," she continued triumphantly, "when could you bury him?"

"And," said Adam, "what do we do with the halter rope?"

"You have only my word," Uncle Joe said, "that the halter on the horse had a cut rope, and you have only my word that I didn't meet Leigh when I was coming home from the station, kill him, and take him home and bury the body then and there."

"The time won't work out right, Joe," his brother said. "It's no use, you can't trump up a charge of murder against yourself. It isn't good enough. Now I want you, Jack, to go tell Pearl that I want to talk to Ellen here. I think you had better not stay here, Joe. You can trust me to treat Ellen squarely."

"I must go and see about dinner." Aunt Prue's mind ran automatically along the lines of food.

When she had gone the others were silent, each thinking on the problem before them. Just what had happened that Thanksgiving eve? Outside the sun shone with the beneficent warmth of spring, as an early fly buzzed at a window. Sunday quietness brooded, unmindful of the disquietude of men.

The minutes ticked away. An uneasy feeling crept over the people waiting in the quiet room. Then Pearl stood in the doorway her face flushed, her red hair awry. "Ellen's gone," she said.

Where Is Ellen?

Ellen had given the twins their usual morning attention and their midday lunch, had put them to bed for their naps, and been sitting beside them turning the leaves of a book, when Mrs. Grimes had last seen her. Mrs. Grimes had been in the next room with Peter, who was nearing the grown up age of five years had waited to eat dinner with the family. Aggie had been in the kitchen and had not noticed Ellen going out that way. Pearl had been in her own room above the dining room and Uncle Joe had been asleep in the bedroom downstairs. Despite the concern into which the household was plunged, the atmosphere that Adam had thought of as Sundayness persisted. It was not merely the negative calm of the cessation of weekday occupations. It was a positive thing, an abstraction difficult to define, but unmistakable.

Little Con had come down the stairs and awakened Uncle Joe, just before he had joined the others at their conference.

When Pearl had gone to tell Ellen to go down, she had found baby Prue still sleeping, Con's empty bed, and in the other room, Peter gravely telling Mrs. Grimes a story. "Once upon a time there were four little bunnies and their names were Flopsy, Mopsy, Cotton-tail and Peter, and they lived in a handbag underneath the roots of a verrry big fir tree. Now you tell it."

Pearl had gone from room to room, all over the house, finishing at the door of the parlor with the disturbing announcement that Ellen was not to be found.

"I tell you Ellen's gone," Pearl repeated. "I've looked all over. She isn't here."

A.T. had appeared startled and worried. Jack's face, as he stood looking into the room over Pearl's shoulder, expressed "I told you so." Uncle Joe alone had not seemed worried by Pearl's news. "No need to get excited," said Uncle Joe. "She probably went out for a walk. She'll be back in a little while."

"She knew dinner was almost ready," Aunt Prue said. "It isn't like Ellen to be late to meals. Not that she eats enough to keep a cat alive. She wouldn't want us to wait."

The food Mrs. Leeds set before her household that Sunday shortly after one o'clock was of its usual excellence, and by the time they had finished, all were ready to hope that Uncle Joe's opinion that Ellen had only gone for a walk by herself and strayed farther than she had intended was the explanation of her unannounced leave taking.

Now, the dinner having been duly eaten, Adam and A.T. followed Uncle Joe to the barn, where he had odds and ends of work to look over. Joseph Leeds kept the Sabbath strictly, but he could never resist inspecting machinery or other gear when time threatened to hang too heavily. A.T. was looking into the box stall where Leigh's mare had been kept since Ellen came to stay at Uncle Joe's. It was empty. They trooped to the stable yard. There, Paul Spencer arrived with disquieting news.

The doctors had found that Leigh had been strangled to death and Bruger, nettled by his failure to find Hulda, and feeling that he had been tricked into going to search for her, was coming to question Ellen and Uncle Joe.

"Ellen isn't here," A.T. said.

"Skipped?" Paul asked incredulously.

"We don't think so," A.T. replied, "but what is Bruger going to think?"

"Ye gods and little fishes!" Paul said. "What a lot of deducing he will do when he finds out Ellen isn't here."

"It may not be so bad," A.T. observed. "I wanted some more time to pursue a different line of investigation and it may be that Ellen being away will put Bruger off for a bit. Where are you heading for, Paul?"

"Going home to get a bite to eat. The sheriff is having his lunch at Wrayley's now. I'd just as soon he didn't know I came here. There's no law against it, but you know how he is."

"Go in and let Aggie give you something to eat," A.T. instructed. "Then go to Wrayley's and come back with Bruger. When he finds Ellen isn't home—if she isn't here by that time—persuade him to get up a hunt for her. I will oppose the idea and that will help him get started."

"All right by me," Paul agreed, and left toward the house.

A.T. summoned Adam and Pearl to further conference. "Adam and I had hoped to do a little fishing today," he began slowly. "We won't be able to do it now, but it seems a pity to waste so fine a day. Would you two like to go for a ride?"

"Why, yes," Pearl's answer was hesitant, "only it seems as though we ought not to bother about enjoying ourselves and the day, when things are so bad here."

Adam was watching the older man closely. "Is it something you want us to do somewhere else? Do you suspect that Ellen has gone to some particular place and want us to look?"

"It's something I'd like to have done, yes, but I doubt that it will help to find Ellen. I think Ellen will be back. There's no place where she can go without being seen, except to the woods. It would be no use for her to go into the woods unless she contemplates suicide. I don't think she will do that. I mean that I don't think she will actually commit suicide. She may be thinking of it. She may even plan to do it, but I'm pretty sure that she won't. No, either she has done just what Joe says she has, or she's hiding away, hoping to get a chance to leave the country unseen. That's virtually impossible now. There are no trains until morning. The newspaper folks are waiting now to get the doctor's verdict on the cause of Leigh's death. All the Bangor, Portland, and Boston papers that come out in the morning will have accounts of what has happened here today. If Ellen had taken a car and could get as far as Bangor or even to Millinocket tonight, she might not be recognized and might be able to get away. But she would need money, ready cash. I doubt that she had more than fifty dollars by her in cash. What would she do if she did succeed in getting to Boston or New York?"

"There's folks in Canada she knows," said Pearl. "but she wouldn't leave without her children."

"She would have a lot of difficulty getting across now, with or without the children. And what story do you think she could tell them? Remember that Ellen is proud. Would she go to friends anywhere and say, 'I'm running away because I'm in a difficult position at home, and I want you to keep me'?

"What I have in mind had nothing to do with Ellen. I wanted you to go to Tom Wells' camp and talk to old Charlie."

A.T. had risen from his chair and was pacing the floor with quick nervous strides. "I don't want to think that Tom Wells is a murderer. I don't like to think anyone is. But any remarks made to the sheriff may be heavily discounted. I know as well as he does that Leigh was murdered. I don't see how Tom could have done it. There isn't any doubt that he went to camp that Wednesday night. Or that he came back by train Thursday morning. What I want to know is, did he stay at camp all night? To have killed Leigh he would have had to travel ten miles in the woods and the dark to get to Leigh's place and ten miles back through blinding snow, as well as dark and forest. It would be slow and heavy going. The trip from the camp would not be impossible, a good man on snowshoes could do it in a little over two hours, or two and a half.

"But if Leigh was killed that night, it must have been after midnight, because Rush met him alive then. Then there would be the burying, which would take a good bit of time, even for a powerful man, and then the ten miles back with the snow to bother. It would take twice as long as the trip this way. I don't think it could be done, even by Tom, unless he went straight to the station from some point in the woods on his way back. I believe the train was late that morning on account of the storm, but even so, it doesn't look reasonable. Say he left here a half past one in the morning, which is putting it too soon by half an hour. He would have to be at the station by quarter to seven allowing for the train being fifteen minutes late. It's possible, but if he did that he couldn't have spent much time at the camp. Charlie would know, even though he wasn't there that night."

"How?" asked Adam.

"The amount of wood burnt, for one thing, the food eaten for another, and a dozen and one little things. Now if Charlie suspects that you're getting information about Tom's movements that night, he won't tell you a thing. You'll have to be circuitous and canny. Get Charlie to talking, to telling tales. It may be difficult now, but it will be impossible if Tom didn't spend the night at the camp.

"Well, how about it, are you willing to give it a try?"

"I am," Adam said promptly.

"So am I," Pearl agreed. "Not that I think anything will come of it, because I don't think Tom had one single thing to do with the killing of Leigh, or the burying of him either. What would you do if we found that Tom wasn't at the camp that night?"

"Scout around and find out where he was if I could. If I found enough to go before the grand jury with and ask for an indictment, I could possibly do something, but it's doubtful. The Army won't surrender a man on vague suspicions that he's mixed up in a murder, and my suspicions are vague, probably unfounded, certainly not provable now. Tom did not have any love for Leigh, but there were others who cared as little for him. I'm not expecting much from your inquiries, but I'm not overlooking any bets."

It was a relief to get away. The North Road was straight, hard and smooth. The air delightful; cracks and miniature upheavals marked the action of frost along the roadway, but these holes were easily avoided. Adam remarked on its excellence.

Pearl explained, "This is what we call 'state road.' It's a deep bed of heavy stone, covered with crushed rock and gravel, topped with tar. It stands the racket. After we turn off this to the side road, it won't be nearly as good as this, and after we leave the car, we'll have to walk two miles on a woods road which will be fearful. It isn't going to be a picnic and it's going to be a wild goose chase. I can feel it in my bones."

"I don't know," Adam replied. "It strikes me that Tom the silent would be my logical suspect. He hated Leigh. He loved Leigh's wife, and you put the idea in his mind yourself."

"Rats and piffle, also any other expressions of ridicule you can think of. I hated Leigh some myself, so did Ellen, as did Uncle Joe, so did Henry Delong, and probably a dozen other fathers and husbands. Uncle Joe cared more for Ellen than Tom ever did. Uncle Joe was around there that night and Tom was miles away. Oh, I know, you will say all the more reason for suspecting Tom, because he seems to be free from suspicion, to have an alibi, but you're just being smart when you do that, living up to the best tradition of fiction and all that sort of hooey. Use your common sense. Tom goes to his camp eight miles by railroad, two miles by snowshoes, ten miles by the trail through the woods from Leigh's house to the camp. He comes back by railroad the next morning. It doesn't make sense."

"It's possible, isn't it?"

"It's possible, maybe, under some conditions, but it's absurd under any. A.T. wouldn't consider it for a minute I'm sure if he wasn't right up against it and worried to death about Uncle Joe."

"Well, let it be until after we see this Charlie. Who are you picking for a suspect?"

"Henry Delong. I never thought he killed Beatrice. She just died, poor girl, but he had motive didn't he, and when it comes to alibis, who knows that he was at the mill that night?"

"That's true enough, but if he did it how did the fur coat get to that empty camp?"

"I don't know. Maybe Hulda put it there. She might do almost anything."

"Is she insane, and if she is, why is she allowed to be at large?"

"Dr. Little says she isn't violently insane, and isn't likely to be. She has always been considered harmless, and it would be needless cruelty to confine her in an asylum. She is queer of course and not right in her head. I wonder where she was today, and I wonder where Ellen is, I've wondered and wondered, and worried and worried, until I don't know that I'm just right in my own head half the time. I wish I could stop thinking about it."

"You might think about me for a change," Adam suggested. "You know I was anxious to get sent up here so that I might see you. You know that I wanted to see you and why. Can't you think about that for a little while?"

"I don't know, Adam, I did think about it a lot before you came, and I was glad you were coming. Then all this trouble came upon us, and I just seem numb. If Uncle Joe is tried for murder, murder, Adam, you may not feel the same, you may not care so much for me when I am the niece, almost the daughter of a murderer. You told me how you felt about murder."

Adam passed a car so closely that its driver flung angry words on the wind. "I am an awful prig sometimes," he confessed remorsefully. "What friend Bruger would call a natural-born fool. I still do have a horror about premeditated murder, but if Mr. Leeds did kill Leigh Wells, it wasn't that. It just couldn't have been. It was unintentional or justifiable homicide, if there is such a thing, but whether he did or didn't makes no difference in the way I feel toward you. I'm going overseas, I don't know when, just as soon as I get the word. I'd like to take with me the assurance that you cared for me. That if I came back I'd have a chance."

Adam said no more and for the space of many minutes there was silence.

When Pearl answered, she spoke slowly, somberly. "Back in New York I was sure of myself, sure that I loved you. Now, I am not sure of anything. I care a lot about you. Yesterday it was spring and you were coming, and I was glad. I'm still glad you are here and my eyes tell me it is spring now, all this, looking about over a landscape, flooded with golden sunshine, tells me everything is the same, but I can't feel it. I'll try and think it out before you go if I can, Adam."

"I understand, Pearl. We won't say any more about it now. Rest a little if you can, and just don't think about anything."

"Easier said than done," Pearl answered. "I wish I knew about Ellen. It isn't like her to go off by herself. I'm scared about her."

"The horse is gone," Adam said. "Perhaps she just went for a ride."

"What horse?" Pearl asked, puzzled.

"The mare, Lady. The stall is empty. No steed in sight."

"That almost makes it worse. Ellen might go for a ride, but it isn't something she does often. I've been haunted by something I read somewhere. 'Flight—suicide is a form of flight.'"

"But Pearl, why think that her going away, out into the sunlight, is flight? If A.T. thought she had run away, would he try to have the sheriff hunt for her?"

"Is he going to do that?" Pearl's eyes opened wide in alarm.

"So he said. I doubt he expects him to find Ellen anymore than he expected him to find Hulda."

Pearl's eyes lightened. "Hulda!" she said. "It didn't matter whether the sheriff found Hulda or not. Maybe A.T. doesn't think it matters whether he finds Ellen or not."

They came soon to the road that turned to the west and the woods. It was, as Pearl had predicted, rough and muddy in places. Its only virtue lay in the shortness of the distance they had to travel over it.

"Never mind," Pearl comforted, "this isn't a patch on the walking we will have to do." Again she proved a true prophet.

Physical activity, however, proved to be a welcome change and the hike to the camp, skirting mud holes, climbing over fallen tree trunks, avoiding the debris left by the winter snow, was pleasant in spite of its difficulties.

The camp stood in a clearing, half grown over with bushes and weeds. Bunkhouses and hovels, built of logs and rough boards, were dilapidated. The cook shack and office were in good repair. The cook shack with a bunkhouse attached was Charlie's quarters, and Pearl led the way to its door and knocked. Receiving no reply she called, but the woods were hushed and drowsy. No answer came from within or without. Pearl pushed open the door and entered, and Adam followed cautiously into the gloomy interior, half expecting some weird apparition to confront them. Above a long table, where twenty men might have been seated, tin plates and cups, many of them dark with age and use, hung in a rack. At the left of the door sat the cook stove, coffee and teapots atop. A red squirrel scurried away, popped through an open window at the back and stopped outside on a sapling to chatter a protest at the intrusion.

"Do you suppose," Pearl's manner was faintly reminiscent of Aunt Prue, "that we have come all this way on a fool's errand? Where is everyone today?"

"Everyone seems to have taken to the woods today, and them as were in it have either left or gone deeper. I vote for a seat outside while we rest and wait the coming of the lord of the manor."

"What time is it?" Pearl asked absently, sitting on a convenient stump.

"Three-thirty."

"We can't wait forever."

"Not nearly that long," Adam agreed.

Pearl discovered that she was tired. Adam declared that he was thirsty.

"See if there's water in the pail in there with the long-handled dipper in it," Pearl advised.

"Water there, but it's stale and flat," Adam reported.

"Then Charlie didn't just go to the spring, he went somewhere else. If you want a drink bad enough you can go to the spring for it. You follow that path."

"I'll do it, and while I fetch the Adam's ale you'd better find a more comfortable place and rest. You look all in."

"I am and I will. I'll go inside."

When Adam came back from the spring, Pearl was seated in a rocking chair fashioned from a barrel. She drank, gave him a smile of thanks, and rested her head upon the chairback.

At four o'clock Pearl, somewhat rested, became uneasy. "We ought to be starting back. I don't like waiting."

"We can't go back with our mission unaccomplished," Adam reasoned. "Is this where Tom stays?"

"The office is his camp, over there."

"It's rather quiet and restful here now. I can understand anyone coming here in the summer and in the hunting season, and the necessity of having someone here to prevent fires and all that, but ye gods, think of staying here all winter."

"They don't, unless there's some lumbering operation somewhere about. Charlie came out last year long the first part of December."

At four-thirty Adam suggested they have a look at the office.

"It's locked and Charlie has the key," Pearl told him. "We'll wait just one more half hour and then we'll have to go. Do you carry a jackknife in your pocket?"

"You might call it that, a Boy Scout would blush to own it but it serves my modest needs. Why?"

"I thought you would make a whistle for me. I haven't had one in years."

"How do you do it?"

"My word, your education was neglected. Here, I'll show you. Cut a willow branch about three-quarters of an inch thick."

Adam looked at the bushes. "What does willow look like without leaves?"

Pearl laughed. "City boy." She proceeded to cut a piece about 4 inches long.

"You wield a wicked knife, girl," Adam said.

Pearl then showed Adam how to slip the cylinder of bark off the branch. "Now you place a cut like this." Pearl then slipped the bark back over the wood, set the beveled edge to her lips and blew. The whistle was shrill and clear. "Oh boy," she cried, "It works!"

"I'll say," Adam was as enthusiastic as Pearl. "Let me do it."

Adam blew a blast. They looked at each other and laughed.

All at once, as though he had dropped from the sky, Charlie was before them.

"Hello, I didn't know anyone was coming today. By damn, sorry to be away when company come. Come in, come in, have a cup coffee."

"We can't stay long, Charlie, we ought to have started home an hour ago. Didn't like to go away without seeing you. I brought Mr. Stillman up to see the camp. He was here last Thanksgiving, and Tom was going to bring him up then if things hadn't turned out wrong."

"I've been over on the dead water lookin' for fires." Charlie ignored the lead Pearl had given. "Hallelujah, folks are careless."

"I wouldn't think there would be much danger of fires now," Adam said.

"People from town go fishin', then find a place back on a ridge where it's dry to cook the beefsteak they brought along. Leave the fire and Hallelujah, first thing anyone know dry ridge all blazin'. By damn."

Adam was casting about in his mind for a way to get the information they wanted when Pearl forestalled the questions he might have asked.

"Charlie, there's something I have to know. Did Tom stay here all night the night before last Thanksgiving?"

The old woodsman looked at the girl, his weather-beaten face with its deep-set eyes and bushy brows suggesting some animal of the woods he inhabited—not a ferocious animal, a gentle, kindly one.

"Yes, ma'am, he did. If anyone is figuring that Tom was anywhere else that night they're figuring wrong. It was like this. I went out that night sorta late and I met Tom on the way in, jest by the field there where the path starts into the woods. I come back in, next day along about three in the afternoon. Tom had gone, long before that. I knew he had gone early because his snowshoe tracks had snow in, but mind ye, there was only one track, just one from the office there to the hovel where he fed the chickens I had here and on out the road to the station where he took the train for home. He had left in a hurry and when he come back up the next Sunday he told me that hadn't slept so good the first part of the night, but that when he got to sleep he slept sound until about six, when he woke up all of a sudden and felt that he had to get back home. That's the truth, by damn."

"Thanks, Charlie, that's what I had to know. They found Leigh's body last night, did you know?"

"Hallelujah!" The way Charlie said it, it expressed amazement and wonder. "Where?"

"Buried in his back yard. We really have to get started back. Walk along and I'll tell you about it."

The dusk gathered about them as they walked. The way was long and the mud more sticky. Charlie left them at the clearing's edge. It seemed an age after Charlie left before they reached the parked car, beside the road near a deserted farmhouse.

The rough road leading out to the main highway was rougher, narrower, and more crooked than it had been on the way in.

When they reached the smooth straight highway that would take them up hill and down dale at a good pace and to the the waiting folks at home, darkness had quite fallen.

As they topped the crest of a hill halfway home they saw far ahead where the dark of the sky merged with the deeper dark of the wooded hills, little climbing stars, yellow and dancing, but so bright as to **pale** their sisters in the sky above them.

"Forest fire on August Mountain," Pearl gasped. "I know that's what it is, I saw one from here a few years ago and it looked just that way."

"Hallaleujah," Adam murmured.

"A forest fire is no laughing matter," Pearl returned grimly, "but unless there's a long dry spell it won't be so hard to check now."

The rest of the way home they watched from every hill top.

"It's miles away," Pearl muttered. Adam drove and said little, feeling the spell the region had put upon him. This night, the girl at his side, the silent forest depths, the everlasting hills about them were all but the overtones of a dream, whose deeper tones were suffering, fire, and death.

On the road above the cemetery, where the street lights began, they overtook a horse. Without rider or saddle, it walked sedately toward the barn. As the lights of the car shone on the animal, Pearl gave a little startled gasp. "That's Leigh Wells' mare. What can she be doing here?"

Murder by Persons Unknown

The car drew slowly away from the horse, which kept steadily to the business of getting home.

"Just go on," Pearl said, "She'll follow."

As they drove into the yard they saw A.T. pacing with slow tense strides, in the shadow of the front of the great barn. He came swiftly to meet them, just as the side door of the house opened, silhouetting Bruger in the light at his back.

Pearl spoke swiftly to A.T. as he came to the side of the car. "Lady, Leigh's mare, is loose up the road, coming this way."

"Anything on her?" A.T. Asked.

"Not so much as a rope. Do you suppose—?"

"Can't suppose anything now. Get Bruger back into the house with you and I'll look after her. Some of our folks have returned, anyway, Bruger," raising his voice as the sheriff came near.

"Sorry to be away so long, Sheriff, that is, if you wanted us," Adam said.

"I didn't want you exactly," the sheriff replied rather ungraciously. "I do want to know where you've been and what you've been up to."

"Come on into the house," said Pearl, "and we'll tell you all about it. I'm starved. We were delayed and haven't had a chance to eat."

This was not strictly true. Pearl felt just then that she would never desire food again, but knowing A.T.'s wishes she determined to get Bruger inside before the mare came home. Probably, she reflected, the mare, which had been brought to the Leeds place when Ellen had moved there, had simply broken out of the pasture, where she had been turned out for exercise, and in accordance with her training was now coming back to the barn.

"Didja see anything of Mrs. Wells on your travels?" Bruger inquired, a note of sarcasm in his voice.

"Hasn't Ellen come home?" Pearl countered, surprise in her voice, dismay in her heart. She had hoped that during their absence Ellen had come back, that she would find her in the house with an explanation of her unannounced expedition.

"No she ain't come home, and she won't come home if you ask me. A.T. is a slick lawyer, all right, but he'll have his work cut out for him if he thinks he's goin' to keep me from finding that woman and arrestin' her for murderin' her man. Way down below Danforth last year a squaw let daylight through the injun she was married to, jest got peeved at him and drilled him clean with a forty-five. I didn't hear anyone putting up a holler about, she couldn't a done it, poor thing, and all that sorta guff. It makes a difference to some folks, who's who, but not to me. An' anybuddy that helps a murderer to escape is accessory after the fact, jes as much as the one that buried the body, don't forget that, you folks."

"I assure you," Adam said stiffly, "that while I don't believe for one minute that Mrs. Wells killed her husband, neither Miss Jameson nor I have been assisting in any melodramatic flights from justice."

In the living room Uncle Joe sat before the fireplace, looking fixedly at the empty grate, as though he saw there all the dead fires of a long and busy life.

Aunt Prue sat beside him, her hands idle, her expression grim and anxious. She rose nervously to greet Pearl and Adam. "Where have you been all the afternoon and did you see anything of Ellen?"

"We went for a ride, and walked in to Charlie's. We didn't see anyone except Charlie. I thought Ellen would be here before we got back. Where do you suppose she can be?"

"I suppose she can be lost, and wandering around in the woods, or dropped into one of the bog holes in the swamp. I suppose she can be in any danger at all and her own folks be powerless to help her because the sheriff here has just one idea in his head about her, and that is that she's run away."

In spite of Bruger's blustering, he stood not a little in awe of the Leeds family and had conceived an enormous respect for the opinion of Aunt Prue, a respect he was not willing to admit but which nevertheless influenced him. He endeavored now to set himself right with the lady of the house. "The woods have been full of men looking for Hulda most of the day, Mrs. Leeds. If Mrs. Wells had gone out there and been lost, seems to me some of them would have found some trace of her.

And since they came back all the able-bodied men and boys for miles around have gone down through the old tote road to August Mountain, to fight the fire there. Besides, Mrs. Wells knows these woods. She was brought up right along side of them, wasn't she? Where would she be likely to go to git lost?"

"Where, indeed," sniffed Aunt Prue. "Ellen never was one to wander by herself in the woods. She wouldn't have gone into them at all if she hadn't been half out of her head with worry. But since you know so much, where could she have gone?"

"That," said the sheriff, nettled in return, "is what I wish you people would tell me. Here I am, trying to investigate a murder, and all the help I get from the murdered man's family is 'You must think this and you mustn't think that,' while the chief suspect does a bunk."

A.T. entered the room, giving the sheriff a designedly portentous look. "Here's a funny thing, Burger, that mare of Leigh's just came wandering home, without saddle or bridle, but I'm pretty sure she has been ridden today, and through bushes, too. Want to come take a look?"

"Not even a halter on her this time, I suppose." Bruger's sarcasm, like his walk, was heavy and grim as he left the room.

When he was gone, Adam and Pearl turned eagerly to the couple by the fire. "Now tell us what has happened while we were gone," Pearl said.

"Dr. Little finished the autopsy, got a jury together, and reported that Leigh was murdered by a person or persons unknown. You know, just the usual verdict. Little says that he was strangled, and Rush agrees with him. I'm practically under arrest now," said Uncle Joe, wearily, still keeping his eyes on the empty grate.

"But Uncle Joe, how can the sheriff do that? He just said that Ellen was the chief suspect, and she's gone. Why does he pick on you?"

"As I understand Bruger, he is casting me for accessory after the fact. He thinks that I buried Leigh and that I've sent Ellen away. I wish I had. I wish I had sent Ellen away weeks ago. Hulda warned me, told me that I should but I only thought it was part of her crazy notions. She's full of fancies that come from living alone there in the woods."

"They didn't find her?" Adam asked.

"Hulda? No. They won't find her until she's ready to be found. What shall we do about Ellen? I hate to think of her out there alone, maybe hurt, hurt in body as well as mind. What did Arthur mean about the horse?" asked Joe.

"Lady came down the road just behind us," Pearl told him. "A.T. wanted to look her over by himself, before anyone else saw her. That's why we came on in so that the sheriff would come in too."

"Ellen hasn't ridden for years, has she, Prue? I can't think why she would ride Lady, anywhere. I think I will go out and see about it," Joe said.

"And you children must be hungry." Aunt Prue led the way toward the kitchen, "Come on out and have supper. Aggie went to church, Mrs. Grimes is with the children, and Jack went with the firefighters."

"I wouldn't think that there could be a bad fire after that shower last night," Adam said, devouring cold meat and bread and butter with pickles, with an appetite that shamed him under the circumstances by which these, his friends and hosts, were surrounded.

"August is seven miles or more away from here. Thunderstorms follow along the river and if they come this way they seldom strike there too. It's drier there on that rocky hillside than it is most anywhere else around here, gets dry quicker in the spring. There's a little lake at the foot of the mountain. It's closed to fishermen but a lot of people go there just the same, sneak in and get a few fish. It's always been a bad spot for fires. The timber isn't worth much right there but if a fire gets started this time of year and we happen to have a long dry spell it's pretty hard to keep it from spreading unless it's put out right away. I'm glad they didn't find Hulda. If Ellen is wandering around in the woods anywhere I'm glad Hulda is in the woods, too."

"From what I saw of her," Adam said, "I don't think it would comfort me much to know that she was loose in the woods with me."

"You mustn't misjudge Hulda. You've only seen her under trying conditions. She isn't a bad sort of woman and if she has crazy spells, goodness knows she has had enough to make her that way."

"I've been wanting to ask about her. Pearl just hinted at a story. Is it a mystery of any sort, or is one permitted to ask about it?"

"There's no special mystery about it. I suppose we are all so used to it that we don't think of it's being of interest to anyone. Hulda isn't her real name. She's really Mrs. Marion Wilkinson. She's not much older than I am. Her father was an officer stationed at the garrison at Houlton, years ago when there was one there. I don't remember much about that, myself. I know that Hulda's mother was dead and that she was educated in a convent in St. John. Her father died while she was there and after she was through school she went to Houlton with a girl who studied at the convent with her. She met a man there and they became engaged to be married. Then on the very eve of her wedding, at least close to it, the man married another girl.

"Then Wilkenson, old Julius Wilkenson, who was a plausible rascal, happened to be in town on one of his 'business' trips. Somehow he met her, and told her a tale of his castle in the woods, making it sound, I suppose, like a romantic medieval fortress. She eloped with him on horseback and he brought her to a squalid log cabin, miles from anywhere, and presented her to three half-grown and half-wild sons as their stepmother. Then the baby girl she had two years later died just after her first birthday. Old Julius died too after a while and the boys grew up and went away.

"The youngest one is good to her, has tried to get her to come out and live among folks in the village, and when she wouldn't he built her a new cabin there, a real nice little house it is with water piped in from a spring and everything as good as one could ask for. But the harm had been done to Hulda's mind years ago. She doesn't care about the house, and she wanders about just as she had for twenty years. Folks give her things and she can have whatever she asks for at the stores. Her bills are always paid without question by the stepson. He has a good position," Prue concluded.

"It's a queer and tragic story," Adam mused. "There must be something about the great forest which gets one as the sea is said to call some people."

Pearl responded, "Partly that and partly just clinging to what you are used to. Aunt Prue, what are we going to do, what can we do? Do we just have to sit still and do nothing at all while Uncle Joe and Ellen are tried for murder?"

"We don't have to do quite so badly as that, Pearl. There isn't much we can do. Arthur wants us to just 'sit tight' as he calls it, and not to be discouraged if things look pretty bad after the hearing tomorrow. He says it may end by having Joe tried for murder, and that's bad enough, although Joe and I could stand it I think, and come out all right. But if something terrible has happened to Ellen, Joe is just going to give up. Joe's weird in some ways. He's afraid Ellen did kill Leigh and he would rather be tried for it than her, but if anything has happened to her, he's going to feel worse than any murder trial can make him, because he will be bound to think that he might have taken care of her better than he did. If Pearl and I were jealous sort of women we should be jealous of Ellen. Joe is more protective of her than either or both of us, I think."

"More than me, maybe, Aunt Prue, but not more than you. I think he's felt all the time since Ellen was married that he might have prevented her marrying Leigh and so avoided a lot of unhappiness."

"Ellen was always headstrong. I doubt that we could have kept her from marrying Leigh. Well, it's too late to think about that now. All we can do is what Arthur says, sit tight and trust to him."

While they talked, Aunt Prue had been deftly busy. No trace of the supper was left. It looked like magic to one who watched her effortless and efficient clearing up. Now she led the way back from the living room, where A.T. for once sat silently by while his brother talked. "But I tell you, Sheriff," Uncle Joe was saying, "we didn't know a thing about Ellen going away by herself. We only decided she had done that because it seemed to be the only thing she could have done. Now the horse comes home, and it's plain to see that she's been ridden. A blanket has been strapped to her back and she's been wearing a bridle. She's been in the woods. Now the pasture is over that way," pointing to the northeast, "and the mare was there, turned out there this morning, not for feed, she was fed in the barn and turned out for exercise. Ellen could have gone down there and ridden her into the woods up that way on some errand or other, and then perhaps she slipped the blanket off maybe wanted it herself to sit on. Suppose she hitched the mare by the bridle reins, and went for a walk in the woods for a few minutes. You know that mare is cranky. If she didn't want to stay hitched, she would get out of that bridle easy. She came down the north road, Pearl says." In his eagerness to make a point, Uncle Joe had quite forgotten that it was his brother who had brought them the story of the loose mare and that Pearl had not mentioned it to the sheriff. A.T. said calmly, "I told you that, I think, Joe. I'm quite sure that Pearl didn't mention it."

"I also am quite sure that Pearl didn't mention it," Bruger mimicked A.T.'s statement, "and her not mentioning it is all of a piece with the rest of it. You haven't mentioned anything you could help mentioning, none of you, from the night Leigh Wells was killed. You all know something, but you haven't mentioned it."

"If you've finished, Sheriff, shall we hear the rest of what my brother was going to mention?" A.T. asked, not at all ruffled by the sheriff's outburst.

"I just wanted to point out that Ellen might have been somewhere to the north of town all day, and not have been seen by the men who have been in the woods, because they were looking for Hulda off to the west and south. She might not even be in the big woods at all. She may be lost or hurt in the woods beyond the pasture. That patch is three or four miles square, and it doesn't take much woods to get lost in sometimes. I want to go there and see if I can find Ellen. You come with me, Bruger, then you'll be sure that I won't run away."

"I can't be sure of anything in this case, but I'm not goin' to be led away on a wild goose chase to the woods while some of the things you folks would forget to mention happen here. No, I stay right here and you stay with me, Mr. Leeds."

Rebellion was writ large on Uncle Joe's face. "While you refuse to go or send someone to hunt for Ellen she may be suffering all sorts of things. How would you like it to be lost at night?"

"I did not refuse to send someone to hunt for Mrs. Wells. If you can think of anyone who can and will go out tonight to hunt for a woman who may be lost or may not be, you can do better than I can."

"Here's where I am one up on you then, Sheriff," A.T. said carelessly. "Bet you a nickel, I can raise half a dozen men in fifteen minutes."

"Go right ahead then. See what you can do."

A.T. went to the telephone and called a number; presently he could be heard in conversation. "You, Mitch? A.T. speakin'. Mitch, Joe is afraid that Ellen has been lost in the woods beyond the pasture. He can't go out to hunt for her himself, can you get Henry and three, four other fellers and go have a look? Good enough, Mitch, good enough. Yes, you come to the house and tell us if you find anything."

A.T. hung up the receiver, well satisfied. "Now don't worry any more about that, Joe. Mitch will search as thoroughly as possible, and if nothing is found and Ellen doesn't come back by noon tomorrow, we will get out a regular crew, right, Bruger? And now I think we had better all go to bed."

There was little sleep at the Leeds home that night. Adam pondered many things. Pearl alternately worried and hoped. Uncle Joe waited anxiously for some word from the searchers in the forest. Aunt Prue worried about the whole situation and more especially about Uncle Joe. Jack did not come home from the firefighting crew. It is to be hoped that Aggie prayed. As for A.T., the morning showed that the night had brought counsel if not content. Bruger spent the night in alternate naps upon the living room couch and fits of watchfulness when he tried in vain to detect any surreptitious movement of the inhabitants of the quiet house.

The Confession

Morning brought another clear and sunny day, with breakfast prepared by Aggie, who under dire threats from Aunt Prue refrained from lifting her voice in song. Jack arrived tired and grim, reporting the fire under control, and a discouraged Mitch arrived from the pasture woods, reporting their lack of success.

Burger placed Joe under arrest. The court hearing was to Adam a most interesting affair. Held in an office that was not small, but not large enough to allow many spectators, it lacked the formality of a trial, yet the proceedings had an air of tremendous import, a dignity which needed no support from mere formalities.

Trial justice John Willoughby was white of hair and of scholarly mien. An older man than A.T., he had, before his retirement from the active practice of law, opposed or supported A.T. in many a court case. Now he presided over this arraignment with an air of quiet decorum.

"The purpose of this hearing," said the justice, "is to decide if there is just cause to send this case to the grand jury, and to determine if bail will be granted."

"What charge are you bringing against your prisoner, Sheriff?"

Bruger, who sat beside Uncle Joe upon a long wooden settee at the right of the justice's desk, rose.

"I charge Joseph Leeds with the willful murder of Leigh Wells, on Thanksgiving eve of last November."

A.T. looked at Bruger with lifted brows. The sheriff had seemed so sure that Ellen was guilty. Did he think that both were guilty, or had he decided to charge Joseph Leeds only?

Pearl, sitting in a chair among those facing the justice's desk, felt her heart plummet to lie like a lump of lead in the pit of her stomach. She had thought that Uncle Joe was to be charged with accessory after the fact, for burying the body and protecting Ellen. Pearl looked at Aunt Prue, sitting beside Uncle Joe, and wondered if her heart too was behaving strangely. If it was, that redoubtable lady gave little sign. She sat quite still and only the clenching of her hands in her lap showed that she heard the awful charge.

"What evidence do you bring in support of this charge?"

"I can prove, your honor, that Mr. Leeds argued with the victim on the night he was killed. I can prove Mr. Leeds was at the scene of the crime when it was committed. I can prove that he was able to commit the murder and that he had motive for the crime. I can prove that Mr. Leeds had great love for the victim's wife who he raised since infancy and more than enough reason to hate the man who treated her so poorly. Taken together with other facts which I need not go into at this time, I believe there is ample reason for holding Joseph Leeds for investigation by the grand jury with regard to the murder of Leigh Wells."

Bruger was well satisfied with himself. Adam wondered if he really thought he had a case against Mr. Leeds. Did he have witnesses to prove what he alleged or was the man's colossal conceit leading him to make a statement that could not be backed up? He noticed that A.T. did not seem especially disturbed.

The justice addressed Uncle Joe. "Mr. Leeds, what have you to say in regard to the charge the sheriff brings?"

Uncle Joe rose slowly and spoke haltingly. "Your honor, I did not kill Leigh Wells. It's true that I drove by the Wells home late on the night of November 23rd last year. I admit that I might have been able to commit a murder, but I did not do it."

The judge opened his mouth to speak, but what he might have said was not to be disclosed at the moment.

There was a stir in the corridor. The crowd that had gathered there, seeking for admittance to the already filled room, parted to allow the entrance of a curious procession. Ellen Wells entered, disheveled, her pale face streaked with dirt and scratched by briars, followed by Hulda, a black lace straw hat with a mushroom crown, its side decorated with a crimson velvet rose, upon her head, and the little white dog under her arm. Ellen stumbled forward. "Uncle Joe didn't do it. He didn't do it. I did it myself."

Uncle Joe moved as though to protect her, to shield her even from her own confession, but Aunt Prue caught the girl in her arms and steadied her upon the seat at her side. "Nonsense, child, hush, you are all upset. Don't come home to tell us such absurd stories."

But Ellen rose determinedly to her feet. "It's true, Justice Willoughby. May I tell you all about it?"

The kind old eyes, under the thatch of white hair, looked steadily on the girl. "Unless A.T. objects, and I don't think he is going to, you may."

"That night, just before Thanksgiving, Leigh had promised to come home early so I could go down to the stores. I wanted to buy some little things, just little things. He said he would come home and stay with the children and if I would be ready to go when he came I could take the team and go."

"I was ready at half past seven and I waited and waited. He didn't come. I put the children to bed and I tried to read. Then I tried to sew. I even tried playing solitaire. Then it got to be ten o'clock and I thought that if I didn't do something I would go mad. It wasn't just that one time, you see. It was like all the times before when he had promised things, rolled into one. I got the things ready and began to iron some of the children's clothes. There are always children's clothes to be ironed, when you have three. About eleven o'clock he came in the front door and through the sitting room. He just stood there in the door with his cap pushed back off his head and grinned at me. Then he said in that sneering way of his, 'Not ready yet?' I had the flatiron right at my hand. It was only warm; I had just finished pressing flannels. I just threw it at him as hard as I could. He caught the string on the light cord as he fell, and the light went out. Then I heard little Prue having croup and I rushed up the stairs. He must have staggered outside and fell in that snow drift and died. So you see it was me, I killed him, not Uncle Joe at all."

Ellen sat down weakly and Aunt Prue slipped a comforting arm around her.

A.T. spoke, "May I ask Mrs. Wells one question, your honor?"

"You may."

"If," said A.T., very gently to Ellen, "you killed Leigh with your little flatiron, can you tell me how it came about that he was strangled to death before his body was buried in his own back yard?"

The Hearing

Ellen Wells stared intently at the questioner, unbelieving. Her lips, suddenly grown stiff, strove to form words as she looked at A.T. In her eyes the last spark flickered out, leaving darkness without luster. Then she began to crumple as a fragile flower wilts when bruised by a rough hand.

Prue opened her arms to catch Ellen as she fell, but Uncle Joe had not waited. He caught Ellen's inert body in his strong arms and cradled her there.

Justice Willoughby stood up, saying, "We will halt these proceedings for ten minutes, Miss Gray," speaking to his secretary, an elderly woman whose name was an apt expression of her appearance. "Joe, bring Mrs. Wells into my private office. No one else will leave the room during this recess."

Whispers began to break the amazed hush that had fallen upon the room. Suddenly Hulda's voice was heard, high and scornful. "Fools! Fools, all of you! Do you think a woman is made of steel? I'd better have let her die than have her suffer this torture."

A sort of grim bafflement was stamped on A.T.'s face. "Why did you bring her here, Hulda?" he asked.

"I couldn't keep her back. We were going through the trees when the sheriff took Joe from the house. She ran down the road after the cars. I couldn't stop her."

Adam was trying with all his might to straighten the situation in his own mind. A.T.'s abrupt question had nullified Ellen's confession. If what she had told were true, and Adam believed that it was, she might know as little of the real circumstances of her husband's death as anyone else. But was that possible? Could Leigh have been killed and placed there so close to the house without Ellen's knowledge? And if that was so, who could have done it? He glanced at the sheriff's face and knew that Bruger did not believe it. He looked at A.T. but learned nothing at all of what might be going on behind that impassive yet expressive face. Had A.T. expected Ellen to react as she had to his question? It seemed to show that Ellen was innocent, but was she?

Adam's mind slipped into a half reverie, searching, searching for the solution to an incredible situation. He wished that he could see the faces behind him, could judge from them the temper of the crowd that filled the room and blocked the doorways. Unable to do so, he scanned the faces of those who sat at his right behind Mr. and Mrs. Leeds. Henry Delong was there, old Mitch beside him, two old men, grizzled and gnarled, roughly dressed, faces seamed and scarred, eyes that saw many things and looked upon them emotionlessly. Beside Henry and Mitch, sat a younger man, a man who bore the same stamp, yet was different with the difference of youth. "Vane Young," Pearl told him in answer to a whispered query, "foreman at the mill."

Ellen and Miss Gray returned to the room and resumed their places, Ellen beside Aunt Prue and Miss Gray at the justice's right where she picked up the pencil and notebook she had been using, quite as though all this was a matter of course. Ellen had washed her face and done something to the curls that clustered around it. She had regained a measure of self-control, a hint of hardness, of purpose.

"Do you wish to change anything in your previous statement, Mrs. Wells?" the justice asked.

"No," Ellen answered clearly, "I did throw the iron at him. I did not strangle him."

The sheriff started to his feet, hot words bubbling to his lips. The justice waved him back and continued to address Ellen.

"Will you tell us what happened during the rest of the night?"

"Nothing, so far as I know. I came back down to the kitchen in just a few minutes later. Leigh wasn't there."

"Was anyone else there?"

"No."

"Had anyone been there? Was the door open, or were there any traces of anyone having been there?"

"No."

"What did you think had happened?"

"I supposed Leigh had just been knocked down, and that he had got up and gone away."

"You didn't look around any?"

"No."

"Why?"

"At the time, I just thought he left because he was angry. I thought that if Leigh had gone, he must be all right, and I was worried about the baby."

A.T. addressed a question to the sheriff. "Are you satisfied that Mrs. Wells had nothing to do with the death of her husband?"

"Satisfied? Not by a long chalk, I'm not. I wouldn't put it past you to stage all this." Bruger made a sweeping gesture which included Hulda.

"I'm not so infernally clever as all that." A.T.'s voice was acid.

"Willoughby, I want them both held. She has confessed to an attack on her husband's life." said Bruger truculently. "I have a warrant for the arrest of Mrs. Wells for complicity in the murder of her husband. Shall I read it?"

Ellen looked questioningly at A.T.

He smiled encouragingly at her. "You may consider it read, Sheriff," he said.

Again Adam's mind slipped into the world of half thoughts. Had it all happened just as Ellen said? Then who had met Leigh Wells somewhere in that snowy night and strangled him to death? Who had brought his body back to his home and buried it?

Still pondering the matter of how and who, Adam heard through the fog in his mind the voice of the trial justice stating gravely his conclusion that the circumstances allowed only one decision, that Joseph Leeds and Ellen Wells, who had also been placed under arrest, be held to appear before the grand jury at its next sitting in November. And A.T.'s voice, carefully controlled, asking, "Will you admit them to bail?"

To Adam, suddenly alert to what was going on, it seemed as though the justice's momentary hesitation meant refusal. To the sheriff it must have seemed otherwise because he was instantly on his feet with a protest. "Your honor, this is a murder. You can't admit these people to bail."

The justice's calm was broken not one whit, but his voice had a tiny edge as of sharp, exceedingly sharp steel. "Whether or not I accept a bond for the appearance of persons before the grand jury is entirely in my province to decide, Sheriff. There has been a murder committed, so far you and I agree. But as to whether or not the people who have been accused by you committed the deed, is not for this court to decide. Our only concern today is whether there is cause to bring their case before the grand jury. I have decided that there is cause, and have ordered that Mr. Leeds and Mrs. Wells shall appear before that body at its next session." Justice Willoughby turned from the sheriff to A.T. "The features of this case are peculiar. Am I right in thinking that neither Mr. Leeds nor Mrs. Wells are in very good health?"

"You're right, your honor."

"Then I cannot see wherein the ends of justice would be served by committing either of them to jail and I will accept on behalf of the state, a bond of five thousand dollars from each of them as a guarantee of their appearance before the grand jury."

Adam and Pearl left the building together. Adam's preoccupation with things that happened during his former visit to Edenville was so great that coming out to the spring sunshine was a distinct shock. They should, he felt, have stepped forth into snow and darkness. "Should we wait for the others?" he asked the girl at his side.

"No, let's walk home now. I want to think. They'll be some time making the arrangements about the money, and it's eleven o'clock now. They'll bury Leigh at two o'clock. I suppose Ellen did what she thought was the right thing when she told about knocking Leigh down with that flatiron, but it seems to me that she has put Uncle Joe in a worse position than he was before. She's kept it to herself all these months. I think she might have kept still a while longer."

"But she really thought she had killed him, and she couldn't know that he was strangled. She had been wandering in the woods all the time the autopsy was being made and she didn't know about Little's report."

"I suppose not. Everything has gone absolutely wrong about the whole thing from the very first."

"Everything is always wrong in a case where a murder is mixed up."

"How very brilliant you are sometimes, Adam."

"Sorry, you know I confessed to being the particular sort of fool who would say something like that. I've been doing some heavy thinking, and I can't figure the thing out much. It doesn't seem possible that Ellen could have strangled Leigh and buried him that night. It must have been some job for a man, let alone a rather small woman.

"Then too, if he came home at eleven o'clock as Ellen says, and Dr. Rush met him going that way, he must have survived the flatiron because he was driving away from home an hour later. If he was killed somewhere else and not buried that night, where was the body hidden? There was a pretty thorough search, you know. And that fur coat must have been left in the deserted camp before morning because whatever tracks were made were obliterated by the snow that fell after it was put there. If somebody killed him in the woods why would they bring the body back to his house and bury it there? It might never have been found in the woods. And then what becomes of the cut rope and the vanishing halter?"

"I don't know, I really don't know, the more I think about it the more involved the whole thing is."

"Now look here, Pearl, if it had happened this way—I'm not saying that it did mind you and I don't believe Uncle Joe is a murderer any more than you do—but suppose Leigh did not go home when Dr. Rush met him on the bridge, say that he turned down Elm street and went to the Delong place. Perhaps the girl there was already dead, perhaps she wasn't, but either way, we will say that Leigh has a bad scare. He wants to get away in a hurry, so much of a hurry that he doesn't untie the halter just slashes it with his knife and drives away, back across the bridge, meeting Dr. Rush again. He's excited and in a hurry, doesn't answer the doctor's hail.

"Meanwhile, Uncle Joe has been called to the station and when he's finished his business there he drives over to make sure Ellen is all right. Perhaps Leigh had already calmed down and gone home, perhaps Uncle Joe got there first. But let's say that Leigh had arrived home and that he and Ellen had quarreled. She had knocked him down and choked him. When Uncle Joe got there there seemed nothing to do but to get rid of Leigh's body so together they take it out and bury it in the easiest place and also the most secure place, because no one would think of its being there. Then Uncle Joe could get home about the time he did get there."

"I don't believe it," Pearl stated, "it's horrible."

"I don't believe it either, but Bruger would, and he will attempt to prove something like that."

"But he can't prove it."

"Can A.T. disprove it?"

"I don't know, but he can do most anything. Unless Bruger can really prove something like that and bring witnesses to back it up, A.T. can make it seem so absurd to a jury that they will give Ellen and Uncle Joe the benefit of the doubt."

Adam responded, "And leave everyone else in doubt too, with half of the people believing that they are guilty and only A.T.'s cleverness has saved them."

"I don't see that it's as likely as you said that Leigh went home just as Ellen said and that after that he met Dr. Rush on the bridge he went back to the Delong's and was killed there. Henry might have been at home, you know. No one saw him at the mill as far as anyone has been able to find out. Anyway, if Ellen and Uncle Joe did it, who put the fur coat in the camp? Uncle Joe wouldn't have had time to do that. Suppose Hulda was at the Delong place. She might have been. She says she wasn't out that night, but nobody can prove that either. She and Henry might have buried the body and either one of them might have taken the coat to the camp. I'd say Hulda did that. Perhaps Beatrice was in shock and wandered out into the night after they had gone and left her alone. Henry blamed Leigh for Beatrice's death so he could have killed him and buried him. Maybe Hulda planted the coat. It's hard to understand anything Hulda does. They could have done it. Then Hulda stole the halter, so it couldn't be proved that Leigh had been there that night. She found Ellen in the woods and got her to confess. Now, you pick flaws in that theory," Pearl concluded triumphantly.

"It's good," Adam agreed, "darned good. Of course, Hulda would have known that Leigh was strangled, and she didn't seem to know that. I saw her while A.T. was asking Ellen about it. Do you think she is clever enough to have acted as though she didn't know if she did?"

"I don't know, and I don't really believe it happened that way at all, but it's a much more satisfactory theory than yours. I don't see why, if Bruger has to have someone to have done it, he couldn't have picked on Henry with Hulda to help as well as Uncle Joe."

"Bruger is a bit of an anarchist," Adam pointed out. "To him Mr. Leeds and Ellen represent the moneyed ruling class. He would rather get something on one of them than on a more humble subject. To give him his due, I doubt that he knows he feels that way, but it's plain to an outsider."

"You know I was mulling over things in my mind and I partly missed Ellen's story of her trip to the woods. It was about as we thought, wasn't it?"

"Yes. She was pretty badly upset and slipped off by herself. She saw Lady in the pasture, and just followed a vagrant impulse and thought she would go for a ride. Put a bridle and blanket on the mare and went to the pasture woods. Then she got to thinking about Hulda, and thought she would go and have a talk with her. When she had ridden into the woods on the other side of the road a ways, she heard people and didn't want to be seen. It was the men the sheriff had sent to look for Hulda but Ellen didn't know that. She was with the children, you know, while we were talking. She tied Lady by the bridle reins in a thicket, and took the blanket with her into another. The flies bothered the mare and she got restless, slipped the bridle by rubbing it against a tree and ran away. If any of the men got a glimpse of her they weren't especially surprised to see a loose horse in the woods there and didn't try to stop her. So Ellen was afoot and alone, in the woods.

Adam continued, "It is the easiest thing in the world to get lost, especially if you are excited anyway, and Ellen isn't used to the woods, like some girls. Hulda found her after dark, when the men left to go and fight the fire on August Mountain. She kept her all night and brought her home this morning. I don't know why she kept her there. She could just as well have brought her home last night. Of course, Ellen was pretty well done out, but I doubt that that was the reason. That's the trouble, no one can get at Hulda's reasons for anything. I think she plays on her reputation and gets away with a lot of stuff."

Back in the room where the hearing had been held, the business of bonding had been completed, and Uncle Joe found a moment for a word alone with the justice. "I'm greatly obliged to you, Willoughby. I had hardly dared hope for bail being allowed."

Justice Willoughby polished his spectacles reflectively. "I had a precedent, Leeds, you know, but you really should thank Bruger. I was so determined to be influenced by no personal considerations that I was in danger of bending over backward, until Bruger brought me upright with his few well-chosen words." A grim smile touched the corners of his stern mouth. "Unofficially, Leeds, if you want any help there's plenty in this community that will give it to you. I'm glad that you will have an able defense."

Aggie had hurried home. As Adam and Pearl opened the side door, a voice from the kitchen raised in song, smote upon their ears, *"Choose now, choose now, on the right or wrong side where stand you."*

"Oh, for Pete's sake, Aggie, hush," Pearl called. "The others may be here any time."

"There's a time to rejoice and a time to weep, Pearl Jameson, and this is a time to rejoice. Didn't that trial just the same as show that our folks didn't do it?"

"Good heavens, no, Aggie, it just showed that nobody knows anything yet."

"Well, I should call it a victory for the right. They weren't sent to jail anyway." Aggie resumed her work, but modified her song to a lower and more subdued key.

Jack, coming in, wore a look of reprieve. "I wasn't called and lots of other folks weren't either. Do you think that means I won't have to give any evidence?"

"I think it just means that neither side wanted to disclose any more than they had to," Adam answered.

Pearl added, "Just don't talk and be ready to help A.T. when he needs you."

"But nothing I can tell will help that I can see."

"It may when the time is ripe. Just let things slide for now." With sage advice to youth given, Adam went to his room, leaving Pearl to meet the others when they came home.

Little Peter, having been told that his mother would be home soon, waited in the doorway and greeted her with an ecstatic hug. "I'm glad you are home," he said sedately. Pearl, watching those chubby arms clasping his mother's neck, felt again that leaden drop of her heart. Peter's mother could do no wrong in Peter's young eyes, but in the future, Ellen could be tried, perhaps convicted, of the murder of Peter's father. No, it couldn't be. It just couldn't be.

That noonday dinner was a somber meal. When they had finished, A.T. pushed back his chair. "Adam, I suppose it's necessary for you to get away today." Adam assented. "Then if I go now and call the people you hoped to see, you can take my car and drive down to Houlton and see them. Leave the car there and go on just as you planned."

"I thought," said Pearl, "that I would drive Adam down. Will it be all right for me to, or do I have to go to the funeral?"

For a moment no one spoke, then Aunt Prue said firmly, "I don't think you need to go. I'm not going myself."

Uncle Joe looked with troubled wonderment at his wife. "No, Joseph," she answered his look, "I'm not going. I'm going to send Mrs. Grimes with Ellen and I'm going to stay with the children."

"But don't you think Peter—" Uncle Joe hesitated to put his thought in words.

"If you mean, do I think Peter ought to go to his father's funeral, I do not. It is a great pity that once he was buried with so little ceremony, he ever had to be buried again with such ceremony as there will be. I am not going to persecute myself to go and listen to a minister praying, people singing dolorous hymns, and all the people who can get in whispering among themselves about the family. They've said so much about us in the newspapers and out, that a few more words to the effect that such and such members of the victim's family were not present at the last rites will make very little difference." Aunt Prue left the room with colors flying.

A.T. laid his hand on his brother's shoulder. "Prue still has her spunk, Joe. We'll come out all right yet. Now I'll go and telephone, and then

Adam, I want a few words with you before you go."

Half an hour later Adam had said his farewells to the rest of the family A.T. stood by the car where Pearl was already behind the wheel. With a last handshake, he said, "You know what is necessary and you will do it if it's humanly possible?"

"I'll do my very best," Adam answered.

"I'm putting my hope in you, young man, and now there's that funeral. I wish I had Prue's spunk."

And so it came about that while a harassed preacher attempted the difficult task of saying as few words as possible in an awkward situation, while his hearers sat in silent endurance before him, while all that was mortal was placed again to earth, while youths played in the afternoon sunshine of a beautiful May day, a gray-haired, apple-cheeked woman rocked a baby with golden curls, in a pleasant upstairs room, humming half-forgotten lullabies. And Peter, building marvelous castles with his blocks upon the floor, wondered why tears ran down his grandmother's cheeks.

May It Please the Court

It was the Monday after Thanksgiving. Pearl Jameson was once again waiting for Adam to arrive. He was expected to testify for both the prosecution and the defense. Pearl indulged herself with trite thoughts about the inevitability of time, the slow grinding of the mills of the gods, the difference between the weather of this November and that of last year when she had met Adam Stillman at the station in the beginning of a storm both physical and metaphorical, insofar as the house of Leeds was concerned. Then she had been eagerly awaiting Adam's visit; now fear made it difficult to feel pleasure. Then she had been joking with Tom; now Tom is fighting a war in France. Then snow had lain thick upon the ground; now there was almost none. The flurries that came at night melted the next day. "Each noon burns up each morning's chill, Each morning's snow is gone by night," Pearl murmured as she pulled her wraps closer around her.

Joseph Leeds had been in jail for the past two weeks, his bond revoked after the grand jury indicted him as the murderer of Leigh Wells. The charges against Ellen had been dismissed, since the evidence showed that Leigh had not been killed or even badly injured by the iron.

A.T. had telephoned. They were all to come to Houlton in the morning to be there when court opened. Pearl's mind was consumed with hope that the trial would be speedily finished.

Sitting in the courtroom was not entirely a new sensation for Pearl. Like most of the young people who had been at school in the county seat, she had visited court, at different times. Then she had sat in the gallery that ran across the back of the room, among the more or less interested spectators, and had regarded the groups about the judge on the bench as actors in a play. When the play was amusing it whiled away time that must be spent somehow, and when the case before the court was dull, she and her friends, like the grown ups, slipped away to find more enjoyable occupation. Then she had entered by way of the stairs in the rear of the room. Now she was one of the actors, one of the groups at the front of the courtroom.

The courtroom looked different from Pearl's perspective the next morning. The place where the judge sat, instead of being only a little above the floor as it had looked from the height of the gallery seats, now seemed vastly elevated like a throne. Before it but upon a lower level were the seats for the clerk and the stenographer, and lower still, as though descent had been made to the common plane, the chairs for the prosecuting attorneys were grouped about a table.

Beyond the table in the center of the room was the space enclosed by a horseshoe-shaped rail, whose open end faced the bench, where those in the legal profession were seated. "The bar" they had jokingly called it in those old carefree days. Inside the bar too, was the reporter's table. A young man was already seated there, spreading out papers and pencils.

There were three doors in the wall opposite the gallery. In the center was the one that opened just behind the judge's bench; to the right the one through which A.T. had piloted Aunt Prue, Ellen, and Pearl. Between this door and the judge's bench sat the court messenger. The third door was at the left of the judge. Through it juries were wont to file solemnly in and out, going to their deliberations, and returning to give their decisions. The seats for the jury on a terraced platform were to the left of this door, ranging at right angles to it, down the side, almost to the boxed-in enclosure called the prisoner's dock. Between this third door and the judge was the witness stand, boxed-in like the dock, with a gate in the side and a step up to the chair where one might sit if unable to stand while they answered such questions as counsel might propose.

Pearl, Aunt Prue, Aggie, and Ellen sat just outside the rail, close to the end that faced the door the jury used. Adam and Jack sat on either end of the women. Just in front of them and a bit beyond was the table at which counsel for the defense would be seated.

All this was familiar to Pearl, familiar and yet because of the present circumstances, vaguely unfamiliar. The long, uncurtained windows on either side of the room, the sheriff's seat on the one hand and the criers on the other, midway down the walls, were oppressive like sentry boxes, before the walls of some grim place where menace dwelt.

Lawyers were coming in, filling the seats inside the rail. Spectators were beginning to crowd the back of the big room and the gallery, for the word had gone abroad that there would be doings at the court-house that day and who would miss a human drama acted by people of prominence and tendered to the public at no extra expense? Well advertised too, Pearl thought, watching strange faces appear at the press table. Bangor papers, Portland papers, Boston papers eager to give their readers so welcome a change from the fare of war news, which since no American troops were in action yet, lacked the poignant savor of personal interest.

Pearl counted the windows in the opposite wall mechanically, one, two, three, four, five, six, three above the sheriff's seat, three below. Outside, snowflakes were beginning to float lazily earthward. Through the windows bare branches could be seen etched upon a smoky sky. Same old windows, no change in their numbers. Same old human characteristics: curiosity, love of the spectacular, and desire for escape. That was what this meant to many, perhaps most, escape for a time from the humdrum. This might take their minds from their own petty frets and discomforts, those folks who crowded the space allowed to those who came to look on, but for the actors there could be no escape, nothing but the play until its grim finish, and then, escape, or more thralldom.

No escape certainly, unless the real murderer of Leigh were found. If Uncle Joe were found not guilty, there would always be that feeling of suspicion, people would be saying here and there where they were met together, "Of course Joe Leeds got off, but you know I wouldn't be surprised— someone must have done it." There would always be the shaken heads, the tongues thrust in the cheeks of those who admitted that there was really no evidence against him.

The courtroom was full now. Justice Willoughby, seated by courtesy inside the rail, since he was no longer in active practice, bowed to Aunt Prue and smiled cheerfully. Pearl felt her spirits lighten ever so little. West, the county attorney, and Michael Sawyer, attorney general for the state, seated themselves at the table below the bench. A.T., smiling genially at all about him, sat at the table just in front of Pearl. It was evident that A.T. was well liked by the reporters. The stoop in A.T.'s shoulders had become more pronounced. The lines in his face were even deeper. The clerk was busy with papers for a minute, then the door behind the bench opened and everybody stood up. The court crier in his sentry box beside the prisoner's dock lifted his sonorous voice, "Hear ye, hear ye, hear ye, all persons having business before the Honorable Justice of the Supreme Court of the State of Maine, now held at Houlton in and for the County of Aroostook, may come forth and declare it and they shall be heard."

To Pearl, waiting tensely for something to happen that was vital to the only case in which she was interested, the following hour seemed only a jumble of unrelated procedure. The clerk read from the report in his hands, the lawyers leafing over similar reports, mumbled a few words in reply. Or the judge asked a question, "State versus so and so," the clerk would say, an attorney would stand up and make a cryptic reply, then quite clearly, "The State versus Joseph Leeds"—and A.T. rising to address the judge, "Your Honor, if the prosecution is ready I move for immediate trial of this case."

West and Sawyer signified that they were willing, and the judge declared a recess of fifteen minutes.

Few people left the court room. A young man, sandy hair and grey eyes, eminently correct in dress and deportment, came to sit beside A.T. and was introduced to the ladies. "Alexander Hewett," A.T. said. "He's going to help me out a bit on the defense." Ellen and Pearl smiled at the young man.

"I remember Sandy Hewett," Pearl said. "You were at school, a lordly junior, when I was a freshman, I think."

"Something like that," the young man replied.

"One of the Bingfield Hewetts, aren't you?" Aunt Prue inquired.

"Yes. I was admitted to the bar just last year."

A.T. and his junior conferred. The seats beyond the door at the opposite side of the room began to fill with talesmen. Witnesses were taking seats, which had to be cleared for them in the row behind Pearl. She heard a voice protesting to someone, "Ef Mist Joe say—" then a warning "shhh," and the judge came back to his seat. The sheriff rapped on the board before him and the judge directed that the prisoner be brought in.

There was nothing spectacular in the entrance of Joseph Leeds to the court where he was to be tried on the gravest of charges. His hair was as snowy white as the flakes that whirled occasionally outside the tall windows of the room, his eyes as clearly blue as the sky above when snowflakes have ceased to fall and the clouds that dropped them vanished away. His clothes were conventional and unassertive. If his face was less round and ruddy than it had been a year before, his step was no less firm and his carriage no less upright than it had been then. When the clerk read forth the indictment charging that he did willfully and with malice aforethought kill and slay one Leigh Wells, his answer to the question "Are you guilty or not guilty?" was spoken firmly and clearly. "Not guilty," he said, and a breath ran over the crowded room, as though its inhabitants had found respite from a pressing anxiety.

The business of empanelling a jury was, to Pearl, tedious and the whys and wherefores of their selection or rejection past all understanding by the lay mind. The first one selected was by name Anthony Morse. He was, Pearl decided, medium, just a medium sort of a man who declared in a medium sort of a voice that he had formed no opinion of the case and was not personally acquainted with anyone connected with it. By reason of being first selected he became foreman of the jury. Then in succession came others, this one challenged by the defense, that one challenged by the prosecution, this one admitted, that one excused by the judge. One said that he had formed an opinion and so was disqualified. One stated that he had read a little about the case but had kept an open mind and was, strangely enough, it seemed to Pearl, admitted.

Only once did Uncle Joe show especial interest in the panel. A man who answered to the name of Hussey Rogers, read from the slip by the clerk, came forward, making the usual answers in regard to knowing nothing about the case on trial. Uncle Joe leaned forward and looked intently at the man, his blue eyes growing icelike. "I challenge this man," he said. "Excused," said the judge. "Hussey Rogers excused," droned the clerk and drew another slip.

So it went until the panel was full, and twelve men sat in the terraced seats at the left of the door by the witness stand. Twelve good men and true they might be but Pearl's chief thought about them was that all the others, like the foreman, were medium. Their mediumness varied somewhat. It was quite true that they did not resemble one another in features or in stature or in dress, but there was about each of them a lack of distinctiveness, of anything that set them apart from their fellow men. There was no escaping the fact that they were—just medium.

A.T. seemed well satisfied and the county attorney not dissatisfied with the selection. Pearl wondered if mediumness might be a good qualification for a jury. A.T. might have enlightened her on this point, but she did not ask him.

The hands on the clock pointed to half past twelve when the jurors had sworn to well and truly weigh the evidence presented to them, and a recess was declared until half past one.

As the exits from the courtroom poured forth humanity into the chill November air, Pearl found herself and Ellen confronted by reporters and cameramen. Aunt Prue and the others had lingered briefly for a word with Mitch. Pearl considered flight, but A.T. came to the rescue. Stepping to the front he thrust his head forward, hunched his shoulders until their natural stoop became grotesquely exaggerated, stepping first on one foot then on the other until he resembled the proverbial hen on hot bricks, and issued an invitation, "Take my picture boys, I'm used to it and I like it. You can send in a lotta bunk about brilliant former attorney general defends his brother, you know the line, it won't be new, but there won't be anything else new about this case either, so you had better hang on the tag about startling developments hourly expected.

"That's better," as the cameramen regretfully shut up their boxes, "and here's an honest to goodness tip. Be around when West puts Hulda on the stand and you'll get some copy. Thanks a lot, and if you don't bother the ladies, I'll give you anything I can, when I know it."

"That's a deal, A.T.," one of the men replied, and the groups around the steps dispersed, the reporters to seek more fruitful fields, and the others to eat and rest before the afternoon's ordeal.

"I'm glad they weren't more persistent," Pearl said. "I really don't care to be blazoned on the front page of the newspapers."

"You probably won't escape entirely, but you needn't mind. Not all of the reporters who will be around will be as easy to deal with as those were. They know me, and they would rather not offend me. They're good fellows. I'll help them when I can, even if it does mean throwing Hulda to the wolves. I may be able to have Bruger accompany her."

The county attorney was bald and bespectacled. He gave his opening statement in a voice that was mild almost to the point of monotony. "May it please the court"— antiquated phrases, the prescribed method, mustn't get away from formality—"We will show how this man did on the night of Nov. 23rd of last year, meet his victim and argued with him…under cover of the darkness and storm, how he strangled him…lied about a halter in an attempt to throw suspicion onto another…hated Leigh Wells…wanted to prevent him from leaving town… knew the land and where to hide the body…" It was the voice that was becoming a torture to Pearl, would it never become animated with feeling, would it remain level and cool? The words signified little, a strangled man, a buried body, death, crime, storm and darkness—words, just nothing but words, but the voice flowed on, numbed, enveloped, became soporific.

Like a person in a nightmare Pearl saw the thing that haunted her, the thing from which there was no escape: Uncle Joe, alone in the night, his heart hot with resentment, grasping a throat with sinewy hands, squeezing out the last gasping breath of his victim, digging, digging, digging in snow and frosty earth, tumbling into the grave the lifeless body, covering it from sight with indecent haste and driving away to his home, to creep silently into bed, leaving wet footprints and sopping footgear to accuse him.

The voice ceased and abruptly the nightmare was gone.

"Your Honor, and gentlemen of the jury." A.T. was giving his opening statement. "Before I present to you the evidence that will clear my client and brother of the hideous charge which has been lodged against him, I wish to dispel from your minds any idea that may have entered them as a personal bias on my part, because the prisoner at the bar is my brother. I give you my solemn assurance, that were the prisoner not related to me in any way, I would still, in the interest of abstract justice,

seek to free him from the least shadow of this monstrous and prepos-
terous charge that has been lodged against him. I believe Joseph Leeds
not only guiltless of the charge of murder, but also that he possesses no
guilty knowledge of the manner or the time or place of Leigh Wells'
death. This being the fact, without any regard whatever for relationship, should I shrink from his defense because he is my brother? You
will agree with me that I should put forth every effort to cause you to
see the truth, disregarding entirely any plea of brotherhood, except the
universal call of the brotherhood of mankind to see that right shall not
be perverted and that justice shall be done. Will you too put from your
minds all thought of the fact that this man stands in blood relationship
to me and remember only that the innocent must not suffer for the sins
of the guilty?

"I cannot point out to you the murderer of Leigh Wells and say,
'There is the man who has shed the blood of another,' I can only show
you that the prisoner at the bar is not that man, that he is incapable
of bloodshed, that he sought to keep the home of his foster daughter whole and without stain. If in that seeking, circumstances have so
conspired against him as to bring him to his present position, I know
you will be able to reread those circumstances and send him forth to
continue a life which has been devoted to doing good to others.

"The prosecution will attempt to show you that Leigh Wells was planning to leave town on the night when he met his death, that Joseph
Leeds knew of his plans and was determined to thwart them even at
the cost of murder.

"The defense is in entire agreement with its worthy opponent insofar
as its evidence shows that Leigh Wells had laid his plans for a getaway.
We will, indeed, show you conclusive evidence that this was so and
why it had become imperative that very night for him to leave.

"But Joe Leeds did not know on that night why Leigh Wells must get
away at once. He did not murder Leigh Wells."

Sheriff Bruger was the first witness. As he raised his right hand the
clerk mouthed with the contempt of familiarity, "Do you solemnly
swear truth whole truth nothing but truth swelpyougod?" Bruger nodded, said "I do," and stepped into the witness' place.

He looked, Pearl thought, uncommonly like a man selling tickets to a side show, or the barker leaning out over the railing about a raised platform, as he spieled. She stifled a nervous giggle. She was more than a minor actor in this play, she had written the prologue, that night when she talked with Tom Wells at the station. Had she incited Tom to murder? But no, it wasn't Tom. Tom had gone to camp, gone to find peace in the forest. It was Uncle Joe who was being tried. Perhaps she had not written the prologue after all. Perhaps she had only told to Tom some of the things that had seeped into her mind from the atmosphere at the Leeds home. There had been something odd, or had she imagined it?

Bruger was telling his story—Leigh Wells disappeared the night before Thanksgiving a year ago. The sheriff's office was not notified until after dinner the next day. "I wasn't able to get on the ground until the next morning, and then I had another death to investigate. I sent out all the usual notices about Leigh Wells, railroad and police, and instituted a thorough search of the Wells house and premises and of the whole countryside but the only clue we could find was the fur coat which was brought in and which Mrs. Wells identified as belonging to her husband. I went out and inspected the camp where the coat was found. It was about three miles from town and there were no tracks about it except the ones made by the people who brought the coat in."

But something seemed wrong with the picture. The sheriff wasn't running true to form. He wasn't spieling. He was telling his story quietly. There was a trace of unsureness, a hint of regret in his manner as he looked at the man in the dock. Pearl too looked at Uncle Joe. Then she understood Bruger's changed attitude. He had been living in close association with his prisoner. Bruger now had doubts about his guilt. Inevitable! What effect would this have on the jury?

Bruger continued, "The search for Leigh Wells or his body was kept up all winter but nothing came of it until the body was discovered this spring buried in his own back yard. There was the mark of a blow on the head but the medical examiner said he was strangled. I found that Mr. Joseph Leeds had been absent from his home on the night when Leigh Wells was killed and although I was not able to question Mr. Leeds about the matter, I found that he was on very unfriendly terms with the murdered man. Had quarreled with him only that day, in fact. I also found that his whereabouts the night of the murder would bring him into contact with the murdered man. Mr. Leeds claimed that he hung a halter with a cut rope in the Wells' barn, but it mysteriously disappeared. I arrested Mr. Leeds and brought him for a hearing before trial justice Willoughby of Edenville."

Bruger paused and West asked that the coat in question be recorded as Exhibit A.

"When you found the body, Sheriff, did you get the impression that it had been buried with great haste, or did it appear to have been buried deeply? Can you describe the grave?"

"The grave was shallow, I'd say the burial had been made in a hurry. One hand stuck up above the surface, a hand with a ring on it."

West said monotonously in A.T.'s general direction, "Cross-examine."

"I would like to ask the sheriff," said A.T., crossing his hands beneath the tails of his coat, "if he did not perceive a connection between this case and the case of the unfortunate Delong girl which he investigated at the same time?"

"I thought at first that there might be some connection, since they were eager to convince me that Leigh Wells had been at the Delong place, but decided later that there was none."

"Did you then preserve the bit of rope which was found hanging to the railing at the Delong house?"

"The piece of rope which you said belonged to the end of the rope on the halter which was alleged to have been on the horse which Leigh Wells drove that night?" the sheriff inquired sarcastically.

"The same," A.T. cheerfully agreed.

"I have the piece of rope in my office, but since the halter was not found and no one saw it except the accused, I cannot see what bearing it has on this case."

The judge turned a bleak look upon the witness as though to admonish him to guard his speech but A.T. ignored both judge and witness. "I'm glad you kept the piece of rope," he said blandly, "because," reaching for a parcel on the table beside him, "I have the halter."

The Prosecution

Casually untying the bundle, A.T. held up the simple arrangement of straps and buckles used to fasten about a horse's head. A length of rope, perhaps eighteen inches, dangled from it, and the free end of the rope was cleanly cut.

"I wish," said A.T., addressing the judge, "to enter this halter now as an exhibit. I will at the proper time produce a witness who will identify it as the halter that Leigh Wells' mare wore home on the night that Leigh Wells disappeared."

West intervened, "Your Honor, I fail to see that the halter has any material connection with the case. I object to having this case cluttered up with disconnected evidence."

A.T. responded, "Since the 'disappearance' of the halter led to judgments as to the veracity of my client, I consider it quite relevant."

"Since the defense considers the object in question to be of bearing on the case I shall have to overrule your objection and admit it as an exhibit."

"The defense does so consider it, your honor, and it also requests that the length of rope taken from the Delong railing be brought in later for comparison. I brought in the halter at this point, your honor, because I have no interest in suppressing any bit of evidence, or in keeping the prosecution in the dark as to the defense of my client."

"Good theatre," Pearl commented to herself, "trust A.T. for that."

Dr. Little was sworn and took the sheriff's place on the witness stand. His answers to the questions West asked were curt and to the point, his manner was impatient; Little was not a patient man. "The blow that had been given Leigh Wells did not kill him. The blow on his head made a very slight cut. It would bleed very little. It would have stunned him. Knocked him out for five minutes, maybe ten. The cause of death was strangulation."

"You're positive, then, doctor, that the murdered man was strangled, not smothered, that he was choked to death while he was above the ground, not buried while he was unconscious and smothered by the earth of his grave?" The county attorney's monotonous voice gave the question with its horrible implication, the same inflection it might have given a question about the weather. Its very lack of emphasis made it suggestive of dread possibilities. This, too, Pearl recognized, was good theatre. How long would they keep it up?

"Positive?" snapped Dr. Little, "Of course I'm positive, the body was in a very good state of preservation, and even without the marks on the throat I would have been positive that the man was strangled before he was buried. The indications were unmistakable."

"Were there any other injuries or signs of a fight?"

"There were no other marks of violence on his body, no obvious signs of a fight. But not all fights leave marks, especially if winter clothing is worn. I can only tell you what I know, simply that Leigh Wells was strangled to death sometime last fall or winter."

Little explained to the jury the manner of the strangulation, speaking of carotid arteries and vagus nerves, suffused face, blood-shot eyeballs, endeavoring to make clear a matter which however it affected them, left Pearl with only a feeling of loathing and horror.

West produced two large linen handkerchiefs. Little identified them as the ones that had been wrapped about Leigh Wells' head, one tied about the face like a blindfold and the other passed under the chin and tied at the top of the head.

"When you examined the body, were there any handkerchiefs in the clothes?"

"No."

"Why were the handkerchiefs tied about his face?"

"The way they were tied indicated an attempt to close the eyes and keep the tongue in the mouth and the mouth closed. Also they were tied in such a way as to cover the face and keep the dirt from striking it."

"Wouldn't you think that was an unlikely gesture for a murderer?"

"I have no way of determining how likely that gesture would be."

"But it would indicate, would it not, that the murderer was not a hardened criminal, that this was his first crime, and that being a man of tender sensibilities on ordinary occasions, he was moved even in the commission of a brutal crime to observe such decencies as possible?"

A.T. seemed undisturbed, but the judge admonished, "Facts, Mr. West, not thoughts."

"It indicated absolutely nothing to me except that someone had tied up the face before the body was buried."

West had finished. A.T. was asking the doctor a question.

"Would anything you found in the examination of Leigh Wells' body indicate whether or not the body was buried immediately after death?"

"I found nothing at all to indicate whether the body was buried immediately after death or whether it was buried a week or two afterward. It was frozen within a few hours of death, and there was no indication of successive thawing and freezing."

"Then the body might have been buried at any time providing it was placed where it would remain frozen?"

"Yes."

"How long after death did the freezing take place, Doctor?"

"That is a question I cannot answer. The body was placed in the position it was found within a short time after death, likely but not necessarily in the grave. Freezing might have occurred at any time after, provided that the body was kept at a very low temperature."

"Was the left arm held in the position you have described by freezing?"

"No. Rigor was well established before freezing began. The arm was set in its position by rigor mortis."

"Dr. Little, would it be possible to remove a coat from a body that was stiff from either rigor mortis or freezing?"

"Yes, possible, depending on the position of the body."

"Would it have been possible to remove Leigh Wells' fur coat after rigor mortis was complete?"

"No. Not without tearing or cutting it."

"How soon after death was the coat removed?"

"Not more than a half hour, maybe less."

"That's all." A.T. sat down.

Dr. Rush, called to the stand, corroborated Dr. Little's evidence and told of meeting Leigh Wells twice on that Thanksgiving eve, once at about eleven o'clock and again at midnight.

"How are you able to fix the times of these meetings?" West asked.

"I had a call, shortly before eleven o'clock, to a patient on the North Road. It was about eleven when I met Leigh Wells as I crossed the bridge going north. I was at my patient's home less than an hour and it was about midnight when I came back. I met Leigh driving away from home."

"You spoke to him both times?"

"I spoke to him both times but the last time he didn't speak to me."

"Did you think that was queer?"

"No. It was snowing very hard then. I was in a hurry to get home. Wells was a man who pleased himself as to whether he spoke or not. Besides, he might have said something I didn't hear. I thought nothing of it."

"He seemed just as usual then. Not sick or hurt in any way?"

"Yes, just as usual."

"And you're not able to fix the times of these meetings exactly?" West asked.

"Not to the minute."

A.T. took up the questioning.

"You said, I believe, doctor, that you got no reply when you hailed the man driving Leigh Wells' mare north on the bridge at midnight. Am I correct?"

"Yes."

"It was snowing hard, was it not?"

"It was."

"The man was well muffled in a fur coat. Were you able to get a good look at his face?"

"Why, no, I don't suppose I did. I hadn't thought about it."

"Then it's possible that some other man might have been wearing Leigh's coat and driving his team?"

"I suppose it's possible. I had not doubted that it was Leigh. His failure to answer was entirely in character."

"Indicating only that if it wasn't Leigh, it was someone who might know that he might not answer a friendly hail if he didn't feel like it. So that if it comes to a point of positive identification, you are not able to say now that you are absolutely sure that it was Leigh Wells?"

"I've thought all along that it was Leigh I met. I never considered the possibility of its being someone else. I guess I could have been mistaken." Dr. Rush looked anxiously at A.T. "It must have been Leigh."

"But you are not absolutely sure, now?"

"Who could it have been?"

West was instantly on his feet, "Your Honor!" But the judge interrupted, "Strike that last answer from the record. You may restate your question to the witness."

"Can you state positively that the man you met at midnight of Nov. 23 a year ago driving Leigh Wells' mare was Leigh Wells?"

"Answer yes or no," directed the judge.

"No."

"That's all," said A.T. and resumed his seat at the table.

The first day of the trial was finished with the testimony of Dr. Rush.

Wednesday morning, directly after the crier had finished his "Hear ye, Hear ye, Hear ye," the questioning of witnesses was resumed.

Gerrish Jotham, cashier of the bank that handled the Wells finances, testified that on Nov. 22, 1916, Leigh Wells had drawn from the bank $9,344, almost all of the available funds of the Wells Mill at Edenville on that date.

A.T. questioned him briefly. "Do you remember what sort of bills you gave to Leigh on that date?"

"Only that they were of large denomination except for about two thousand dollars, which was in smaller bills."

"Do you know whether or not any of that money has passed through your hands since you paid them to Leigh Wells?"

"As to the smaller bills, I can't be sure. $7,400 of the larger ones were deposited again on November 28th."

"By whom?"

"Joseph Leeds."

A shocked murmur ran through the courtroom.

"To whose account?"

"To the account of Ellen Wells."

Vane Young, foreman at the Edenville Mill, testified that on Nov. 23, Leigh Wells had placed in the safe at the mill office $1,304.54, money to meet the payroll on the following Saturday, saying that he might be out of town over the weekend.

James Eastman, potato buyer, Edenville, told of overhearing a quarrel near Sleeper's store on Thanksgiving eve, a year ago. He was not able to state the time with any certainty, other than "after supper and before bed." Eastman was a spry little man. He was emphatic in his testimony that he heard Joe Leeds and Leigh Wells arguing, and he made a good impression on the jury.

A.T. might, Pearl thought, have objected to his account of hearing Leigh say, "I am not leaving, you old goat, and I'll go home when I'm damned good and ready," but A.T. seemed quiescent, almost as though he was taking no notice of Eastman's words. "No questions," he said when West gave him the opportunity to cross-examine.

Amos Cooke, station agent at Edenville, was called and testified that on the night of Nov. 23, 1916, Joseph Leeds had been sending out a lined car loaded with potatoes in the care of Ike Jennings. Jennings had failed to appear and he, Cooke, becoming anxious since on account of the snow he had orders to send the freight out at 12:15 rather than at 12:30, had telephoned Mr. Leeds between 11:45 and midnight, telling him that Jennings had not shown up. Mr. Leeds had come to the station and telephoned to Houlton asking a man there to take on the car with others in his care. Mr. Leeds had put the call through from his office and had left the station a few minutes before the freight had pulled out. It might have been five minutes or it might have been ten. He couldn't be sure.

A.T. taking his turn at questioning, asked, "Did you see Leigh Wells in the ticket office shortly before the Bangor train left?"

"Yes."

"What was he doing?"

"He bought a ticket for a woman and then stood around and waited until the train came in."

"Was he wearing a fur coat?"

"Yes. He was wearing that fur coat." Cooke pointed to the coat upon the clerk's desk. "I had plenty of chance to look at him. He wore that coat."

"Isaac Jennings," droned the clerk, "Hold up right hand, solmly swear truth whole truth n-but truth swlpyougod?"

"You were engaged to take a car of potatoes to Boston for the defendant on the 23rd of November last year, were you not?" asked West.

"Yes, I was."

"Will you tell the jury what happened that prevented you from going?"

"Well, you see it was this way," Ike began. "I was on my way over to the station along about half past ten that night, I thought I'd get along pretty early, so's to be around on time. Along by that strip of road this side of where Joneses live on Ford street—"

"That is the road which runs to the right off the main highway just beyond the Edenville Bridge, is it not?" the county attorney interpolated.

"Yes, the road that leads around to the old ford below the bridge. Well, just when I was goin' along there some fellers come up behind me and grabbed me. I fought, but they threw a blanket over me and tied me up, put me on a sled, and took me way out to a house on the B road. They left me there tied up 'til along about four in the morning and then Old Man Lawler found me there and let me loose. I come home as soon's I could and if I knew who the fellers was I'd a persecuted 'em for it. They lost me a good job an' jest about ruined my reputation."

"You never found out then, who was responsible for this outrage upon your person?"

"I ain't got no idea," Ike confided, and since A.T. declined to cross-examine, Ike was allowed to step down.

"Eben Lawler," called the clerk. Pearl looked across to where Jack sat hunched in his chair with averted eyes. Poor boy, he had kept quiet about seeing the kidnapping because of shame that his father should have been mixed up in anything so disreputable. Ike Jennings might have been telling the truth, but not the whole truth, and it was likely that Lawler would do the same.

Lawler was rotund with scanty hair and a walrus mustache. His voice was a nasal whine. West asked questions in his level monotone. Lawler answered, whining through his nose. His story divested of much hedging was that on the morning of the day Leigh Wells disappeared, he was approached by two men, Shorey and Camp, with whom he had only a slight acquaintance, that they had a proposition that he should help them play a trick on Ike Jennings. They were to kidnap Ike. All Lawler had to do was to drive the team and to let Ike out of the house where they would take him, on the day appointed. They wouldn't hurt Ike, just have a little fun with him. They would pay Lawler ten dollars to just drive the team so as to leave them free to tend to Jennings. He hadn't meant to do any harm, thought it was just a joke.

Shorey and Camp were both in the army somewhere, had been drafted. Yes, he did know that they had worked for the Wellses, and yes, he admitted reluctantly he knew Leigh Wells was at the bottom of the kidnapping business. No, he didn't know what he wanted it done for, he thought it was only a joke. He didn't know Ike was going out with potatoes for Mr. Leeds. He would not have done anything to injure Mr. Leeds, nor any of his folks; he thought it was a joke.

Here West put in evidence a deposition given by Shorey at the army camp where he was in training. The deposition stated that he, Shorey, had been hired by Leigh Wells to get Ike Jennings out of the way on the night of Nov. 23rd. With the assistance of Camp he had done so, and according to instructions from Leigh had gone to the mill that night some time before midnight to receive his pay. After waiting in vain until after midnight for Leigh to meet him, he went in search for him. He had driven by the railroad station just before the freight train had pulled out, and had seen Leigh driving the mare. Leigh had not seemed like himself. Shorey had demanded his money and Leigh tossed him a wallet without speaking or getting out of his sleigh. Shorey counted the money and went on his way. He would have stopped, but he had no real need to talk with Leigh, he just wanted his money. It was snowing hard and Leigh seemed bent on getting along. He had seen Henry Delong about the mill but had kept out of sight, not wishing to be seen. Camp's deposition was fundamentally the same and both were accepted into evidence.

Zachariah Sleeper took the stand and stated that he was a storekeeper by occupation and that he lived on Sleeper Street, the road from the main highway to the station. On the night of Nov. 23, he heard a loud, angry voice in the street before his home. It was about a quarter past midnight and he was in bed but not sound asleep, being wakeful because of having a cold in his head. He got out of bed and looked from the window, shoving it up regardless of the cold so that he might see. He could discern what he believed to be Shorey shouting and Leigh's team driving off toward the main road. He heard no more calls and went back to bed. He was carefully questioned as to how the window faced, how far he could see, how he fixed the time.

Asked in cross-examination if he had been able to identify either of the teams or their drivers, he admitted that he had not been able to do so positively.

Sleeper's wife corroborated his testimony as to hearing the sounds and looking from the window.

During the lunch recess Pearl told Adam that she dreaded being called to the stand.

"We've both been in the courtroom the whole time. Is no attempt made here to exclude witnesses before they are called?" Adam asked.

"Sometimes, I suppose," Pearl said listlessly. "What would be the use in my case? When Paul questioned me I told the truth. I have almost wished since then that I had denied all knowledge of what time Uncle Joe came in."

"What did A.T. say about your testimony?"

"He says my testimony won't hurt Uncle Joe. He says I must be straightforward and impersonal. I wish I had never woken up. They are trying to show that Uncle Joe had plenty of time to kill Leigh."

"I think some of those questions about rigor may have been to cast doubt on that theory."

"Perhaps. But this whole thing makes me miserable."

Pearl was still turning matters over in her mind, wondering if West meant to show that Leigh had arranged the kidnapping and planned to take Ike's place at the last minute and so get out of town, when she heard the clerk call her name.

Mechanically, she went through the formality of the oath and took her place in the witness box. Aware that all eyes were centered on Pearl, Adam looked away from her and regarded Joe Leeds. Some people, on trial, became detached from themselves, as though it were someone else in the dock. Was Joe Leeds like that? He appeared to be. As though he were a spectator, interested but not vitally concerned. A protection against too great a suffering set up by a certain type of mind. Did anyone know what thoughts and feelings stirred behind the calm front of the man listening the testimony?

Adam's eyes were drawn irresistibly back to Pearl. Outwardly she was calm and correct but inwardly she was thinking of what A.T. had once said about the way he would leave town if he wanted to go without being discovered. Leigh would not go to the station until almost time for the freight train to pull out, and then he would slip into the car. He could tell the agent that he had brought Ike over and left him there, or no, people would suspect when they found him gone, the train crew would find that the car was fastened on the inside and he could call through the door that everything was all right, then they would not know but that Ike was inside. He would be safe for six or eight hours and the crew would be changed on the freight at northern Maine. If he wanted to leave the train there he could, with damage to the potatoes of course, or he could go on to Boston and lie his way through. It was quite possible that a clever man could get out of town just that way. The main plan would be the same, the details might vary. West was trying to show that Leigh was driving to the station, not knowing that the freight car would leave earlier than he thought, and that Uncle Joe had been there and started back. Pearl came out of her daze to realize that West was asking her something.

"On the night before Thanksgiving, last year, Miss Jameson, you were wakeful, were you not?"

"Yes."

"You knew that Mr. Leeds was out during the night?"

"Yes."

"Did you know what time he came home?"

"Not the exact time."

"You didn't hear him come in."

"No."

"Was Mr. Leeds home at 3 o'clock in the morning?"

"Yes."

"Was he home at 2:30?"

"I think so, I'm not sure what time I waked up. He must have been home when I waked."

"What did you do after you waked up?"

"I was restless and went to the kitchen to get a drink."

"Was it three o'clock then?"

"No, I had gone back to bed when I heard the clock strike three."

"Does the clock you heard strike the half hour?"

"Yes."

"You did not hear it strike at half past two."

"No."

"Were you quite certain that the clock was correct?"

"Yes."

"What time did you use to check it with?"

"I checked it with railroad time that day."

"Then you can only be sure that Mr. Leeds was at home some time before three a.m."

"He might have been home much earlier," Pearl protested, wishing with all her heart that she might lie outright, that she dared to lie, hoping that the incident of the wet socks had not reached West's ears. She hoped in vain. West's smooth voice continued its questioning until the whole story was out, and the jury knew that Joseph Leeds must have come to his home not earlier than 2:30 in the morning of Thanksgiving and that it had taken him two and one half hours to come home from the station less than a mile away.

Uncle Joe flashed her a look of encouragement as she stepped down from the box, and Aunt Prue patted her hand as she resumed her seat beside that good lady, but Ellen looked at her accusingly. Ellen needn't, she would have lied if she had dared to lie, if she hadn't been sure that a lie would find her out. Uncle Joe and Aunt Prue would want her to tell the truth, would understand that she had to say what she did.

A.T. had not asked her any questions, and there had been no reproach for her in his face. There wouldn't have been, of course, he wouldn't have shown it if he was displeased. He had told her that the truthful course was the best one and she could feel that he approved of her, although her evidence had been vital to the prosecution. She sensed a difference in him now when Ellen was called to the stand, an anxiety. Why? Surely Ellen had nothing to tell as damaging as her testimony had been.

Now Ellen was taking Pearl's place in the witness box. Adam scanned the faces of the men in the jury seats, then brought his attention back to Ellen, an appealing figure, slight and pale; as the defendant in the case Pearl thought she would have been invincible. Even a jury of unimaginative men would have declared her guiltless. But was she? Ellen preserved a resolute self-control, but nerves and heart had been strained to concert pitch for many months, and she could not hide her purpose to help the defense at any cost while she witnessed for the prosecution. Neither could she hide her hatred for the murdered man, the man who had been her husband. Would West be able to convict Joseph Leeds because of the witnessing of this greatly loved daughter?

Understanding began to glimmer in Pearl's mind. The jury—it was not just an assembly of reasoning men. They would react, not weigh. In Ellen's hatred of Leigh, in her desire to shield the defendant, they would sense guilt, but not her own guilt. Even an unimpressionable jury would have been unable to resist altogether the appeal of the slight figure, the golden curls peeping from beneath the sober hat, the pale face and tear-weighted eyes. These men would feel that if she killed Leigh she might be justified, but would they justify Uncle Joe in doing it for her? Possibly, but it seemed to Pearl more likely that they would only be assured of his guilt but fail to justify him. To her own mind Uncle Joe's white head was more appealing than Ellen's golden one, but the jury was composed of men, average men. Unless A.T. were able to create a counter impression they would, in spite of all pleas to weigh the facts, decide the case by the impressions they had received.

West began, "Mrs. Wells, why did you hide the fact that you injured your husband on the night of his disappearance?"

"I thought—it didn't matter. I thought he wasn't badly hurt."

"What time did your husband come home on Nov 23rd?"

"I don't know exactly. About eleven."

"Tell the jury what happened." Ellen faced the jury. "Leigh came in. I was ironing. He laughed at me. I threw the flatiron at him. Then I heard the baby having croup. I ran upstairs."

The very baldness of the statement gave it pathos.

"Yes," West prompted. "What happened next?"

"When I came back downstairs, Leigh had gone."

"What effect did the blow with the iron have?"

"Leigh fell."

West waited a moment before he put the next question.

"Had your husband threatened to leave you?"

"Yes."

"Would you have grieved if he had done as he had threatened?"

"Yes."

West seemed mildly surprised. "You felt no affection for him?"

"No."

"Then why would you have cared if he left you?"

Ellen's lips were paper white, and she spoke with difficulty. "He said he would take Peter."

"Your son?"

"Yes."

"Did you believe he would do as he said?"

"I was afraid."

"You surely did not think that your husband would take a small child from your care, did you?"

"Yes, I did."

"Had you talked the matter over with Mr. Leeds?"

"No."

"Had you told anyone of these threats or of being afraid?"

"No."

"You telephoned to Mr. Leeds the night that your husband was killed, did you not?"

"Yes."

"What time did you call him?"

Ellen put her head in her hands. "I don't know. I can't remember."

"Can you remember the other things that happened that night?"

"Yes, but some things are all mixed up."

"Miss Jameson has testified that the telephone call to Mr. Leeds came around 5 in the morning. Does that help you to remember?"

Ellen spoke slowly. "I telephoned when I woke up and found that Leigh had not returned."

"Did you ask Mr. Leeds to come over to your house?"

"Not exactly, but he offered to come do the chores."

"Did you tell him that the baby was sick?"

"He already knew that."

"Then why did you telephone?"

"To tell him Leigh wasn't at home."

"You said in the confession which you attempted to make at the hearing last spring that you went upstairs and stayed there after you had knocked your husband down. In this trial you have said that you came back down the stairs and found that your husband was not about. Which statement is correct?"

"I stayed upstairs for awhile, then I came downstairs and saw Leigh was gone, so I went back upstairs."

"And you saw nothing of your husband, nothing to tell you how badly he was hurt?

"No. There was no blood. Leigh was strong and healthy. I assumed he just left."

"And you made no further attempt to find out where he had gone?"

"No. It wasn't unusual for Leigh to leave us. He came and went on his terms."

West was an astute prosecutor. The witness was becoming exhausted but not her possibilities. The questions went on.

"You saw nothing unusual or out of place on the floor?"

"No."

"Mrs. Wells, did your husband give you the money that was deposited in your account on Monday, November 28th?"

Ellen hesitated, and then answered reluctantly, "No."

"Where did you get the money?"

"Uncle Joe found it on the floor of the kitchen when he came over in the morning."

"Did you see him find it?"

"No."

"And you did not see the money the previous evening when you came downstairs to look for your husband?"

"No, I couldn't see that well. The kitchen light wouldn't go on. I had only the light from the sitting room door to see by."

"But you had light the next morning. How—"

"Uncle Joe fixed it. The string had simply pulled off."

"Mrs. Wells, you are under oath, remember. Do you say then that this wallet was on your kitchen floor and you did not see it until Mr. Leeds called it to your attention the next day?"

Ellen was not to be trapped. "I did not see the money, any money that night. Uncle Joe called me after he fixed the light. I came downstairs. He showed me the money then. I asked him to take care of it."

Pearl hoped that West was overdoing it. If he pushed Ellen too far, he would arouse resentment against himself in the minds of the jury, which might react against the prosecution. It was hard on Ellen, Pearl reflected, but the effect might be favorable.

West, however, knew when he had gone far enough. A.T.'s questions for Ellen were brief. She answered affirmatively that Leigh was wearing his fur coat at 11:00. Was Joe in your house between 11 pm on the 23rd and 4 am on the 24th? Have you ever seen Joe fight physically with any man? After Ellen's answers in the negative she was excused from the witness stand, spent and dejected, and court was adjourned.

The next day began with questions about the search. Adam himself was called and told of the finding of the fur coat. "There were no tracks in the snow leading to the camp?" West asked him.

"No, that is, there were no fresh ones, there was a faint line of depressions nearly filled up which Mr. Leeds said was an old snowshoe trail. I know very little about snow tracks myself."

Back in his seat Adam heard more testimony about the weather conditions that fateful night months back, how it had begun to snow in the early evening, had snowed fitfully until nearly midnight, how the storm had increased in violence from midnight until near the morning and cleared away after daylight had come.

If Ellen had spoken truly, it might well be that Leigh Wells had picked himself up from the floor and left the house, either in a rage of resentment or with an idea of revenging himself by disappearing, without saying a word to Ellen. In any case, he must have left the house because Dr. Rush had met him driving away around midnight, and he had tossed the wallet to Shorey at about 12:15. Then if he had been killed somewhere in the town why had his fur coat been taken to a deserted camp in the woods and left there? Perhaps to make it appear that he had gone to the camp and been killed there?

Pearl looked at her watch; 4:20, perhaps the court would be dismissed now, but West was saying something about calling one more witness and the clerk said, "Mrs. Marion Wilkinson."

Who was Mrs. Marion Wilkinson? The name did not click for an instant, then Hulda stepped forward. She was not in a happy frame of mind. She had taken the fascinator off her head and now carried it over the arm that was wont to encircle the white poodle. She had been obliged to leave the dog outside in the care of a deputy and was disgruntled at the deprivation.

"You found the body of Leigh Wells, last May, did you not, Mrs. Wilkinson?" West began smoothly.

"I found where it was buried."

"How were you able to find it?"

"I knew it was there somewhere."

"How did you know?"

"I smelled death in the black trees."

"Was that the only reason you knew where to look?"

"I didn't know where to look. The smell of death hangs around a long time where there's big black spruces."

"What do you mean by the smell of death?"

"I mean what I say, even water can't hide the smell of death. The water hates the smell and tries to wash the smell away, but the spruce trees love it, they hold it."

"Then you mean to say that you had no other way of knowing that Leigh Wells was buried where he was except this smell of death."

"I didn't need any other means. Dwellers in the woods learn to smell, learn to know where death has passed. Learn many things you know not of. The smell of death was strong about the place all winter, even while the snow covered the grave."

West's calm demeanor did not change. "Please describe finding the body."

"When the snow was gone, I looked and just before the light had failed I found a hand and a ring. I rubbed the stone and it winked its red eye. It winked, I say."

"What did you do next?"

"I went and told Joe. That's all. Now I'll go and get Toto. He's frightened without me."

"Just a minute. Why did you go to Mr. Leeds when you found the body?"

"Joe knows things. He knows what to do. He's not a woods dweller like me but he knows things."

"What did you think Joe knew?"

"Why can't I have my dog in here?"

"Dogs aren't allowed in here. What sort of things does Joe know?"

"A lot more than ye do."

"You must answer the questions, Mrs. Wilkinson," cautioned the judge.

"Fool questions," Hulda snapped, "about what people know and don't know."

"Mrs. Wilkinson, do you know what contempt of court means?" the judge asked gravely.

"Anyone who attends this court knows what contempt means. You try Joe Leeds for murder. Joe Leeds! Joe Leeds did not kill Leigh Wells. The trees know. The water knows, and A.T. knows."

For a little space there was complete silence in the courtroom. The darkness outside became almost vocal. The light within oppressively still.

"Move to strike from the record," said West, looking slightly shaken.

"The last answer of the witness is to be stricken from the record," the judge directed. "Any more questions, Mr. West?"

"No, your honor."

"Do you wish to cross-examine the witness?" he asked A.T.

"No, your honor."

"Your honor, at this time the prosecution rests."

"And faith they need it," Sandy Hewett whispered in Adam's ear.

The Defense

Reporters crowded around A.T. "What about it? Is the old woman crazy? Do you know who killed Wells?" A.T. held up his hands in a gesture of surrender. "Easy, boys, easy, one at a time. You have a story, don't you? Ought to make good reading."

"But we can't use that stuff now, can we?"

"Well, I should say you could if you handled it right. The doctors say that Hulda isn't crazy. As to the statement she made, she made it, I didn't. Use your heads, and shoot your stuff. If what she said was true and I had an ounce of proof, do you suppose my brother would be standing trial? Walk softly, gentlemen of the press, remember that useful word 'alleged,' and that Hulda's irrelevant remarks were stricken from the record."

"Who's Hulda's candidate for Thomaston, A.T.?"

"You'll have to ask Hulda that. And if she should tell you, which isn't likely, remember it's the unsupported opinion of an old woman who while she isn't insane, has her mentality warped by years of trouble and loneliness."

Sandy Hewett, leaving the courtroom in A.T.'s wake, said for the ear of his senior, "West made a mistake in putting Hulda on the stand, didn't he? Why did he do it?"

"I hope he made a mistake," A.T. answered soberly, "but I'm not so sure. He did it because Bruger insisted that she might reveal something of advantage to their case. Bruger had that idea firmly implanted in his mind somehow. The idea hasn't flowered which is as I had hoped. I've made allowance for poor soil too. It may be turned to our advantage. It may prove to be a boomerang and come back to rest at our feet."

Aunt Prue seemed not at all excited by Hulda's statement. She had perhaps appraised it correctly, when she said wearily, "She was provoked by having to leave her dog, but she couldn't have told anything of any advantage anyway. She may suspect someone we don't suspect but if she really knew she would have said so long ago."

"But who is it, Aunt Prue?"

"I don't know, but I suppose Arthur does. It's Joe who's being tried."

Pearl restrained her curiosity until after they had eaten supper at A.T.'s house where the family was quartered. Ellen went straight to the children's room.

Pearl asked A.T. the question that had been in her mind ever since that moment in the courtroom when Hulda had made her declaration. "Do you know who killed Leigh?"

A.T. was tired; no strain of all his years in the courtroom had equaled this strain of defending his brother against this charge, to him absurd. He knew Joe, but that was of little avail unless he could somehow make the jury know him too. How could he show them how impossible it would be for his brother Joe, even in a moment of wrath to strangle and bury, to drive away into the night and leave a clue at a lonely camp to divert suspicion? Now he spoke wearily.

"Knowledge is so small a thing. In my heart I think I know who did it. In my heart I know that Joe didn't. Yet on the face of evidence, the one who did it could not have done it and Joe might have, so don't ask me any more questions. I'm going to try and rest, Pearl, and you had better do the same. I think we will clear Joe. If only he had come straight home that night. All the same, I think we can do it. We have to do it, and we have only the facts at hand to use. I can secure the benefit of the doubt, but I want more, much more. I want to prove his innocence. Good night."

A.T. opened his defense by saying, "Your Honor," dignified obeisance, about face, "and gentlemen of the jury: You have heard one side of this case. Circumstances have been presented to you in a certain light. A guilty light, which has tinged them as the sunset last night dyed the light in this room. We will now present to you these same circumstances flooded with the light of common sense. Gentlemen of the Jury, you shall see what manner of man the prosecution has charged with murder. I find myself peculiarly handicapped in conducting this defense. I know that Joe couldn't have committed the crime of which he stands accused. But I can almost hear you thinking, 'He's Joe Leeds' brother, he will try by hook or by crook to get him off, innocent or guilty.' This is said of many attorneys who work wholeheartedly in the interest of their client. In most cases it is of no great moment. But in this case, that you may find it easier to lay aside all prejudices in the matter, that you may be able to see the facts we will present without obscurity of my relationship to my brother, I am turning over to Mr. Hewett, junior counsel for the defense, the questioning of our witnesses."

Pearl looked at the judge. Did he feel, as she did, that this move was not so much concession to any feeling the jury might have that he was defending Uncle Joe because he was his brother, as it was a clearing of the handicap of his own reputation? What that speech had meant, Pearl felt, was, "See, I'm so sure of my brother's innocence that I'm willing to trust his defense in the hands of an untried attorney, a beginner with no claim to special expertise." In effect he had rolled back his cuffs and said "I'm playing fair, gentlemen, I have no cards up my sleeve." It probably was a clever move, but suppose Sandy Hewett should blunder, should fail to create the desired impression?

The testimony of the first three witnesses, called by Hewett, was brief. Sophronie Smith, boarding house mistress, identified a photograph shown her as the woman she had known as Miss Foote. She testified that Leigh Wells had associated with Miss Foote "inappropriately." Miss Foote had left her place the night before Thanksgiving, a year ago, saying that she was to spend the holiday in Bangor.

The conductor of the train on which Miss Foote had made her departure told of taking her ticket to Bangor, but said that at Houlton the lady had said she was too sick to travel that night and had left the train. He had taken special notice of her that night because of the rumors about her, and the events of the next day had fixed her conduct in his mind.

A New Brunswick official, called in at the expense of much red tape, told of apprehending the woman whose likeness was shown in the photograph at a secluded farmhouse near the St. John river, where the man who was posing as her husband had died on the 25th of December, 1916. The woman had a little more than six thousand dollars in her possession, nearly all of it in United States currency. She was now in jail in Canada, accused of spying for the enemy, specifically of gathering information as to the type and location of resources, including wood, available for the war effort.

So that disposes of the Foote woman, thought Pearl, and conjecture as to the bearing of testimony she had heard gave her food for thought during the recess at midday, so that the food she ate was given no thought at all.

Justice Willoughby was called and under his eye not so many sounds were eliminated in the repetition of the oft-administered oath.

Young Alexander Hewett had the makings of a fine attorney in his composition. His voice and appearance were pleasing, his manner businesslike and unemotional. Under his questioning, the witness having established his status in the scheme of life, stated that he had known Joseph Leeds since both were young men, that he had had business dealings with him as well as social contact, and that he had found him honorable and just.

"Will you tell the jury of any business transactions between yourself and the defendant during the past several years?" Hewett asked.

"In December of 1913 I loaned Mr. Leeds five hundred dollars, taking a six-month note secured at Mr. Leeds' own request by an insurance policy."

"Would you have taken an unsecured note for the loan?"

"I would have loaned the money to Mr. Leeds' based on his word alone had he not pointed out to me that life was an uncertain matter at our ages, and insisted that the policy secure the loan."

"So you feel Mr. Leeds is trustworthy and honest?"

"There are few men that are more trustworthy. I've never known him to prevaricate."

"Was the note paid at the end of six months?"

"Yes."

On cross examination, West asked, "You have stated that you were a personal friend of the accused; did that personal friendship enter into the fact of your allowing him to stay out of jail?"

Hewett half rose in his chair, but an almost imperceptible nod from A.T. caused him to sink back to his seat while the answer came clearly.

"Only insofar as it prompted me to refuse bail, lest I appear to be favoring an acquaintance until the sheriff so obligingly reminded me that the matter was entirely at my discretion."

Mrs. James Waller was called to the stand. Her testimony was that she, a widow with small children to care for, had been in very reduced circumstances in November a year past. She had received on the eve of Thanksgiving a turkey and all the things to go with it from some unknown source. Someone had left the package at her door, knocked, and gone away. She had known that the things were meant for her because her name had been on the package. She was sure that Mr. Leeds was the donor because he had a reputation for doing such kindnesses for his neighbors in need, but when she had seen him on the street and attempted to thank him, he had turned her thanks aside with some pleasant but noncommittal remark.

Gregory Dempster, placed upon the stand, had much the same story to tell.

West did not cross-examine either of these witnesses. His manner suggested that he considered their testimony trivial and beside the point. Horace Petty, clerk at the Sleeper general store and market, told of selling to Mr. Leeds two or three turkeys and fixings on the eve of Thanksgiving, every year for at least seven years. He always, he said, looked for Mr. Leeds to come in along about closing time and buy out the last of his stock of fowl.

Miss Agnes Jones was called to the stand, and again Pearl felt a queer little shock of amazement. Aggie, of course, was Miss Agnes Jones, but how strange the name sounded called forth in that formal manner, under such grim circumstances, yet there she stood. Aggie, gaunt and prim, preternaturally solemn, hid her long skirts behind the walls of that absurd little stall that was called the witness stand.

"Have you been a member of Mr. Joseph Leeds' household for some time, Miss Jones?" Hewett asked.

"I've worked for the Leeds family for twenty years," Aggie said, "and I must say there aren't any better folks in the country than they are."

The reporters revived. There might be something here. Pearl was impatient and half annoyed until she scanned again the faces of those ordinary men in the jury box and remembered that they would feel and render a verdict from their impressions.

"Did Leigh Wells visit the Leeds home frequently?"

"He used to come a lot when he was courting and right after he and Ellen were married, but lately, I mean before he was killed, he hadn't been there for six months, I guess."

"Was he cordially treated when he did come?"

"Oh, yes, even when he wasn't wanted he was treated well."

A ripple of laughter, quickly hushed, ran about the room.

"Confine your remarks to the answering of questions, Miss Jones," admonished the judge.

"Yes, your Honor, I'll answer just the best I can."

"Will you tell the jury what you know about the night Leigh Wells disappeared?"

"Yes, that is, I don't know anything special about that night. Leigh and Ellen had been asked over to dinner the next day but they weren't coming. We had company though, that young Mr. Stillman from New York come to see Pearl. She was home from there. She went to the station to meet him. After supper Joe went out and so did Jack. They was late getting in, and Pearl was fidgitin' all around the place."

Hewett asked, "What happened next?"

"After the menfolks came in, everybody went to bed, but I didn't go to sleep very soon. I heard the telephone ring. After I got to sleep I slept like a log and when I got up Joe had gone over to Ellen's to see about Leigh."

"Had you ever heard anyone in the Leeds household make threats against Leigh Wells?"

"My stars, no, I'd heard a lot of talk about Leigh's goings on, but threats? That's not their way."

West did not cross-examine; perhaps he felt that Aggie had said enough.

When Aggie had been seated once again among the other witnesses, court was dismissed.

A great weariness enveloped the household at A.T.'s home. There was little of talk, and despite early retiring, little sleep.

The first witness called when court opened on Friday morning was Mrs. Prudence Leeds.

Aunt Prue looked ill. The white lace at her neck and wrists shamed the dinginess of the court room. She faced the throng with brave gravity, but Pearl saw her furtively slipping the worn gold ring on her left hand back into place and knew that it had grown too large for its once plump finger.

"Will you tell the court what happened on the night before Thanksgiving a year ago, Mrs. Leeds?" Hewett asked, a shade more deference in his manner than he had shown before.

"As I remember it was just about as Aggie, Miss Jones, has said. Joseph came in a few minutes after eleven, Jack came home just a little before him. I've tried to remember times exactly, but it's hard to be sure to the minute after so long."

"Did you know where Mr. Leeds intended to go that evening?"

"In a general way, yes."

"But you did not know exactly what he was doing."

"Object, your honor, to the form of that question," West said.

"The court considers that a statement, Mr. Hewett. Restate it as a question please."

"Did you know that Mr. Leeds was providing food for people who would otherwise go without?"

"Yes."

"How did you know?"

"That's a difficult question to answer. Joseph was never one to boast of good deeds, but I knew his custom on Thanksgiving eve."

Hewett knew that further pursuit of that line of questioning would bring objections from West and rebuke from the judge. He changed to the telephone calls.

Aunt Prue had been asleep when the call had come from the station, and had waked when Uncle Joe was dressing to go out.

"Do you know what Mr. Leeds wore that night, whether it was a fur coat or not?"

"No. I didn't get up and Joseph put on his coat after he had left the room."

Hewett continued to question, skating as closely as he dared to the thin ice of irrelevancy and eliciting little save a picture of tranquil domesticity.

Aunt Prue knew that Uncle Joe had come in before the clock had struck half past two.

West's brief cross-examination brought out that Aunt Prue was aware that Joe was unhappy with Leigh's treatment of Ellen, and did not want him to abandon his family.

On redirect, Hewett established that the defendant had never threatened Leigh Wells in his wife's presence, and that she did not know of any plan that Leigh Wells had made for leaving town.

Knowing Aunt Prue's forthright habit of speech, Pearl had half expected that she might be led to express a few candid opinions. She realized that it had been more expedient that Aunt Prue had exercised restraint.

Mitch came next. In his picturesque Canuk speech he had identified the halter by certain straps which he had attached to it in an attempt to prevent the mare, Lady, from slipping it from her head. "She's bad, that one, ver bad," he explained. "She's let ears go flat, she's rub top of head, go loose, tie head with check rein, she's shake, shake, snap. He's broke." He had only fixed the one halter, and was positive that this was the one which had been on the mare that night.

The rope end taken from the rail by the Delong house fit the halter rope. As to how or when the halter had disappeared, Mitch knew nothing. "I nevare see heem more again," he insisted, "and ef Mist Joe say she's hang, she's hang."

Joe's Testimony

Why did A.T. make so much of the halter? Was it important, or was it all just a bit of A.T.'s stage management? Pearl was so deep in puzzlement that she did not hear the next witness called and sworn.

She came out of her fog of preoccupation to hear the man she knew as Godfrey, the man who ran the farm for Uncle Joe, saying, "Work had eased up on the farm and so I went over to the Wells place to look after things around there a little, bank the house and so forth." He had found the halter at the bottom of the grain box. The box had been full when the barn was searched. Knowing that A.T. wanted the halter found, Godfrey decided to empty the grain box. He had found the halter and turned it over to A.T.

"How long ago did this happen?" Sandy Hewett asked.

"Wednesday. Jest the day before Thanksgivin'."

"Did you recognize the halter?"

"No. Never seen it before, but I know the mare Lady, and I had heard that a halter was missin'."

"Did anyone suggest to you that you should go take care of things?"

"No. Joe, Mr. Leeds, he said some time ago that when work was slack he wished I'd go over to the Wells place and fix things up a bit."

"He did not suggest that you empty the feed box?"

"No."

"Was the halter buried deep?"

"Pretty deep, yes."

"How do you suppose it got in there?"

"I reckon it fell off the hook and the mare musta been messing with it. I heard she hated that halter. Somehow it ended up in the feed box and then someone added grain without noticing. Not much daylight that time of year, so it's not always easy to see in the barn."

"Your witness, Mr. West," said Hewett, and sat down.

Close pressed by West as to the fortuitous nature of his find, Godfrey simply repeated his story. West gave it up.

The rope taken from the rail by the Delong house was shown to fit the halter rope.

Hewett offered the deposition of Tom Wells, taken after the finding of the body of his cousin, at the National Guard camp downstate. Tom had already gone to war when Leigh's body was discovered. He stated that he had returned from his woods camp, where he had spent the preceding night, on the morning of Thanksgiving in 1916; that he had assisted in the search for his cousin; had been present at the Delong home when the body of Beatrice Delong was found; that he had seen the end of the halter rope tied to the railing; had been present at the finding of the body of the baby.

Little that was new in that, was Pearl's thought, and by some strange association of ideas there drifted to her mind the interior of the church at Edenville and the preacher reading the psalmist's words of crushing his enemies.

Adam was again called to the stand, and Hewett, through skillful questioning, endeavored to show that Joe Leeds had no prior knowledge of the events at the Delong house or of the location and condition of Leigh's body. West objected repeatedly and used his cross examination to distinguish between fact and opinion. Once back in his seat Adam wasn't sure if his testimony had helped at all.

"James Wrayley," called the clerk.

Jim Wrayley ran his gnarled right hand over the stubble on his face, extracted the cud which he had been ruminating, and seeing no proper place to deposit it, shoved the hand in his pocket, then rubbing it down the side of his trousers leg before he raised it to take the oath.

Under Sandy Hewett's questioning he gave the information that he had a lifelong acquaintance with horses, kept a livery stable, and drove a hack to the station, summer and winter. In the summer he used a Ford, in the winter he drove horses.

"Did you make some tests of the time it takes to drive over the road marked on the map, from the station to Joseph Leeds' house?"

"Yep."

"Will you describe the tests you made, for the jury?"

"I drove over that road after dark in a storm, three different times this fall. We ain't had no sleddin'. I had ter use a wagon. Once I used a hoss of my own, once I had Leigh Wells' mare, and once I had Joe Leeds' hoss."

"How long did it take you to make the trip?"

"First time, with my own hoss, it took an hour and twenty minutes. Next time, with Joe's hoss, it took me a hour and a half. Last time, with the mare, it took me a hour an three quarters. It was rainin' hard that last time. Had to go pretty slow."

"Did you have to go as slow as you would have on a stormy winter night?"

"Object, your Honor."

"Is this an attempt to introduce expert testimony, Mr. Hewett?" asked the judge mildly.

"Yes, your honor," Hewett smiled at the judge.

"You may ask for an expression of opinion as to the time under the proper conditions," the judge ruled.

"Mr. Wrayley, judging from your experience, how long would it take to drive over the route outlined with a horse and sleigh, in a stormy winter night?"

"Wal," Wrayley scratched his ear meditatively, "It might be done in an hour and a half, but then agin it might take two hours, if a feller was lookin' for somethin'."

"Your witness."

If West could ever be said to thunder a question, he thundered now. "How far is it from the depot to your place, Mr. Wrayley?"

"'Bout a mile."

"How long does it take you to drive that distance?"

"It depends. Sometimes in the winter when the road is broke out in good shape it takes ten minutes; when it's been snowin' a while, it takes maybe fifteen; and when it's been snowin' and still is and dark in the bargain, I 'low twenty minutes and start to the station half an hour before train time so's to be sure an' git there."

"If it takes twenty minutes to drive a mile, I would expect most of your passengers could walk and save time."

"They can suit theirselves," Wrayley averred, and was excused.

The judge declared time off and such of the assembled participators and spectators as wished went forth in search of food.

When once again the business of the court was resumed a sense of refreshed attention pervaded the atmosphere. Reporters were in their places. Inside the horseshoe rail of the bar the space was filled with attorneys and others whose position in the scheme of affairs entitled them to privilege. All space without was filled. Those who were fortunate, sat; those who were obliged to, stood. By some mysterious means the word had gone forth that Joseph Leeds would take a stand in his own defense.

Within was breathless interest. Without, the westering sun still riding high in the heavens threw the shadow of bare elm twigs across the lower panes of the tall window across the room from the jury. Pearl's eyes strayed often to that window, emblem of the world outside.

Uncle Joe's eyes were steady, his step firm as he took his place in the witness box and at the request of Sandy Hewett gave his version of the happenings of the night Leigh Wells disappeared.

"After supper that night," said Uncle Joe, "I went out to look after some errands. It's true that I met Leigh near Sleepers store. He seemed excited. I advised him to go home. I told him that I had heard of Miss Foote's departure and that if he had any idea of following her, he had better give it up. I got home a little after eleven, and heard that Ellen had told Pearl that Leigh still wasn't home. I didn't notice the time particularly, but I went to bed right away. Then before I was asleep, ten minutes perhaps before midnight, Amos Cooke telephoned that the freight was leaving earlier than had been scheduled and that Ike Jennings had not come to take over the key to the car I was sending out. I got dressed, harnessed up, and went over to see about it. There wasn't time to locate Ike, so I telephoned from the station asking Harvey Munroe to take the car over at Houlton. I gave the key to the brakeman and started to drive back. Since I was out anyway it occurred to me to check a few places for Leigh. I drove along to the mill, but the office was dark and the door was locked. I didn't see Henry Delong, but was not surprised at that because he might be anywhere about the mill, or in the boiler room away from the storm and cold.

"I hoped that it might be that Leigh had gone home after all and decided I would go on around by the back way and find out. I figured I'd rest easier if I knew he was home. When I got to the barn, I went in and found that the team wasn't there so I knew Leigh wasn't home either. The house was dark and I thought that Ellen was asleep and there was no need to wake her, but I was worried.

"It didn't seem possible that even Leigh would leave town, driving on a night like that one. I drove on up the drive way and turned, pulling out of the road a bit to where the bushes made a windbreak and waited a while to see if Leigh would come. I don't know how long I waited, but not very long I suppose, because it was very disagreeable sitting there. There was one more place where Leigh might be and I decided that I would drive by the Delongs and see if the team might be hitched outside. I drove on toward the bridge, turned right just before I reached it, and on past the houses there. I saw nothing living. Everything was dark and wrapped in the storm. The old bridge there is only a foot bridge, and I didn't like to chance the ford so I came back to the bridge and on home. When I got back to the main road a horse and sleigh had just come across the bridge and was going on up the hill toward Leigh's barn. I could only see it vaguely, but was satisfied from the general outline and the sound of the bells that it was Leigh's mare. I didn't want to talk to Leigh. I only wanted to know that he hadn't decamped. I was mightily relieved and I went home and slept."

Uncle Joe paused. Hewett asked a question.

"Mr. Leeds, when did you last see Leigh Wells alive?"

"The night before Thanksgiving a year ago, when I talked with him near Sleeper's store."

"Will you point out on the map on the wall behind you the exact route you covered that night after you left the station?"

Uncle Joe traced the route.

"Did you see or meet anyone from the time you left the station, until you reached home?"

"No."

"When did you first learn that Leigh Wells had not returned to his home?"

"At about five on Thanksgiving morning, when Ellen telephoned to me. I was confused until I realized that the mare came home by herself again."

"Will you tell the jury of your movements on Thanksgiving day?"

"I harnessed up and went over to Ellen's. The mare was standing in the shelter of the shed. She was blanketed and the halter was in place with the end of the rope dangling. The robes were turned up over the seat of the sleigh and loaded with snow on the top. I unhitched the mare and put her in the box stall, fed her some hay, and hung the harness and the halter on the hook back of the stall. I milked and fed the cow.

"I looked all around the barn and the shed, but could see no trace of Leigh having been there. I brought in firewood and realized the kitchen light wasn't working. One of the connecting wires had been pulled from the contact. I fixed the wire and when the light came on I saw an envelope with money on the floor. It seemed likely that Leigh had dropped it there. I called Ellen down and showed her the money. Ellen does not like having large sums of money in the house so she asked me to hold it for her. When Leigh had not turned up by Monday, I deposited it in her account.

"After I left Ellen's house, I went to the station and telegraphed to my brother in Houlton. On my way there I met Paul Spencer and told him that Leigh was missing. I asked him to make what inquiries he could without making too much stir. Tom Wells came down from his camp on the morning train and I took him over to his house. We went from the station the same way that I had gone the night before, by the mill and across the bridge there. I let Tom out and went on to Ellen's. It was slow going because we had to break the road all the way. We saw no one, but there were tracks in the snow leading from the mill toward Henry Delong's house.

"Ellen had telephoned to Mrs. Grimes and found that she was home. So I went to her place and brought her back to Ellen's. Then I went home."

"When did A.T. arrive?"

"Arthur came up on the morning train from Houlton. After dinner Arthur, Mr. Stillman, Tom, and I went out to see if we could find any trace of Leigh. We picked up Spencer and drove to the Delong place."

"Why did you go there?"

"I believe it was Paul's suggestion. He was with Arthur and young Stillman. Tom and I followed them."

"Did you join in the search for Leigh Wells or his body, Mr. Leeds?"
"Yes."

"Did you make any search last spring after the snow had gone?"

"No. I didn't believe Leigh was dead. I thought further search for his body useless."

"Did you know what Mrs. Wilkinson had found when she came to your home on the evening of May 3rd last spring?"

"I did not."

"When did you know where the body of Leigh Wells was?"

"When I saw the hand with the ring on it that night."

"When did you learn of the quarrel between Leigh Wells and his wife on the night when he disappeared?"

"When she told it in court after the body was found."

"Were you present when the body was disinterred?"

"No, I had gone home."

"Have you any knowledge of any circumstances bearing on the death of Leigh Wells, which you have not already stated?"

"No."

West questioned every point in Joe Leeds' story, questioned but could not shake. He contrived to express doubt but stopped short of openly accusing perjury.

Why had Mr. Leeds taken the roundabout way to the Wells home? How could it be that he was so little in his daughter's confidence as to not know of her quarrel with Leigh? Why was he afraid that Leigh Wells would leave town if he knew so little of his daughter's affairs?

Pearl pondered upon the latter problem, but only for a moment. Ellen, whatever she suffered, would complain to her family only when the last extremity was reached. Most of what Uncle Joe knew of her troubles and of Leigh Wells' intentions, he would know only from town gossip. We're like that, Pearl admitted to herself. Would the jury understand that reticence? Perhaps they too were of the inarticulate.

The shadow of the elm twigs crept up the window panes, up and up, like distorted writing on a giant page, a mystical message written upon the page and erased as soon as the hand moved on.

That evening at A.T.'s house Ellen and Prue retired early. A.T. turned to Pearl and Adam and said, "I'm going to talk to you like the pseudo uncle that I am, to Pearl at least. I fear we have done great harm by trying to be noble. Ellen tried to confess and I fear it made Joe look more guilty. Joe has been noble and it may send him to prison for the rest of his life. He would not allow me to try to create doubt by naming others whom he did not believe were guilty. I have been a sentimental, soft-hearted ass. Pearl has given up her life in New York."

Pearl began to object.

"No, Pearl, don't think that I see no good in your coming home and standing by. It has been a comfort to all of us. You've been a brick. But whatever the result of the trial, you must live your own life."

"How could I possibly leave if Uncle Joe is convicted?"

A.T. turned to Adam, "Do you want Pearl to come back to New York?"

"I want that more than I can express."

"Pearl, I am trying to tell you not to make a needless sacrifice to the gods of sentimentality. You are young. Ellen is young. Joe and Prue and I are old. To the old tragedy becomes endurable because we know that it cannot last forever."

"No, A.T." Pearl said. "It is youth that brought about this trouble. It's not fair that age should bear its weight. When I think of Aunt Prue living there with Ellen, living every day with the constant reminder of the cause of Uncle Joe's imprisonment, can I do anything else except to stay with her and help if I can?"

"Yes, you can go away and give those two a chance to grow together in sharing a common sorrow. Ellen isn't the cause of Joe's misfortune, and Prue doesn't think she is, any more than you do when you stop being sentimental and use a little common sense. Prue does not want to feel like she has spoiled things for you in allowing you to stay with her. Pearl, you must sacrifice your sense of duty and make Prue and Joe happy by returning to the life you had chosen and loved.

A.T. stood up abruptly. "And you, Adam, see that she does it."

Adam thought, but did not say, that making Pearl do anything was not within anyone's power.

Gentlemen of the Jury

The next morning began with the judge asking if A.T. was ready to begin his summation. Adam saw a look pass between the brothers. A.T.'s eyes were pleading, and Joe gave a slight shake of his head. A.T. rose slowly from his seat to argue the case for the defense. He swept the courtroom with a comprehensive glance before he faced the jury. Confident in manner, yet assuming nothing of arrogance in his confidence, he spoke simply as a man to other men.

"Gentlemen, our case is before you. You have heard our witnesses. You know the estimate others put upon the character of Joseph Leeds. You have heard a man who holds a high position, who is known as the soul of honor, state that he considers Joseph Leeds' word as good as his bond. You have heard the humblest among us, without any reservation, avow that if Mister Joe says a thing, it is true, and Joseph Leeds has stood before you and told you of the happenings of that night of storm and misery. Can you in the face of all this evidence, doubt his sworn story of that night?"

A.T. was in deadly earnest. He sought to impress upon the jury his own faith, impress it so strongly that it would still sway them after they had heard the other side of the story.

"The prosecution has told you, would have you believe, that on that night, Joseph Leeds, fearing that the husband of his foster daughter was about to desert her, suspicious that he had planned to leave that night to follow Miss Foote met Leigh Wells in the dark of night and strangled him. Gentlemen of the jury, let me ask you, was this possible? The defendant is an old man. His supposed victim was young and a man of great strength. The blow on the head, which he had received before his death, was not a severe injury. We know this from the medical evidence. Is it within the bounds of reason to suppose that, providing these two men had met, the weaker strangled the stronger, got him into a sleigh, drove him to his home, dug a grave and buried his victim, drove four miles through the night and the storm, planted the fur coat in the deserted camp and drove back a distance of three miles to his own home, and all this in the space of two hours and a half?"

A.T. was facing the jury, all his mannerisms, his little affectations gone, the stoop in his shoulders was only a faint suggestion. He was putting into this appeal every ounce of his personality.

"The state would have you believe that this man, who had spent the eve of Thanksgiving in a kindly deed, who had gone to his home and to his bed with only concern for the happiness of others in his heart, arose an hour later to go forth, meet a fellow man and kill him. Why? The prosecution presents to you this paradox, that because he desires to preserve the home and the honor of his daughter, he kills his daughter's husband. Because he wished to prevent a departure, he made that departure irrevocable.

"You are men like Joseph Leeds; you shall judge if this improbable, seemingly impossible conduct was a fact or only a clutching at the straws of circumstance, by misguided officials."

"I point out to you that Dr. Rush cannot positively say that the man he met driving Leigh's team north on the bridge was Leigh. And that Shorey's deposition leaves the matter still in doubt. In the storm and darkness, someone might have, without much difficulty, passed himself off as Leigh Wells in that brief encounter."

"If that was done, that man, whoever that might have been, was the murderer of Leigh Wells. Thwarted in his plan to escape on the freight train, that man drove to the deserted number one camp in the woods, headed the mare for home, and left the coat he had worn as a disguise and vanished into the night and storm."

Pearl watched the jury. A.T. was not talking down to them; he was, Pearl realized, by means of the everyday speech and reasoning of the countryside, talking them up to him. She lost in this watchfulness the trend of A.T.'s plea but caught it again as he spoke of the halter.

"It may seem to you that I have made much of a simple matter in stressing the importance of this halter. My friends, while no one can testify to having seen Leigh Wells with any certainty after Dr. Rush met him on the bridge that first time, when he was going toward his home and perhaps toward another place, that halter, with its rope cut cleanly in two, and one of the severed ends left hanging upon the porch rail of a desolate home, is a mute witness of one of the places where

Leigh Wells visited on the night when he was killed. The cut halter rope proves that Leigh was at the house of a man who hated him and blamed him for his daughter's death."

Again Pearl's mind wandered, while A.T. pointed out that parties who were said to have quarreled near the house on the road to the station had not been identified, and stressed once more the character and truthfulness of the prisoner at the bar, coming back to strained attention, when A.T. brought his plea to a close in a voice low and vibrant.

"The state is merciful. It is like a father, but it is a stern father, who in its desire to do only the right may be led into error, even as Abraham of old. It believes as Abraham did that duty may call for the sacrifice of a well-beloved son, and it does not shirk the duty however repellant. Abraham was shown that he had misread the will of God. Good men can misread evidence. I cannot ask you to produce a miraculous lamb for the sacrifice. This well-loved son, Joseph Leeds, is innocent even as Isaac was innocent. I can only pray that you may discern the higher will and show the state that this sacrifice is not desired by the Father of us all."

In the moment of profound hush, which settled over the great gloomy room, there was not even the scratch of a pencil, the rustle of a paper. West rose slowly as one who has just waked from sleep.

The monotone of his voice at first was soothing, its very calmness a contrast to the vibrant appeal which had gone before. Step by step, he went over the case, presented its beginning in the conditions which existed in the Wells home and in the community, Joe's anger over the treatment of the girl he raised, the quarrel between Joe and Leigh just hours before the murder, the testimony that strongly indicated that Joe had heard Shorey shouting at Leigh, that he realized that Leigh had planned to escape on the train to follow the infamous Miss Foote, the ease with which Joe could have caught up with Leigh and taken judgment into his own hands. He was careful to admit the final meeting had not been actually witnessed.

After a while, the voice became a torture to Pearl, but it went smoothly on and on. "The prisoner at the bar has told you his version of the events of that night. It's true that he has an enviable reputation for truth, but is his account credible? Even if he didn't hear Shorey shouting at Leigh, is it likely that his anxiety for his daughter's welfare would lead him to take so roundabout a course to reach her home? It was late at night, a stormy disagreeable night in which to be abroad. He says that he went that way in order to pass by the Wells mill, to see if Leigh Wells was there. It had been more than an hour since he had heard that his daughter's husband was not home. Yet instead of making his way directly to her house, by the main and well-traveled highway, to see if Leigh Wells had come to his home, during that hour, he goes first by a back way to the mill. What does he do there? Go in and search for the missing man? No, he finds the office dark, as it would doubtless be at that time of night and says that he drove on, still looking for the team and waited in the cold and storm to see if the man he sought would return.

"Gentlemen of the jury, I put it to you that his story is too great a strain upon human credulity. He was distressed and harassed by his knowledge of the treatment of his daughter at the hands of Leigh Wells. You have heard the story of the blonde woman who left the town that night. You have heard that it took him over two hours to get home from the station. He was not driving around looking for Leigh Wells, he was killing and burying him. The defense would have you believe that Mr. Leeds did not have the physical strength to overpower a younger man. I would remind you that the victim had recently been knocked unconscious. He was likely taken by surprise. Mr. Leeds is a farmer; his arms remain strong from years of farm work. You have heard that after the first few days he did not search for Leigh Wells. He did not search, not because he thought Leigh had left town, but because he knew the man was dead. It was not Joseph Leeds' object to keep Leigh Wells from leaving his wife. What he was determined to do was to prevent the man who became his victim, from following the blond woman. He attained his objective."

Pearl had felt a sense of security when A.T. had concluded his plea to the jury. She had felt that A.T. had won them completely. Now, she felt a numbing weariness, shot through with fear. She saw the jury following with intent interest the utterance of West's level voice. She felt that they were being drawn into a sort of hypnotic spell, that their verdict must accord with the words flowing toward them with such calm force.

West continued. "The State prosecutes this case in no spirit of vindictiveness. It seeks only justice. We have come far from the day when the law demanded an eye for an eye, a life for a life. Yet we have not come, and shall never come, to the state where we condone murder.

"You cannot declare a murderer guiltless. He may have led an admirable life up to the time of his crime. His victim may not have measured up to your standard of manhood. These things are not the issue. The vital question for you is whether or not Joseph Leeds is guilty.

"The evidence has been presented to you. The state awaits your decision in full confidence that you will not shirk your duty."

When the judge began his instructions to the jury, it was like a release from bondage. The judge was fair, terse, and straight to the point. He stripped the case to its essential evidence, explained how that evidence was to be judged and a verdict reached, exhorted them to be faithful in the discharge of their duty, saw them shepherded from the room, and retired to his chamber.

Uncle Joe was taken back to his cell, and the reporters left to file their stories and inform their papers that the verdict was expected soon.

Pearl, not so confident as they, had a moment of terror lest the jury might spend the night in their chamber. Visions of sitting there in waiting all the rest of a lifetime formed in her mind. But no, the court had not been dismissed, and they could only wait. The state and county attorneys conferred in solemn whispers. A.T. sat stonily looking at nothing at all. Sandy Hewett merely waited. Outside the wind had begun to moan. Pearl looked again at the darkened window on her left and sat suddenly bolt upright in her chair. The writing shadow had returned. Not cast by the sun now, not moving up the pane, back of the great elm a street light glowed, a branch cut square across its beam and tossed in the wind, wrote once more its fantastic message. "The moving finger writes." Pearl looked away, back at A.T.'s stony face. Did he pray? The wings of time grew weary, faltered, and ceased from flight for the waiting ones.

The Verdict

Justice Willoughby put his hand upon A.T.'s bowed shoulders and spoke quietly to the waiting family group. "Let's go to another room and wait." They followed him silently along the corridor to a room that was occupied by a reporter and Hulda. The reporter, Robert Sharron, said, "I'll arrange for some food to be sent in."

Ellen shuddered as though the thought of food repelled her. A.T. nodded assent. Aunt Prue said, "That's good of you, sir. It will hearten us."

Aunt Prue sat down in a chair as though her limbs could no longer support her. Ellen's eyes burned. Would there ever be tears, Adam wondered, to quench that burning? Pearl's hair caught the light making her face more pale, her eyes more deeply shadowed.

"Do you think they will let me see Joseph?" Aunt Prue asked.

"Sure they will," Justice Willoughby said. "I'll go over with you as soon as you've had a cup of coffee."

"How long—" Ellen began. She did not finish the question and no one answered the implication.

Sharron ushered in the waiter. Coffee and sandwiches were placed on the table. Hulda grabbed several sandwiches and left without a word. Aunt Prue finished her coffee in one bitter draught. She stood up and announced with gentle dignity that she was ready to go. Justice Willoughby placed his untasted coffee on the table and escorted Prue out. At the door she turned and said as though in apology, "I may not be able to see Joe much more."

A.T. said to the group, "This feller is Robert Sharron, a newspaper man and a good one, but I suspect him of mischief. Have you been talking to Hulda?"

"Yes, I have."

"You didn't get any copy, did you, Sharron?" A.T. had slumped again in his chair.

"No. I got no copy I can use at the present time," Sharron admitted, "but I got a light on something which has caused me much puzzlement. You know me well enough to know that if I say none of it will see print until the time is right, none of it will. Mrs. Wilkenson insists that Joe didn't do it."

"I'm sure she's right about that."

"She wouldn't give me a name, though she said it was someone who hated Leigh."

Adam said, "That would include quite a few men in this town."

"When I tried to ask about specific people she wouldn't answer me, she just started talking about the woods."

A.T. sighed. "I could have made Joe's defense much stronger by presenting evidence to show that either Tom or Henry had means and motive to kill Tom. Even an unnamed jealous husband or anyone who disliked Leigh could have been useful. Joe refused to allow me to do so. Even alluding to Henry in my closing was not what he wanted. Joe feels that when you have an unsupported theory that may do great harm to someone, you keep your suspicions tight in your own mind. But I fear I've been an arrogant, improvident fool. I couldn't believe Joe was in any serious danger. Now Henry's mind is impaired, Tom is seriously, perhaps mortally wounded, and my brother—" Words, for perhaps the first time in his life, failed A.T.

Time waited with folded wings.

At length came a stir in the corridor and a summons. The jury was ready to make its report.

They were back in their seats in the court room when Uncle Joe was brought in with Aunt Prue by his side. Adam, watching Joseph Leeds while the jury filed in, marveled. Uncle Joe was so calm in the waiting.

All listened expectantly as the question was put, "Gentlemen what is your verdict?"

And the answer—"We find Joseph Leeds guilty of murder."

A shocked murmur ran through the spectators. A.T.'s eyes raked the jury like a sword of flame. Aunt Prue was rigid with shock. Quiet tears ran down Pearl's cheeks. But Ellen—for an instant Adam thought she was dead. All life seemed to have gone out of her. She lived in death, an effigy of a woman.

"The prisoner is remanded to await sentencing," the judge said.

Home by the Fireside

Before the judge had finished speaking, Hulda exploded. "You fools! All of you! I told you he didn't do it!" She fumbled in her voluminous garments. Marching forward she handed a sealed envelope to the judge.

"Hulda, have you been keeping something back all this time?" Anger and surprise conflicted in A.T.'s voice.

"Tom bound me to keep this a secret as long as I could. A promise is a promise. Who would have thought anyone would convict Joe Leeds? Fools!"

The judge stared hard at Hulda and then opened the envelope. He read the message silently and then read it aloud to the hushed court room. "'I give permission for the reading of the document being stored with my last will and testament. Tom Wells, March 17, 1917.'"

Pearl said, "He wrote that a few days before he went off to the war."

"Where is this document?" the judge asked Hulda.

She shrugged, but West rose slowly to his feet. "I believe it may be in Attorney Linburg's office on Hill Street. Many of the men going off to war used his services."

"Get it. Lawyers meet in my office in one hour. The prisoner will remain in custody. Court is adjourned," and the judge swept out of the courtroom.

When Mr. Linburg was sworn in, he explained the papers in his hand.

"On March 17, before he left for the Army, Tom asked me to make him up a will. He wanted it in his own handwriting. That's unusual, but he insisted. Then he took the papers from me and added some more handwritten pages, without letting me see them," the lawyer said. "I don't know what was in those new pages, but I have the sealed envelope here."

"Open it." The judge said tersely.

The lawyer broke the seal and pulled out the pages. "These first two pages are his handwritten will." As he looked at the remaining pages, all in the courtroom could see the shock on his face.

"It's a confession, your honor. A confession to killing Leigh Wells."

There was a stunned silence in the courtroom, and then a collective sigh of relief.

The contents of Tom's letter provided the kind of explosive story that fills the dreams of reporters. The confession was clearly in the same handwriting as the will, and included information that was not known before the body was found in May.

The judge gaveled for order. "I declare Mr. Joseph Leed's conviction vacated and order the defendant to be released."

The sun set and the stars came out as the family returned to the hilltop home that Uncle Joe had feared he might not see again. Within, A.T., Joe, and Prue sat before the fireplace. A.T. spread a newspaper across his knees reading now and then from its pages. The firelight glinted from Aunt Prue's swiftly moving knitting needles and faintly from the kitchen came the fragrance of baked beans and brown bread mingled with song, *"There is a land of pure delight—"*

Upstairs, Peter gravely informed his mother that skis were the thing his heart greatly desired for Christmas.

Adam asked Pearl to go for a walk with him in the moonlight. After a period of comfortable silence, Adam sighed deeply and turned to Pearl. "You know I'm likely to be sent overseas soon."

Pearl nodded with sadness.

"Before I go I want to ask again if you care for me. I want to know if I'll have a chance to win your hand when I come back."

Pearl became quite still. "How could you possibly want me now?"

Adam looked confused. "What do you mean?"

"I'm the one who put the idea of murder into Tom's head. At the church on Thanksgiving the minister read that passage about pursuing your enemies and destroying them. That's what Tom did. I was so relieved when Charlie said Tom had been at camp that night because it meant I wasn't guilty of encouraging a killing. But Tom did do it, and I'm the one who started it all."

"Pearl, oh Pearl, you're not—you can't—none of this was your fault!"

"Leigh would still be alive if I hadn't said what I said," Pearl insisted.

"Leigh would still be alive if he hadn't threatened to harm Ellen! When Tom was struggling to subdue Leigh, I don't think your light-hearted conversation earlier even entered his mind."

"Subdued was part of that scripture lesson also. *Thou hast subdued under me those that rose up against me,*" Pearl added.

"Yes! You see, even in the Bible there are examples that sometimes killing is justified. We should be grateful that Tom had the strength to subdue Leigh or we might have been burying both Tom and Ellen!"

"But surely I bear some responsibility because I said bad things about Leigh."

"Do you have any idea how many people in this community have said bad things about Leigh? If that is the standard for guilt, you have plenty of company."

Pearl looked at Adam and he saw a glimmer of hope shining through her eyes.

Adam said, "Pearl, I care for you. Do you have feelings for me?"

Pearl sighed deeply, "Yes, Adam, I care for you, too. When you come back I'll be waiting for you."

The paper spread upon A.T.'s knees carried screaming headlines. "Joseph Leeds Not Guilty. Confession of murderer, found after the conviction, clears up mystery of three deaths."

A.T. reread the opening paragraph, "The mystery that had shrouded the deaths of Leigh Wells, Beatrice Delong, and her infant daughter for more than a year was cleared away yesterday afternoon. Just after the trial of Joseph Leeds for the murder of Leigh Wells had concluded with the conviction of the defendant, a confession was found written by the murderer, Tom Wells, now dead from wounds received in France."

A.T. dropped the paper. No need to read again the account the news-papers called, "An amazing human document." Tom Wells had come back from camp that night, saw Leigh throw the baby's body into the stream while Beatrice stood outside screaming. He saw the flash of a knife and Leigh driving away quickly. Tom had cut across the fields to Leigh's place with the idea of facing him and making him admit what he had done. He arrived outside the Wells' window just in time to see Leigh mocking Ellen and she hurling the iron. When Ellen fled upstairs, Tom had gone inside and carried Leigh, unconscious, to the shed.

Tom thought that Leigh was dead then. It was when Leigh began to regain consciousness a few minutes later with vile curses and threats of violence to Ellen that Tom had been compelled to restrain him. Leigh fought to get free and his threats toward Ellen increased. As the men struggled with increasing fury, Tom's hands surrounded Leigh's neck. When Tom released his hold he realized that Leigh would never rise again.

Tom had buried the body hurriedly in that secluded spot behind the shed, using tools from the barn and working by the dim light of the flash he carried in his belt.

In Leigh's pocket he had found a billfold with $7,400, which he tossed onto the kitchen floor. Tom donned Leigh's coat and then drove Leigh's team away. He met Dr. Rush but knew the doctor did not realize who was really driving. He didn't find the smaller wallet until he was approaching the train station. He had a closer call in his attempt to escape on the freight train. He encountered Shorey on the road to the station and heard the words, "Leigh, give me my money, you crook!" shouted into the storm. Tom threw the smaller wallet into Shorey's sleigh. He did not know why Leigh owed Shorey money, but throwing the wallet had saved him from discovery.

"Then he decided to escape into the woods. That explains how Leigh's coat ended up so far from his body," Aunt Prue said meditatively.

"It just didn't make sense that someone would kill Leigh in the woods where the coat was found and then bring the body all the way home. It would be far easier to hide it in the woods. After the killing Tom didn't want anyone to see him. Leigh's coat, horse, and sleigh provided the perfect disguise," A.T. said.

Prue said, "He knew once he turned the mare loose she would go home."

"It was easy to leave the fur coat and walk back to his camp," Joe said. "It gave him a good alibi since people believed he had been at his camp the whole time."

A.T. said, "Then before Tom went away to war he deeded his place to Mitch and Delong with enough funds to keep them the rest of their lives."

Joe said pensively, "It never would have occurred to Tom that Beatrice would freeze to death with a warm house right there."

"She must have been out of her mind with grief," Prue added.

Joe speculated, "Tom may have felt more guilt over her death than Leigh's."

A.T. picked up the story. "He had already provided for the burying of the Delong girl, you remember, with room for three other graves there. He made his will, gave old Charlie a life tenure of his camp, and provided for Mitch and Henry. Those things might indicate that he was providing only against the chance that he would not come back from the war. But I believe that he did not intend to come back."

"But you don't think that Tom planned to kill Leigh, do you?" Prue asked.

"No. He wrote that he came back that night, just on an impulse. I believe he did just that. But when he saw Leigh throw that body into the stream, he certainly wanted Leigh to pay for his actions."

Joe said, "Tom's resentment had been building for years. He hated the way Leigh treated Ellen."

"'Rescue the weak and the needy; deliver them from the hand of the wicked,'" Prue murmured.

Joe winced. "Rescue, yes, but I'll never believe Tom wanted to kill, no matter how justified it was."

"That's true. Even after all that went before, Tom wouldn't have killed Leigh if he had just calmed down," Prue said.

"Tom should have just admitted it right away." Joe added.

"If I had known that night that he killed Leigh, before he had buried the body and got away," said A.T., "I could have made it only manslaughter at the worst."

"But," said Joe, in reply, "he might have had to go to prison for several years even for that. I'm glad, Arthur, that you didn't get Tom to confess. I would almost rather have gone to Thomaston myself than to have had Tom go there. It would have been another murder."

"I don't think it would've come to that. It's a well-established principle legally and biblically that some killings are justified."

Prue stated emphatically, "It's certainly easy to believe that Tom would do everything in his power to prevent Ellen from being harmed."

Joe agreed. "Not many would convict a man who was protecting a woman."

Then Prue added, "Poor Tom. I hope his Indian spirit finds good hunting."

Joe asked, "How much did Hulda really know?"

"She had a pretty good idea of the big picture, but I don't think Tom told her any of the details. Hulda is woods dweller, like Tom. She kept the secret because 'a promise is a promise.'"

For a little space there was silence. Then Joe said, "I hope Adam and Pearl get back to New York before the next snow storm hits."

Prue smiled. "I'll miss her, but I'm glad she's going back with Adam."

Joe said pensively, "I always hoped Pearl would be married here at home."

Prue looked surprised. "Did he ask for your permission?"

"Not yet," Joe replied. "But it's only a matter of time. It's easy to see how he feels about Pearl."

"Adam is a fine lad," A.T. said, folding the newspaper and giving it to Aunt Prue. "Here, Prue, put that thing in the family scrapbook. I never want to hear of it again."

Aunt Prue looked at the fire and smiled.

About the Author

Emily Porter Blair was born Inez Emily Robinson in Sherman Mills, Maine, in 1886. She was known as Emily all her life. Aroostook County, Maine—potato country—is where she spent her early life and provided the setting for this story.

Emily married O.B. Porter in 1905 at age 19, and their first child was born in 1906. Five more children followed, one who died in infancy, and the last in 1918, when Emily was 32. In 1925 she divorced O.B., and the next year the whole family piled into two Model T Fords with all their belongings, and the two older boys drove them to Washington, DC, where Emily's sisters had relocated.

She worked for a while selling insurance and then as a secretary in a U.S. Senator's office in Washington. Some of this manuscript was typed on the backs of stationery from that office. She stopped working when she married Ernest A. (Paddy) Blair in about 1930. He was a printer for the government in Washington. He died in 1945.

The household in the city was soon full of various family members, with Emily's sisters and children and their spouses and children living in the house at different times. Than, the oldest son, married in 1929 and moved to a small town in Maryland outside the city, and 1934 he built a house next door for Emily, Paddy, and Eva, Paddy's sister. Eventually he built a smaller one even closer, and Emily lived there after both Paddy and Eva died. Various family members gathered around her again, living in the different houses at various times.

Emily was a writer and a poet. Some of her poems were published in the local newspaper in Maine, and she with her son Hal wrote a mystery, *Three Saw the Murder,* that was published in 1938 by Robert Speller Publishers in New York. Used copies are still available online. Several other partial book manuscripts have been found.

Emily was a small woman, slender, and not quite five feet tall. She died of a heart attack in her sleep in 1948.

About the Editors

Barbara Moyer is Emily's great-granddaughter and Maya's niece. Her father, Frank M. Porter, wrote *Portraits of Love* in 2008. She has found editing to be a fascinating experience, and she has several projects in mind for the future. She is a pediatric physical therapist living with her husband in York, Pennsylvania.

Maya M. Porter, Emily's granddaughter, has been an editor and writer for more than thirty years. She has recently completed her memoirs, *Recognized in Flight*, which includes a chapter describing her grandmother's interesting life. She lives in Fayetteville, Arkansas.